ZION RIDGE DRAMA

A novel by

MELISSA COBB

PUBLISHER'S NOTE

This book is a work of fiction. Names, characters, businesses, Organization, places, events, and incidents are the product of the Author's imagination or are used fictionally. Any resemblance of Actual persons, living or dead, events, or locales are entirely coincidental.

Library of Congress Control Number: 2013944249

ISBN 13: 979-8-9931887-3-7

Printed in the United States of America

Moral Statement

"Beware of the advice you give"

CHAPTER 1 (August)

"Get your dick out of me, you cheating son of a bitch!" I spoke harshly while staring into the face of my husband.

As soon as he opened his brown eyes, the stroking was quickly missed. He stopped taking me in another world to huskily utter, "What the hell is this about? I was about to fucking nut." Popcorn stared down at me while I scooted up from under him. Standing to my feet, I looked at his slimy dick, and responded, "First of all, my name is Shondia, your wife, but you called me Shay that supposed to be baby momma of yours."

As he stood in the middle of the bed on his knees, his dick head swayed as it dripped on the spot where I was. Popcorn looked puzzled as he blankly said between pauses, "What? I did what? What the fuck you say I did?"

I did not respond. Assuming my words finally reached his brain, he loudly proclaimed, "Oh, hell no! I didn't fucking call you her. I hadn't fucked her since the night she got pregnant. You know how fucking long that has been? I know damn well you're not saying I pulled some shit like that?"

"Yeah, Popcorn, say what you want, for I know what you called me," I dissatisfiedly stated while walking off.

"You don't know a damn thing but how to fuck up a good nut right now. So, get your ass back down here. The pussy is good as hell and just the way I love it, too." I still

1

did not respond as I watched his movements. My husband saw that I was not budging. Therefore, he went on to say in a pleading tone, "I need this pussy to get me going this morning. Come on, Shondia. You know you're my coffee. I'm about to add the cream. So, quit wasting valuable ass time. Get back on your back and put the pussy back into position so I can dive deep into what I know is good."

I remained silent and Popcorn became very quiet. I knew he was waiting on me to return to my position, but he knew me well enough to know that if something was bothering me then I wouldn't perform at all. I deeply desired that nut as much as he did, but I went to the bathroom.

Popcorn must have gotten impatient, for in the background I heard him scream out, "Ain't this some bullshit, Shondia, some motherfucking bullshit? In fact, you on some bullshit right now. We both have the day off together and you done fucked it up by some hoe ass shit. Come on back, Shondia, let's talk about what the man in your head said after we finish. Shit, I know who the hell I'm fucking and it's not her. The bitch was a one-night stand that ended in a baby that she doesn't let me see."

I turned on the shower in our master bathroom to drown his voice out. I knew he was off into it and the dick was damn good, but I thought he called me her name. She could be under-handed. To attract men, she pretended to be friendly and then fuck up their relationship, but to women she was a real bitch that needed her ass kicked for playing games. I could understand if she had something going for herself, but she didn't.

2

She had another child by another man, no GED, no job, live in the projects, and no car. In fact, the bitch depends on rides because she can't drive. Above all, he fucked off with her. He fucked off with a damn down grade. Guess if she has a banging body along with good conversation that was all that mattered. I began to laugh as my brain rambled on, "Where the fuck they do that shit at? Lville?"

For some reason, it is beyond me why men love stank ass hoes like that. Then again, our names were similar and maybe Popcorn didn't call me her, maybe I did misunderstand. Quickly, I turned off the water and placed a towel around me. Opening the door, he was, as I figured he would be, lying across the bed still naked. I did not want him because I was still confused in mind about the name thing; however, I knew I had to put on a show to ease the tension.

He rose up to see me, and asked in a mocking tone, "What? You thought you heard me call you or did that fucking man in your head tell you I said something else?"

Sighing, I began to put on a show. Popcorn loves when my hair clings to my face. Rolling my ass seductively, I turned around and exposed a little of my moist back. Peeping over my shoulder, I saw that he sat up and smiled. I knew I had his attention, and the argument was over in his mind.

"Fuck that. Come give me that pussy, throat, or something. Shit, enough of this teasing. I'm already up to do battle," Popcorn demanded.

Seductively, I turned around to make my breasts

3

bounce as the towel dropped. Popcorn licked his lips as his eyes focused on my tan melons. "They need attention, too" I pointed out sexually.

"Bring those fruits to me," Popcorn said loudly in a raspy tone.

I got on the bed and leaned over so he could taste me. Sexually, I moaned with delight. One nipple, then both nipples, Popcorn caressed them ever so eagerly. His tongue spoke a language to my breasts that only they understood. The more he spoke, the more they responded to his verbal message.

All the pulling, tugging, and tongue flicking made my pussy thump with intense passion as his tongue tingled my soul. *I love the way he makes me feel all over, mainly that soft spot between my legs, and the way he dicks me down, Shay couldn't help but to want him.*

Clearing my thoughts, I pulled back and saw that his manhood stood at attention. Grinning, I turned around and put my pie in his face. Like a good boy, his hands were all over my ass as he pulled his dinner closer to his mouth. The first flicker of his tongue didn't do justice as I began to lick up and down on the lean muscle that stood in my face. I thought from within, *I'm going to make this dick sit down and not want to get up in my face again.*

I could tell Popcorn enjoyed his mouth on my pussy too much, and so was I. It was about me taking care of him, not the other way around. Thinking quickly, I tried to pull his desert back, but he was getting up off the bed with it. I couldn't have him do that; therefore, I tooted my ass up further and he finally lay back down.

4

Seeing that he was trying to get me first, I tasted his mushroom cap as my hand wrapped around the stalk. The more I pulled on him, the more his toes wiggled and turned. Popcorn moaned louder than usual, and I knew that it was good, but I planned to make it better. Taking my left hand, I started playing with his balls and from time to time, I put those huge balls in my mouth at once. That action made Popcorn hysterical, as I pulled and tugged on him stronger. Slowly, I let up and allowed him to taste me. Like a hungry child looking for milk, he tasted me as he shook his head back and forth, hungrily.

He's trying to put his face in it, I thought with a huge smile.

As if he was a bad child, I took the pie away from him and went wild on his dick. I tried to swallow his lean muscle whole as my lips went all the way down to the base of the balls. I had to back up some and allowed Popcorn to play in his pussy for a moment. I really needed the break. I went too deep and started choking myself.

"Hell no, don't back up off that dick now. Take all of it, baby. It's yours and yours alone. Get your dick." Changing positions, I got up and placed myself between his legs. Working him a little slower, I heard Popcorn say, "You better not waste a drop of that nut. You hear me? You better not waste it at all." I put my neck muscles in overdrive.

The more I swallowed him, the more his hands pushed down on my head. I could tell that he truly enjoyed himself by the pressure on me. Forgetting all about the intense pressure, his dick began to throb and swell in my mouth.

5

With each pump of his heart, my cheeks appeared to have been stung by a bee as his seed filled my mouth.

Relaxing my face, I allowed his salty seeds to fill my stomach cavity. Like a good girl, I did not waste drop of the precious fluid, for the freak in me would not allow me to do so. Earnestly, I sucked on him, knowing that his nut sack was empty, and the dick was limp. That did not stop me. I needed him to fill me completely. Popcorn tried with all his might to pull me off him, but he could not. He tried to roll, twist, and shake me, but I was on him like white on rice.

"Baby, please, I'm weak already. Fuck, I'm weak as shit. Stop, baby. Please, stop. I can't take it," Popcorn entreated softly.

Still, I would not let him go because he begged for me to drink him and drinking him was what I planned to do. He could beg all he wanted, but I was not letting that dick go until it was exhausted in my mouth from pleasure. I thought he had passed out because he stopped begging and started hitting on his chest. I jumped up off the bed to get a better look at him. My husband scared me.

"Popcorn, what the hell is wrong with you? I wasn't finished getting my Vitamin D out you," I screamed out as if I was in some type of pain.

Sitting up and taking deep breaths, he looked me hollowed eyed to say, "Baby, you were taking my breath away. Shit, fuck. I couldn't breathe and the way you had me, I was about to pass the fuck out or have a heart attack or something."

Smiling, I replied, "I am your wife. Pleasing you is

6

what I love to do. Can't help it, I love the way I make you feel and what I won't do, another one will try."

Finally catching his breath, he replied with a grin, "Shit like that will make me bury yo ass. No other nigga gonna know how you suck or fuck. It's either me, Taylor, Beck or William Herrington Funeral Home. Pick one."

Laughing at him, I responded, "I'm a grown ass woman. You can't put me anywhere if it's not my time. Forget about Beck and William Herrington. As for Taylor's, they are around the corner in Greensboro, so why would I go there?"

Sitting on side of the bed, he chuckled, and replied, "I don't care where you want to go. I know where you are going if you mess up. You better get that shit right with God because I know me, and I know that it's either me or one of them. Honestly, I'm a firm supporter of Beck and the hearse team motto I gave them, "You stab 'em, we grab 'em.'"

"Now I know why I'm still with you," I replied before I went to the bathroom.

"Why is that?" Popcorn asked with a smile.

"You make me laugh," I majestically proclaimed.

"Is that right, Mrs. Shondia Tubby-Collier?" Popcorn questioned with great joy.

"You damn right, Mr. Chadwick Collier," I said as I went in the bathroom to clean myself up.

"Baby, not the government name," Popcorn yelled out to me. Seconds later, Popcorn walked in behind me and took a hoe bath in the sink while I was in the shower. Turning off the water, I heard Popcorn say, "Shondia, I was going to hit the weights, but I'm too weak. I swear you take a lot out of me when you do that. You felt different when I was on the inside fucking you. It's like your pussy is better than before. With pussy and head like that, you gonna have me crazy as hell, more than I already am now."

Stepping out the shower, I spoke, "I don't know about feeling different on the inside, but I am your wife. You supposed to be crazy about me."

"Yeah, it's not supposed to be crazy enough to kill you if you look at another man. Just the thought of you and another man pisses me off," Popcorn spoke honestly.

"Awe, Popcorn, I'm just one woman in a sea of many. Sure, there are many out there better than me. I am an amateur and no way in being a pro," I spoke while drying off.

As if Popcorn heard something, he spat out the mouthwash and stood frozen like he was in a trance. He tilted his head toward me and spoke with an even tone before leaving the bathroom, "Shondia, but you are my wife, pro or not, fuck the many. I don't play with mine. For mine is mine. Those bitches don't mean shit to me and believe me; I had my pick of the litter. That is why I am married to you and not them. At the end of the day, it's the one you come home too. In case you don't get it, baby, my is a personal pronoun. It means belonging to and that is what you are, mine, for you belong to me and no one else. It drives me insane with anger to even think of you being unfaithful to me in any way. I can't handle it if you were to ever give away what we share in this bed, nevertheless, a conversation to any man with other intentions."

8

I stood there as Popcorn left our home, not knowing what to think of the odd conversation I just had with my husband. He had never sounded so sincere about anything and to hear him say that I was his woman sounded scary. Disrupting my thoughts was the sound of a car pulling up on the rocks. Looking outside, I saw a car pull up across the street at Aunt Rose's house. No one lived there but that was where everyone who was anyone went to chill and lift weights.

The passenger door opened, and it was my cousin, Chug. He got out. I then remembered the car; it was one of his homeboy's. As I stood on the steps, Chug said something to Popcorn and then went to the mailbox while my husband walked with him. He pulled out some mail, rummaged through it, and put some back in the box. He tore open a letter and read it very fast as he vigorously shook his head.

"I'll be damned," were the words that came out loudly, drawing attention. Chug handed the letter to Popcorn. My husband read it and started laughing, and then they gave each other a high five.

I yelled out loud as I could as I made my way toward them, "Well, what is making y'all grin like that? It can't be about a scheme, a car, your own place or a freebie, so it must be about a woman."

"Wrong, wrong, and wrong. You looking at a motherfucker who just got in to kill bitches and snitches. Once I get past boot camp, I will be able to make money and have a job with benefits," Chug said as he shook his head with the paper in the air.

"Benefits? That is what the bitches come in handy. Anyhow, who is giving yo ass a job to have a gun?" I asked as he handed me the letter. "The fucking Marines! You have to be kidding me. They must be desperate because they enlisted you to join them," I exclaimed as Chug did his happy dance all over again.

"Right, baby. I thought the same thing because Chug in the military means this country is in a world of trouble," Popcorn said.

Chug cut into the conversation by saying, "Love birds, they need a nigga like me out there. I'm young, black, and have nothing to live for. Shit, that makes me dangerous as a motherfucker."

"Shit, I don't think they know who they got," Popcorn said.

I but in, teasing, "They don't know what the hell or, better yet, who the hell they are letting in these days if yo ass got in. I bet you will take off running if they start shooting at you."

Laughing hysterically, Popcorn added, "He would probably drop the gun and say fuck this shit, I'd rather be back at the Pig."

"I see ya got jokes on a brother. Shit, I'll be getting paid, what more could a nigga ask for? While y'all still here in Winston County, I'll be traveling the world and seeing what else there is out there and not be stuck in a rut" Chug said.

"At least we will be alive and be able to spend our damn bread. You, on the other hand, have to make it out before you can spend a damn thing," Popcorn said to Chug.

"Yeah, Chug, yo ass has a job and you don't want to go to it, and it's just uptown. Shit, you are wasting their time and yours, too," I spoke teasingly with a laugh.

"Shondia, I'm going to get paid mad ass cash to kill fuckers," Chug replied. He further said, "Shit, I'm in there now. If they made a mistake, it's their fault, not mine. Besides, I'm tired of working there, anyway. Bitches need a nigga with benefits and what benefits does the Pig have?" Chug stated.

"I don't know, but it keeps yo ass off the street. Anyway, you think of anything to get out of going to the Pig to work. You might make it through boot camp," I spoke.

"How about off our couch for good? And don't forget those schemes he puts you through, which includes me," Popcorn added

"Man, you honestly think I will endanger my favorite cuz in some type of plot that knowing I would have to face your ass in the end?" Chug asked.

"How many times have you not included her in some type of scheme of yours? That is the question you need to be asking," Popcorn told him.

"Popcorn, that was a long time ago and if I hadn't included her, y'all might not have met. Therefore, all my tricks are not bad as you would think," Chug pointed out to us.

"He is right, honey," I said to my husband as I smiled.

Popcorn looked at Chug, and said, "She does have a point. If it hadn't been for your underhandedness to come to Spay, I would not have met the woman of my dreams. I thank you, at least this once."

I moved closer to my husband and felt joy like never before. He touched me with his words of love. Slowly circling my arms around my husband, I tasted his lips and couldn't control myself.

"You better cut that out before we go back in and have fun," Popcorn said to me.

Before I could respond, we heard, "Let me use your phone, got to hit ole girl up and let her know," Chug spoke as he snatched my phone.

"Is this the same one that you asked me advice on leaving alone?" I said with laughter.

"Yeah, I need to leave her alone, but her money is too good," Chug said.

"Well, use your own phone to call her. I told you if I were you, I'd leave her married ass alone," I stated.

"I'm not you and I will. Shondia, you know damn well I lost my phone. Right now, I need her to do something else for me."

"Well, if she can't get in touch with you, her ass may need to invest in a cell phone so you can keep me out yo business with her and the rest of them," I replied to my favorite cousin.

"I am going to leave her alone like we talked about before. I know ya mean well, cousin, but I have shit to do and she helps me get that shit done," Chug spoke.

"And like I said, if it's wrong, it's wrong, it doesn't matter who it is. If I were you, I would leave her alone. You have asked me, and I have spoken," I stated back to him.

"All bullshit aside, she gives damn good head."

"Too much information, plus, you don't need to be calling that married bitch. Shit, her husband may call my phone back and then what? Don't think I won't tell it," I said as I stood by.

"He ain't gonna do a damn thing because she runs his ass," Chug spoke while dialing her number.

"Yeah, like she running yo ass," I teased.

"Ain't no damn body running..." Before he could finish telling me what he thought, she must have answered the phone because he said, "Hey, baby," as he walked off and turned his back.

I waited a few more minutes and Chug brought back my phone. When I moved away from the driveway, a car pulled up and stopped. I looked and it was my boss, Big Quack. He was in his brand new, four door, candy apple red Cadillac sitting on twenties. It was a nice ride, and he always had to be a showboat.

"Come on over here, girl. You staring like you didn't know who I was in this car," Big Quack said as he laughed.

"Santa, you are not hard to miss, especially out of season and with no reindeer," I joked.

"I traded the reindeer in for eight horses," Big Quack spoke as he laughed.

In response, I said, "Funny, very funny."

"All jokes aside, I brought you the key to the restaurant because I won't be in today. Got to talk to a lady uptown about catering her upcoming functions." I got the keys, and his hands brushed up against mine. He said, "Ooh, black cotton. Girl, you still soft as ever."

I laughed, and said, "Do I make extra money working the function or is it regular pay?"

"Since you family and all, regular pay." As he laughed, he glanced toward my husband.

"What! I may be sick that day. Let the new girl work it," I replied.

"She can, but she can't work it like you," he spoke back.

"Goodbye, Big Quack. I will be there a few minutes earlier. Oh yeah, who else is working today?" I asked.

"So far, just you and her because it is a slow day."

"You know we don't have slow days unless it's a Sunday." I spoke as he laughed.

"Right, but ah, seriously, you can call in someone else if you need it. I trust your opinion."

"I trust you have the money to pay these people because I don't have money to pay them. You are not going to trick me like you did the last time by acting like you wouldn't pay them because you didn't call them," I said as he looked at me.

"Shondia, you need to tell that husband of yours to make some serious ass money," he spoke as he tilted his head back in Popcorn's direction.

"He doesn't have anything to do with my money. And, Quack, you need to pay me more money before I fire my damn self."

"Awe, here we go again about you wanting more money. Sing another damn song because the one you

14

singing stay broken," he said as he pretended to close his ears.

"I know you can still hear me, but I'm serious. You want me to train all these people and expect me to call all the shots. That sounds like a supervisor job to me," I told my boss.

"You are truly right, and I will go up on your pay."

"I don't mean a penny, dime, nickel, quarter, fifty cents, or anything less than a dollar," I laughed as I told him.

"You drive a hard bargain, but in business you are right. Shondia, I don't trust anyone else to run my restaurant if it is not you. I will give you two dollars an hour more and if you do functions, twenty percent on every hundred," Big Quack said as he handed me the paper. I was stunned. "What, you thought I was playing?" He handed me a pen, also.

"This is really why you swung by my house, isn't it?" I asked.

"Yeah, plus, I haven't been on this end of ZR in a minute."

I read over the paper, and it stated all he had said. Looking at my boss, I said, "What's the catch? Why me?" I asked.

"What catch?"

"You heard me."

"Honestly, you are honest and doing right is what you stand for. Plus, you have been there for over two years. Why not you, is the question you should ask?"

"Good answer," I responded as I gave him back the

signed paper.

Big Quack drove off and I was about to go back into the house until my husband called out for me. I walked to the end of our driveway to meet him. "What's up, honey?" I asked him tenderly.

"What the hell Big Quack fat ass want?"

"To give me the key and to tell me that I have a raise," I said as I reached up to kiss my husband.

"That better be all that fat fuck want. Hate to make his family ride slow," Popcorn said seriously.

"Stop it," I spoke to lighten the mood.

"Anyway, what time you get off?"

"I don't know. Big Quack will have me working late because a new girl supposed to start today. Why?" I asked.

"I hope she is good enough to take your place. He's cool as hell, but I don't like the way he stares at you when I'm around. If he does that shit with me around, imagine how he looks at you when I'm not around," Popcorn said.

"I told you before, he and I are just friends and nothing more. His friendship is just that, friendship. He likes flirtier women and women that depend on him. I am neither. I don't flirt and I don't depend on him for shit."

"No, you're not, and that's what makes getting you a higher stake. You are not like the women he usually likes. He knows you are married; he knows that you are top notch, but I will fuck you and Quack up. Is that understood?" Popcorn spoke with laughter as he leaned in to kiss me.

Pleased in his upbeat humor, I smiled again, and said,

16

"Men and women can be friends as long as shit doesn't cross the line. Besides, you have friends I don't like, but I trust you."

"I have not given you any reason not to, but that fat fucker, I have my doubts. I don't trust him. Every time I see him, he talks to me, but I feel like he knows something that I should know, and it bothers me."

"Honey, I can reassure you that he is just a friend. When you are not around and when possible, I do talk about you. The fact of the matter is the job keeps me busy, and I did tell you that the beginning of the year that I will find another job. As of right now, this job at Big Boy's BBQ helps me, help you, help us. So, don't think anything more into it. He knows I love you and only you. I'm not leaving my husband for no body. We have been through a lot to get to where we are now," I reminded Popcorn.

"I know, baby, but I'm a man and I know that you are the type of woman that men like."

"Look at me. I'm kind of thick and I'm plain. No make-up, no jewelry, no fine clothing, and I drive a compact car" I laughed.

"All those are true, but when you want too, you are a totally different woman. You're already sexy, you become sexier. You don't need jewelry or make-up; your skin gives off a glow that shows your inner beauty. I know what the hell I have at home, and I know what the hell I plan to keep at home," Popcorn said as his lips brushed against my forehead.

"All this talk of fucking up is making me look at you from another angle."

17

"You better because you have never seen me pissed off and in my 'I'll fuck you and everyone around you up' mode. Kids and all," Popcorn said seriously. Then I yelled as he was leaving, "I have to go get ready, but remember, I love you and it is you that has my heart, my mind, my pussy, and my throat, for what it's worth. Not my job and Big Quack, for that matter."

CHAPTER 2

I got home from work exhausted and glad that I did not cater with Big Quack for the function uptown. Of all days, they worked the shit out of me at Big Boy's BBQ. The new girl messed up orders, didn't dictate the orders correctly, and I had to go behind her and fix things.

Loudly, I spoke, "Big Quack gonna hear about this shit. I didn't get a raise to fucking work myself. I see why he wants to offer more money. It's a damn job to do all this shit I have to do."

Sighing, I unlocked the door and went in the house. *Big Quack entrusts me, for he knows that I will do my job and try to help the newbie out, but shit, her lack of working is working the fuck out of me. I'm tired of coming home late at night with aching feet and no one to rub them. Shit, something has to give.* I locked the door behind me and pulled off my slip proof shoes. When I finally focused on what was before me, I saw a vase sitting on the dining room table. It was no longer empty; it had red and yellow roses in it. I noticed the trail of rose pedals leading into the bedroom.

The trail went all the way to the bathroom in my room. There was no need to turn on the light because from the door of my bedroom, a lot of light was seen. I assumed it was candles. Focusing more on my bedroom, I went in and saw around the tub railing lit with scented candles. Smiling, I shook my head in surprise. "When and how did Popcorn have time to do this for me? He is always full of surprises."

Stripping off, I soaked in the very warm water and

thought more *Popcorn has to be at work from eleven to seven, how is the water still warm? I know the Wal-Mart overnight stock supervisor did not let him ease out. Then again, he has been there for over seven years.*

My cell phone rang, so I took one hand out the water and answered the phone without looking at the caller. "Hello."

"I see you in the bath water I fixed."

"Yes, how did you know that I needed this pampering? Were you outside and heard me complaining about coming home late and how something has to give?" I said seductively.

"You are my wife. If anyone should know what you need, it should be me. Wish I was in that water with you doing some freaky things to you," Popcorn said in a sexual tone.

"How did you find the time to do this, and you had to be at work?" I asked, for I truly desired to know how he pulled off such a marvelous surprise.

"It's for me to know and for you not to find out."

"So, it's like that now?" I said as I waited on an answer.

"No, but I will tell you this, I do have my ways."

"Honey, thank you and if you were here, I would thank you in person," I said as I closed my eyes and thought about that morning.

"Open your eyes, baby. I don't want you to fall asleep." As if he could see me, I obeyed his command. "I'll be home, and you will be sleep. Guess you will have to thank me another time like you did this morning. That's the killer shit you pulled this morning. My dick getting hard now just thinking about how you made him come to attention."

"If you were here, I would make him stand at ease, too" I laughed while speaking to him.

"I know you can. Don't make me get off from work just to come and fuck the shit out of you," Popcorn said, and I knew he would come.

"No, baby, stay there," I moaned.

"You better be lucky because I know you are tired and can't put up a fight."

"Don't worry, I love you and only you," I proclaimed to my husband.

"I know, baby, just need you to believe that I love you and only you, too. Shay wasn't anything but a one-night stand that turned into a baby. In time, we will have our own baby. Shit, that broke me up from one-night stands," Popcorn said with humor.

"I know. We just have to be patient and continue to enjoy each other before that time comes," I spoke as the warm water soothed me.

"I have to get back to work. We have an eighteen-wheeler to unload tonight. I love you."

"I love you, too, honey. Can't wait to see you in the morning," I spoke before I hung up the phone.

Throwing the phone on the bed from the tub almost made me angry. It was actually sad that Shay wouldn't let him see his supposed to be daughter because he married me. It was not my fault that he never loved her. In truthfulness, I had never seen him until I drove Chug to

21

some house in Spay.

I remembered how Popcorn came outside, and his swag caught my attention. He said something told him to come outside and he was glad he did. I, on the other hand, was nervous because Chug always got me into some type of foolish mess of his. That time, I was glad I came along, for it I hadn't I would not have met the man of my dreams.

Popcorn and I hit it off great. I knew I was in love from our first date. As the months progressed, so did our love. To my astonishment, we didn't rush into sex like most because I had made up in my mind that the next one, I was with would have to have more than money, he would have to have my heart. If Popcorn hadn't showed me that compassion, I would not have given him the time of day. Luckily, he did, and my life hadn't been the same. I was happier and felt more alive than I had in my life.

My only problem was Shay. I personally knew she was full of shit. She did all she could to break us up, but Popcorn told me that he wasn't the only man she was with and if it was his, she set him up. He said he used a condom she gave him because he wasn't going bare in her. I laugh because he was stupid. Women like her would do anything to trap a man using the oldest catch phrase, "'I already have one baby daddy, I don't need another one.'"

To his amazement, she told him she was pregnant, and he denied it like the rest of the men. In wanting a child so bad, he took up the slack and began paying support for her. *Sucker*, I thought. Anyway, he had no idea that she put holes throughout the condom and knew her highest time of ovulation. She told him about that some time down the line.

22

Three months later, I came along and picked up drama. I told him that Shay was his business, but when we got married, she became our business.

The sound of my cell ringing woke me out of my dreamland of Shay. "I fell asleep in the tub." Dreamy, I smiled and yawned. I got out the tub dripping only in time for the phone to stop ringing. It began ringing again and I looked at the caller ID to see it was Chug. *Now, what the does he want?* I thought as I pushed the green button on my phone. "What's up with ya?" I spoke as I yawned again.

"I need you to come uptown to the Mickie D's and swoop me up right now."

I removed the phone from my face to see that it was almost two a.m. "Chug, I fell asleep in the tub?" I said slowly, not regarding what he was talking about.

"Bitch, I don't know where you fell asleep at but come get me. I'll be on the inside eating, bye" Chug spoke as he hung up.

Yawning and stretching, I dried off, put on a sweatshirt, joggers, and my slip in house shoes. Deciding to let the water out when I got back, I grabbed the keys. Locking the door behind me, I got in the car and texted Popcorn before I left the yard in case something happened to me. I had to let the hubby know where I was going. Instantly, he texted back be careful, and to let him know when I get there and when I make it back home safely. Smiling, I started the car and backed out the yard headed toward Shellie Brown Road to get Chug.

When I made it to the four-way stop, I looked at my job and it was black as midnight. Turning my head back, a truck passed as I turned left onto Highway 14 with McDonald's on my left. I pulled into the parking lot and sure enough, Chug was there eating with some younger girl. He appeared to be content because he was looking different than before.

Whatever happened to the married woman? I thought as I parked the car right in front so Chug could see me. Soon as I texted my husband, Chug saw me and gave the girl a light kiss on the cheek. I stared hard because I didn't recognize her. She was short, thick, and had a bob hairstyle that cupped her oval face. She walked out the door, smiled at me, and got into a nice Dodge Magnum. He put his stuff in the thrash and refilled his soda. Chug walked to the car and before he opened the door all the way, I spoke, "You better have my damn gas money and a meal for waking me up this time of morning to come get you from some shit I know you were doing."

"Damn, Shondia, help your cousin out. Let me get in the car first before you bombard a motherfucker. Shit, you see a nigga don't have a car," Chug said as he got in and handed me a small bag.

I looked down at the bag and knew right away it was an apple pie. "I know damn well your ass didn't just give me an apple pie that yo ass didn't eat?"

He glanced at me, and said, "Shondia, calm the fuck down. Bitch, the shit was free, I didn't want it. Damn, you hard as the police on a nigga. I got you."

"Nigga, before we leave this bitch you need to show me my cash," I spoke with humor.

"Let's go, Shondia, I got you," Chug spoke as he

24

looked around like a suspect.

"What or who is your ass running from?" I said, not moving the car.

"Damn, girl, come on, let's go. You ask a lot of motherfucking questions. We could be halfway down the road by now. Put the car in reverse and peel the fuck off."

I started the car, and before I could back up a truck pulled up and blocked me in. I had to hit my brakes quickly. "What the hell?"

"Bitch, you on drugs? Back the fuck out!"

"I would, but a truck is behind me and won't move."

Chug peeped over his shoulder and started cursing. "Shit, damn, it's her. Fuck! I tried to leave before she got here."

"Who? Who the fuck you talking about, dude?" I questioned.

"Michelle. Girl, wheel this motherfucker out of here. This bitch crazy," Chug spoke under his breath as if he wasn't breathing at all.

"Well, get the fuck out and see what the bitch wants. I'm tired as hell and need to get to my bed. So, hurry the fuck up," I said as I smiled at him.

"I told you it's Michelle. She tripping because I stood her up for ole girl. Fuck her. Been there, done that, now back the fuck up. Run over the bitch if she doesn't move."

Chug was not smiling. He actually looked agitated at the fact that the girl blocked my car in. I tried to back up, but she didn't move. She kept me blocked in with her black

F-150. Chug just sat there. When I opened the door to get out Chug reached for me, but I ignored him as I stood by the back door of my car. Staring at me standing outside of her truck was a clean dressed, full-figured stranger.

She was about six feet two, light brown, head full of hanging curls, big breasts and hips to match. The big body looked like she weighed about three hundred and fifty plus pounds. Looking through the rolled down window, I saw my bat was still in the back behind me. *Ooh wee, damn, that's a big bitch.* I went on to proclaim loudly with attitude, "I don't know, and I don't give a fuck, but you need to move your shit."

"In case you don't get it, I don't give a damn. You tell that motherfucker to get out the car. Since he wants to play games and shit, I got one for him. It's called foot meets ass," she replied.

Pointing at my car with my left pointer finger to the spot where Chug sat, I calmly as possible said, "If this motherfucker is in my car, his motherfucking ass in my car. Fuck the shit you talking about. It's irrelevant to me. Now, move your shit bitch before I hit your shit."

"I don't know who the hell you think you are bitch, but I can tell that you're about to fuck up," was her only reply.

I responded by yelling "Excuse me bitch if I look like I give a fuck believe me big bitch, I don't!"
"I don't give a fuck either!"
"Bitch, fuck you and that bullshit coming out your mouth. It's what the fuck ever yo ass want to do but if you don't want this issue don't make this problem. Now you need to

stop talking out your ass and move yo fat ass out my way."

I gave the big body time to move, and she still did not move her truck. I reached in my car for my bat and Chug already knew because he grabbed it as he spoke, "Fuck that get in so we can get the fuck on down."

Looking back at her I shook my right index finger at her, and said, "I tell you what." Getting back into my car, I snatched the gear in reverse and smashed on the gas. Chug stomped the brakes just in time. Before I could trip on him about what he just did, he jumped out the car and so did I. He yelled at her, "Bitch, this Shondia, my cousin. What the fuck! Get your big, ignorant ass out the way before I hit your shit myself. Now, move your shit. She don't have shit to do with what I am doing."

Unexpectedly, I heard a very sincere apology. "Oh, that's Shondia? I am so sorry. I thought she was that girl you been creeping with."

"Just move your shit out my way," was all I could say to her as I got in my car.

Chug got in the truck with her while I parked on the other side. I text Popcorn. *It was going to be some shit at Mickie D's.*

He immediately called me. "What the hell? Who the fuck is bothering you? You need me to get off work? I'm just across the highway."

"Calm down. I'm good now. It's that married woman Michelle that Chug mess around with. She apologized after we had a few words, and he told her who I was."

The phone was silent, then Popcorn said, "I hate it when he calls you to do his bidding. I like him and

27

everything, but he's full of shit. He always has a scheme to mess people around that tries to help him and he is always in some bitch face. He my boy and all, but when he involves my wife in some shit, fuck being my boy. You're my wife first and I don't give a damn who she is or who he is. I protect mine and you are mine."

"Awe, baby, that's sweet," I said in a whispered tone.

"Sweet my ass, the shit is real. Nobody gonna fuck with you, man, woman, or beast. I've worked too damn hard in this relationship to have some dumb shit come up and you get caught up. Fuck that," was his only response.

"I didn't mind because I fell asleep in the tub, anyway. At least his phone call woke me up."

"Big Quack must have worked you? Do I need to talk to that motherfucker about working you so hard?" Popcorn asked seriously.

"No, the new girl he hired did and let me tell you…" was all I got out before he cut me off.

"New girl? Big Quack hired a new girl?" Popcorn questioned.

"Yeah, remember I told you about her before I went to work. Anyway, she kept getting everything mixed up. People were complaining and it was chaos tonight."

Popcorn said in his protective mode, "Well, I had to check on my baby and when you talked about drama I was flipping the fuck out. If you hadn't answered I was coming out there and was ready for who the fuck ever."

"See, that would have been uncalled for. You need to get rid of that goon mentality. Louisville isn't like

28

Chicago; where you from."

"No, it's not, but bullshit is everywhere and I'm not a weak bitch."

We paused for a moment because someone on his end said, "Break is over."

"You bout to go home or take Chug down 397?"

"I doubt I take him home because I don't feel like driving to auntie house this late. I just want to get to the bed and catch some shut eye."

"Go head and let him stay the night and take him tomorrow. I don't want you on the highway this late, anyway. It's not like he is paying you because he is always broke and freeloading off some damn somebody" my husband spoke with concern.

"Ok," I said.

"Go home and get some sleep. I have to get back in here and finish this truck. Love you, babe."

"Love you more," I spoke, but he was off the phone and may not have heard me tell him, so I texted it. Chug walked over to the car and got in soon as we hung up. I asked, "You ready now? Because I'm tired and hungry."

"Well, ya food cold," Chug mentioned as he pointed at the bag with the apple pie in it.

"If you had your bitches under control, we both would be happy now," I stated as I turned the ignition on and put the car into reverse.

Once I got to Highway 14, I went right on 15/25 Highway. Chug said, "Yeah, take me to your house"

"Bitch, that's where I was taking you. You see I didn't go left toward town. Plus, you don't have any say so, gas, food, or control. What I look like pulling up at auntie's house this time of morning with her hoe ass son? She's not about to curse me out for your ass," I spoke as I took the yield North.

"I had to spit game to her ass so she can shut the fuck up. I had to remind that bitch she married," he said to me.

"You need to spit more than game to her ass, you need to spit some understanding, some harassment charges, and an all you can eat buffet," I said loudly with laughter.

Laughing, my cousin said, "Shondia, I don't have time for Popcorn to whip my ass because you opened your damn mouth. Hell, if he knew what type of girl choo choo yo ass was he would cut the fuck up. You undercover, sneaky half-breed bitch." I laughed because it was true. I used to get down and dyke like no tomorrow. However, no one really knew that. Chug broke my thoughts by speaking, "Shit, I'll have to knock that motherfucker out with a stick or something 'cause he would think that I should have told his ass. Y'all married now, all that shit is done and over with."

"You shut the fuck up. You the biggest whore between the both of us."

"For real? You mean I am the biggest whore?" he spoke with humor

"Don't play me, your ass lower your standards so you won't disappoint anyone."

"And?"

"Yeah, and?" I responded.

He spoke with humor, "Your ass would bring

bitches for us both to trick off, so how the hell you talking?"

"That shit was a lifetime ago."

"Bitch, just before you got married does not register a lifetime ago" he laughed.

"Well, that was then," I further stated to my dear cousin.

"Besides, I know what you will do and that is to get your little fat ass kicked because she's a big bitch. You haven't seen the size of her motor until you have seen it naked. Damn!"

The way he said it. I couldn't help but laugh. "Yeah, she is a healthy ass girl. Where you get her at, anyway?" I asked as we passed the Home Gate Inn Hotel on the right.

"I picked her ass up at the Pig" I laughed harder than before. He said with a straight face, "I did I met her big ass at the Pig. She was buying all kinds of ribs, hamburger meat, chicken, and hot dogs. The bitch had two buggies. Shit, I am a little guy, but I can eat like hell."

I asked, "She must have kids?"

"Hell no! That bitch doesn't have anything but a headache and I'm giving her a pill for that," Chug stated with happiness.

"You said she had two buggies of food, I just thought she had kids," I continued as we approached Shellie Brown Road.

"She is married to an older man. She isn't but twenty-seven, and he's about sixty-two and in a chair from an accident," Chug spoke as closed his eyes.

31

"Damn she married her great-grandfather" Chug opened his eyes to laugh.

"Hell yeah, that big bitch wears me out. I know damn well Viagra isn't that good because it doesn't work for him at all, for if it was, I'm going to get me some."

"Your ass will get a heart attack or something" I turned left on Zion Ridge Road.

Soon as I turned into our driveway, Chug said, "She isn't ugly, just big as hell. That is a lot of meat for me to handle, but you know what? That big bitch is a freak. Do you hear me? That big bitch knows how to take pipe like a soldier and trust me, the bitch is past boot camp and now she is starting to get rank."

We laughed as I suggested, "Other than sex, if I were you, I would leave her big ass alone. How many times am I going to tell you? You are young, nineteen to be exact, and have so many opportunities ahead of you. You don't need to be tricking off with older, married women, anyway. Y'all don't know how to hit it and quit it?"

"Tried that, fuck that. Last time I tried to break it off with her, she turned off my damn, whip. A player like me can't go without my phone, but shit, she cut me the fuck off. Plus, she likes the way I ten hut that pussy."

"How are you leaving her alone if you still tackling her? Because if you call calling her up when you get horny leaving her alone, then you have not tried."

"Watch, I'm going to leave her alone soon. She's married and there is no future in a woman with a man. Just watch what I say. Michelle knows that I listen to you. She knows that ya don't like her being married and fucking off with this young dick."

"Bitch, young dick doesn't have anything to do with it."

"She is the only married broad I fuck off with. The rest of my bitches are single and a problem. Those bitches expect me to take care of them. Fuck that! If I take care of them, who going to take care of me?" Chug spoke as he laughed.

We were in the yard when I text Popcorn. I let him know that we were safe and back at the house. We got out the car and I locked the doors. I unlocked the front door and checked the back door. Once Chug sat down, I went in the spare room and brought out some blankets, for he loved sleeping on my couch. I gave him the blankets and turned on the ceiling fan.

"You might as well stay up because Popcorn will be home in a few," Chug said as he positioned himself in the blankets.

"No, I plan to be out like a light when he comes home. I'm tired and have to work. That is something you don't know about," I stated as I headed to my room.

Before I could make it to the doorframe, Chug said, "Thanks, Shondia. You have always been there for me even if you know that I'm up to no good. You try to tell me what is right and before you know it, this big bitch will be out my life. I always listen to you if I were you' scenarios, even if you think I do not. You right, I don't need a married woman, but she's a damn freak!"

I couldn't help but laugh as I spoke, "Well, thanks. If I hadn't been with you on one of your crazy schemes, I never would have stopped being a dyke or doing some other shit. Also, I never would have met the man of my dreams, so thank you, favorite cousin," I said as I closed the bedroom door behind me.

I stripped and replayed the entire scene in my mind. I shook my head. I let the tub of water out, cleaned it out, turned off the lights, and got in the bed. I couldn't go to sleep at first, for it avoided me, but as I closed my eyes, I thought of the man I married and how we fit so good together.

With that in mind, I woke up in the arms of my loving husband. Somehow, safe was the feeling I felt when I was with him. Looking over at him, I snuggled closer, but that was short lived. A knock at our bedroom door disturbed my moment. I pretended not to be awake, but the voice said in an annoying and mocking tone, "I know you're not asleep, I hear you breathing. The sun is up and so are you, so say something, Shondia. Get up!"

Popcorn turned over and lightly opened his eyes. We smiled at each other. It was mornings like those that I anticipated because they were precious to me. Always in some form, my husband made my day when he smiled at me. I felt like I was the only woman he adored. At that moment, his cell phone went off and he looked at me, for it was his baby momma.

"You have a bullshitter calling. Warning, the caller is a bullshitter. I repeat, a bullshitter, a bullshitter. Do not answer the phone. You don't have time for bullshit today. I repeat, no bullshit today," blared from his phone.

"Get yo ass up now," Chug said as I heard him walk

away from our door.

My husband looked at me as I reached over him and answered the phone. "Hello," I said.

At first, she was silent, as she finally asked, "Where Popcorn at? I called his phone, not yours. We will talk later."

Remembering she was full of shit and didn't have sense God gave, I took a deep breath, and spoke, "Good morning to you. My husband is busy at the moment. What you want me to tell him?"

"I want you to tell him that I love the way his wife eats my pussy and licks my ass. Also, tell him that she can't hide the fact that she is a dyke at heart and a good ass dyke at that, which my pussy misses." I hurriedly hung up the phone. Popcorn turned his eyes over to look at me because of the way I smashed the end button on the cell. "She is always running off at the mouth and not saying a damn thing. That bitch!" I innocently announced.

"You know that Old Project motherfucker don't know how to talk to anybody," Popcorn said as he sat up.

"Well, she needs to respect your wife, even if she claims you have a child by her," I spoke defensively.

"Shondia, I know that, and you know that, but an uptown, old project bitch like her doesn't know anything like that. I am still stunned that I got her pregnant. I told you that bitch trapped me, and I fell in it."

"At least the child is the best thing that came out of the one-night stand," I said to help ease my husband's mind.

"I'm going to get up enough money and get custody

35

of the little girl, if I can prove she is mine. Shay walks around her like she is the bomb bitch while the little girl looks thrown away. The shit pisses me off. Then, I can't see her, and she knows I can't make her," Popcorn said as he got off the bed and paced the floor.

"Remember, you asked for a blood test, and you have to wait on the court date. Furthermore, you mean when we get up enough money to get custody. I'm your wife and I am in this with you," I spoke with reassurance.

Popcorn walked over, kissed me, and then said, "You see, I love you and you standing by my side mean a lot to me."

"I am standing by you because I love you. You are my husband. I have to stand beside you if I don't do anything else. The child is innocent unless she gets old enough to allow her mother to poison her about us," I mentioned.

"Cut the mushy shit out and take me to the crib!" Chug yelled.

We looked at the door and laughed. Popcorn, with his pajamas on, opened the door and went in the living room where Chug was. I got up and washed off. Glancing at the time, I saw that it was eight forty-five a.m. *Damn, I have to go to work at ten today*, I thought. Shay's ringtone went off again. I, of course, answered. "Hello."

"Is Popcorn up now?" she asked nicer.

"Yes, he is, and when I see that ass, I'm going to take care of that ass," I spoke, not giving her time to reply.

I opened the bedroom door and threw the phone at Popcorn. He knew who it was because he heard the ringer himself. As usual, he began speaking nice, and then it turned into a yelling match. It somehow always ended up about me and not about the baby. She always called saying the baby needed this or that, but he provided her with it all.

She used the child as leverage and sometimes he falls into the trap. I told my husband if he couldn't see the child or bring her to our home, then just pay the child support and nothing else. I thought it was crazy to go above and beyond, and you couldn't even spend the day with a maybe child and have your wife along. Shay didn't get that I was the wife and not some thought of lover. She needs to let him see little Kenosha and be done with it.

Shaking my head I got dressed, I pinned my hair up and made up the bed. Popcorn walked in, and said, "She wants me to buy some more diapers and another outfit because she has grown out of the ones she has."

"What did you tell her?" I asked, already knowing the answer.

"I told her to take the child support money and do it. She is almost a year old. How the hell can my baby Moochie spend two hundred and twenty-five dollars up like that?"

"Baby, I don't know. It's sad that she doesn't want me near the child. Have I ever indicated that I would do something to her?" I asked.

"Hell no, you will make a better mother. She's just bitter because I married you and didn't stick around to try and fall in love with her. She was a booty call. I was horny and needed to fuck. She came along rubbing on a drunken nigga and damn, here I am caught up in shit." Popcorn went back in the living room where Chug was.

"Damn, this early?" I asked with disapproval all on my face as I stepped out the bedroom door to see them lighting up.

"Baby today is the party and shit, this isn't nothing" Popcorn said.

"You must be taking Chug home because I have to be at work at ten. I don't need to go in smelling like weed," I said as I sprayed Lysol.

"You think Big Quack don't know what weed smell like? That big motherfucker smoke more than the average motherfucker," Popcorn stated with laughter.

"He can smoke all he wants. I don't pay him; he pays me to work."

Popcorn turned to Chug, and asked him, "Want me to swing you by the crib and get you some clothes?" Chug shook his head as he kept doing gang signs to the music. "He has spoken," Popcorn said with laughter.

"I get off early because Big Quack is closing down for his big birthday party tonight."

"Is he getting the guy from The Golden Tri-Angle to DJ?" Chug asked.

"He's not from The Golden Tri-Angle. I believe he is from West Point and, yes, he is. You know Big Quack throws the best parties and people from all over Winston County come out," I spoke with excitement.

"You know those Ackerman, French Camp, and Weir niggas might come out, too. As long as KO doesn't show the fuck up, we good," Popcorn said as he puffed on the blunt and handed it to Chug.

"Kosciusko is not the problem. It's the damn niggas you hang with when you are at home. The ones that will jump stupid over their hood," I spoke as I walked toward the door.

"Who are you talking about?" Popcorn asked.

"For example, those surrounding niggas hang with you every day, all day when you are at home, but they will jump yo ass if you cross someone from their community," I pointed out to them.

"If they jump, they will jump back because Zion Ridge don't play," Popcorn said as he puffed on the blunt.

"Shit, my fam from around the way is down with ZR," Chug added.

"Nigga, please, I know you aren't talking about our cousins. Those bastards are house husbands and won't leave 397 for shit."

"They may not leave for you, but if I call them, they will get on down."

"Yeah, get on down and out the damn way," I responded with a lot of laughter

Popcorn laughed as he choked on the marijuana smoke. Between choking and speaking, we heard, "Damn! 397 like that?"

"Hell no, don't believe that wife of yours," Chug answered.

"Hell yeah. He better believe me, I grew up in the sticks with them," I replied.

Popcorn was rolling on the floor laughing and choking. "You kids have fun. I have to get to work, I

My husband could not respond and left for work.

CHAPTER 3

A lot of people came in all day at work, but they mostly came to see Big Quack. I had to admit, he wasn't bad on the eyes and his swag was on point to be a big guy. He always matched from the caps he wore to his shirt and shoes. He was never off beat and was cool. I guess that was why everybody liked to meet up at his house. You wouldn't think so, but he was down for his community, even if he didn't like them personally.

You would think that someone like him would be stuck up, but in actuality he was a people person. You could be yourself and he knew how to make you laugh. I was surprised that he wasn't in a serious relationship. Most of the women he messed with were younger, but for the most many were discreet.

A loud voice broke my thoughts. "I see you watching me. You like it? Pinch yourself and wake up so you know that I'm real. Stop daydreaming, Shondia."

It was Big Quack's deep, taunting voice. I yelled back, "Yeah, I'm wondering why you are working your mouth and not your hands."

"Uh, other than I'm the boss and I pay you to work, I'm sure Popcorn wouldn't want my hands on you," he said as he bid goodbye to his company.

"Glad you feel that way," I responded with a laugh.

Big Quack began to make his way over to me. I looked at him and grinned because he was no ordinary boss. My husband hung out at his crib, he and Popcorn did a lot of things together, and he even hits the weights just like the rest of ZR click. "You and Popcorn coming to the party tonight?"

"Depends if I am not tired when I get off from here," I said jokingly.

"Work smart, not hard. Make them do it. Your job is to sit back and make sure they do their job. How hard is that?" Big Quack asked.

"It's hard when you hire clueless women to do a woman's job" I said as I nodded my head to the new girl.

"Shit, oh that?" he said as he burst into laughter.

"Yeah, that shit. It's not funny. She has been working the hell out of me since day one and that was the day before yesterday."

"Give her a chance. If she does not improve, you still can't fire her. Just move her to another area," the boss suggested.

"Outside picking up paper might strain her" I giggled.

"You haven't ever lied. She is sorry as hell. I don't know why she working the hell out of you like that."

"Well, what are your intentions? You hired her. I'm just a leader and can't do too much but complain to you about her none working practices."

As he walked off, he included, "That's a good question, but I can tell you this, she gives outstanding ass head."

My mouth dropped. I knew it, but when he walked past her and popped her ass I knew for sure. The bitch got a job because she was fucking him. Well, she could do all that and then some. As long as she didn't fuck with my pay, we were Gucci. Big Quack glanced back at me and started cackling like a mother hen. He knew I was pissed. I was getting worked by her while she got worked by him. *Life's a bitch*, I thought as I prepared to go home early.

When I made it home, Popcorn was already gone. I know he was with the boys, and they were getting high. I would rather stay in because I was tired, but I knew baby momma would be hanging around; waiting to get used. *Typical Shay. Just like her*, I thought as I turned on the bath water.

The water was pleasing to me as the bubbly water soothed my aching body. I was excited because it would be the first party I have attended in a minute since I'd been married. I disliked the fact that my husband and Zion Ridge click would already be high and on their shit by the time the party started. That was the only thing I don't like about Popcorn. He didn't get high unless someone he hung with was with him and since the Shay incident, he didn't get drunk, tipsy, but not drunk.

As I proceeded to get out the relaxing water, the cell phone rang. I knew it was my boo because he was the only one in the phone with a song assigned. With gladness, I answered, "Hello, my love"

"Just checking to see where you at," Popcorn asked.

"I'm here at the house. Just stepped out of the tub, where you at?" I asked to sound caring.

"I'm down here at Big Quack's house helping set everything up before the DJ gets here."

"Are you already dressed?"

"Yeah, Chug bitch ass is down here with me and the

rest of the click. You know we have to represent" Popcorn said.

"Chug is from 397 honey," I mentioned with a huge smile.

Laughing, Popcorn said, "Yeah, and that is why I said the rest of the click."

I laughed because Chug could talk his way out of a fight and not actually fight. He never met a stranger, and he always searched places to lure women out. As odd as it was, they all fell for his lies.

"You are the best thing that came out from 397 and I mean that. Nothing but sticks down that way and surprised you came from Nanih Wayia," my husband modestly announced.

"Keep your mouth off my hood. You know how we do it," I spoke proudly.

"Uh, baby, bows and arrows at a gun fight," Popcorn spoke with laughter.

"Chadwick Collier, cut it out," I said with no laughing.

"Not the government name again baby. Anyway, get dressed and come on down. I got dropped off so you can drive us back. Don't wear anything too sexy, I'll cut the fuck up," Popcorn said before he hung up.

Soon as I hung up, someone knocked at the door. I smiled as I opened the door. Shay licked her lips, and said, "Damn, baby, you always come to the door naked?"

"Only when it's a bitch to eat my pussy," I said as I walked off for her to come in and close the door behind her.

"You said when you see this ass; you're going to take care of this ass. Well, here it is," Shay spoke.

"You come for me or my husband?" I asked her.

"Put it this way, I don't need dick right now; therefore, your husband is not important to me."

"Anyway, he's not here. He's already down the road, so we have to make this quick," I spoke to my lover. I wanted to try something we hadn't done in a while. I placed my back on the seat of the couch with my legs pressed against the back of the couch, exposing my pussy for her view.

"Shit, yo ass ready for my face," Shay spoke with excitement.

Shay got undressed and sat on my face as she faced the back of the couch. Once she put her face between my legs, I quickly reminisced *why I loved being a dyke. There was nothing like eating pussy, clean tasting pussy at that. The more she tasted me, the more I delighted myself in her pussy. It was wonderful to taste her and to have her pussy juice in my mouth, for it made me crazy.*

"Yes, Shondia, eat it up," Shay spoke as she took her mouth off me.

When I heard those words, I knew she was in her zone to cum. I pulled on her more and more as she began to fuck my mouth with her hairy pussy. The more she worked it, the more I worked it because Shay was an easy fuck, but good all the same. We were going at it and enjoying every moment of it. Seeing that she was almost at her peak, I stopped.

"What the hell? I come here for you to get that nut

44

out me."

"Get up for a minute and lay on your back."

She got up and lay on her back. Shay was sexy as hell and I could see why men wanted to fuck her, but at that moment I was going to fuck her. Stepping into the room, I went in the closet and pulled out the strap on that she and I had used many times. When I walked out, she said, "Fuck me good because I don't want another to get this pussy tonight."

With a smile, I tasted her first to get her wetter than she already was. The way her clit poked out at me made me insane as I sucked on it. "Fuck it, Shondia! Get your pussy," Shay called out.

Lifting my head, I climbed on top of her, admiring her hefty breasts. I stared into her eyes as she placed her legs around my waist. Once I inserted my joy toy into the soft wetness, her eyes lit up. I leaned down and kissed her with fever as I moved my body on her. I was in a familiar zone with a familiar lover that made me feel wonderful inside.

The more I plunged into Shay, the more she squeezed and pulled me deeper into her body. We were sweating as I was making her body mine over and over again. "Girl, give me my pussy," I spoke lightly to Shay.

She could not speak, for I was digging deep inside her and claiming her. When she did reach her orgasm, I worked harder than ever. I was in competition with other motherfuckers fucking her and I had to remind her that it was me that fucked her well. All of a sudden, she began to holler out and pull me. I got off her and handed her the strap on. But, as she lay there, I began tasting her again. Shay wrapped her legs around my shoulders as she allowed me to take her higher. I got up and took her position.

"You know you are gonna have to come with it because I lay beside dick, and not just dick, but good ass dick."

"I'm not worried about that. I am sure he can't fuck like me."

Opening my legs, I let her enter me. It was good. I never knew I missed her fucking me so much, but I did. "Shondia, he can't fuck you, he can't fuck you like me," Shay kept saying to me as she made my body reach out for her. When I began to call out, she continued to move faster and faster. It was mind blowing the way she made me feel. "See, that motherfucker can't fuck like me."

"No, he can't, but the dick is good, and you should know, you had him first. That's what made me try it."

"Damn, bitch, I didn't tell you to fall in love with him, but you did. He was to be our fuck boy for us to fuck at will," Shay said as she got up sat on the couch.

"You claim he's your baby daddy and we both know that could be a lie," I spoke as I got up and walked off to the bedroom.

Shay walked in behind me, and we got in the shower. She lathered my back, and I lathered hers. It was times like those that I missed her. We would sing in the shower and play. She made bath time fun. Sometimes, I would like to call her over and have the three of us "play", but Popcorn would not go for that. He was more religious when it came to a marriage. He believed that a marriage was a marriage and not for a threesome.

We dried off, and I spoke, "Why you say you came over?"

"I wanted you to fuck me before tonight."

"You walked?" I asked.

"Yeah, I got dropped off on Shellie Brown and walked over."

"How the fuck you know Popcorn wasn't here?"

"Girl, I make it my business to know when I can get fucked."

"You know we can't keep this up. I'm a married woman to a man I really love."

"Bitch, you were my piece of ass first. I don't give a damn about you being married to that good dick bastard," Shay spoke with distaste.

"Shay, I got married because I fell in love."

"You loved me first, and we will see just how much he loves you."

"Shay, you know that I hate the fact that we can't let on how we feel. We always have to pretend. Shondia that's on you and when you want to let yo husband know about us and what we have. If it were up to me both of us would have you, publically."

"Don't do anything stupid to jeopardize my marriage," I spoke as she put her clothes back on.

"Bitch, you have already messed that up, fuck what a wedding ring says. I can give you one of those. It may not be legal, but you can get one from me."

"Shay, stay in your lane and out of mine," I told her with seriousness.

47

"I will stay in my lane when you get out that married one. Living a damn lie." Shay stormed out the house and went up the road. Sighing, I decided not to give shit about what Shay said. I went back into the room and realized that I didn't have anything out to wear. *Fucking off with Shay was good as hell*, I thought as I began thumbing through my clothes in the closet.

Still undecided as the sun began to set, I grabbed something. Sitting in front of my mirror, I decided to pin up my hair with a head full of curls. Popcorn loved to play in my curls as he messed them up. Making sure a few strands hung, I was pleased with the hairstyle.

Putting on a light coat of mascara, I placed on some small earrings. Taking my time to get dressed, I needed to make sure I would get my husband's attention. I lotion my body with the peach oil he craved so much. Next, I turned around in the mirror to make sure that my thongs fit my ass perfectly, and they were. *This will do*, I thought as I placed on the knee-high black boots with the short skirt and strapless shirt. For the finishing touch, I placed an Indian choker necklace on my neck and sprayed Bath and Body's Twilight in the Woods all over me heavily.

I parked my car at the end of the road and walked up to the party. My husband was the first one I saw, but I pretended not to see him. I walked up turning my head to and fro as if I was looking for him. It was funny because he stood out like he was the only one there. I finally let on that I saw him and began to walk over.

Before I could get closer to him, Big Quack got in my path, and said, "You smell better here than you do at work. You even look better than you do at work. You are making me have evil thoughts. What's the occasion?"

"I'm off the clock and, trust me; I taste better than I look. As for evil thoughts, you have them all day, anyway," I spoke as I went around my flirtatious boss. He followed to walk beside me.

I knew how my husband felt about Big Quack, so I made sure not to walk close and walked fast. I knew Popcorn was pissed, for he could only assume that Big Quack was walking me to my husband, and it was not good. Wearing a big smile, I finally arrived to my husband. He took each one of my hands into his and stepped back as his eyes roamed over me.

"You look and smell good. I'm ready to eat you right now," he yelled out and leaned closer to nibble on my ear. I felt awkward because he was loud, but people didn't pay him much attention. Blushing very hard, I gave him my inviting smile. Popcorn stated as he couldn't take his eyes off me, "You might have to go back home, you're too fine to be out here like this. I know you are cute, but when you dress like this you are a sight for sore eyes, my eyes especially. Just think, all of you belong to me."

It felt good to hear him throwing compliments at me like that. It was not often that he said those things to me because we were too busy during the week. When I was at home he was at work and vice- versa. Then, one of my favorite songs came on. Reading my mind, my husband said, "May I dance with the sexiest woman here?"

All I could do was smile. He knew I liked *Love in This Club*. He led me to the middle of the floor and gave me a graceful twirl as he pulled me close to him. It felt so right. Popcorn and I danced like the night belonged to us, but that all changed when I saw Shay looking good as hell and half dressed. When I say half dressed, I meant half dressed. Her outfit consisted of heels that laced up to her knees, a body dress too small that made her breasts lunge out at you, big hoop earrings, and twisted up, long, brown, curly hair.

Damn, I wish I could taste that right now, I thought as I saw her.

At that moment, the DJ played *Lollypop*. Her and her girls made their way to the floor and began advertising a free fuck for the night. I was actually turned on but didn't let it show. Men surrounded them, even her new boyfriend was there thinking he had the pussy to himself.

"Let me know when you ready to go because you know who is here. I hate to jump stupid on that bitch because she doesn't know how to talk to you."

"I'm not running. We are here together. She wants my husband and not the other way around. So, she will be alright," I said.

"I'm going over here with the ZR click, you going to be ok for a few? I'll be back over to check on you."

"Go ahead, I'll be ok. We are at a party. We are not going to be guarding each other. You know how to act and dance, and so do I," I spoke with confidence.

"Don't let me catch a motherfucker in your face. You my wife and just because I may get high on some weed tonight doesn't mean I am not looking at you. We watch all things," Popcorn said as he walked off.

The DJ played the latest hits. No one jumped ignorant and I really enjoyed myself. I didn't dance, but I rocked to the beat and walked around. Out of the blue, Big Quack stopped the music, and yelled out, "Everybody having a good time? I said is everybody having a damn good time out here tonight?"

People screamed out, "Hell yeah. Turn the music back on!"

He continued to the rowdy crowd as they were pumped and ready for excitement, "Hold on. I'm going to play a few songs for a special lady out there tonight. You know who you are, but does he know who you are?" I laughed because it was funny as hell. I shook my head, for I knew who he was talking about, and it was the new girl. She was there. I felt Popcorn's glaze on me, for I was standing directly in the path of Big Quack's eyes. "The first song is called *Is You Wet Yet?*"

A lot of women screamed out, "My ass wet!"

Right before the song came on, he began flicking his horse tongue back and forth. He wiggled it so fast; I could barely see it and I wasn't drinking. He brought back memories of the way his fat ass tasted my pussy. Shit, I was squirming, but the women became ecstatic as his wide tongue excited them. I, on the other hand, turned my head so my husband did not see the look on my face.

Popcorn rushed over and twirled me around. He grabbed me by the elbow and practically dragged me to the dark part of the party. He did not appear high anymore but outraged. I had no idea what was going on and I didn't know why my husband was acting the way he was. Once we were away from everyone, he questioned in a tone that was unlike him, "What the hell is that all about?"

"I don't know what you are talking about. What was what about?" I questioned back.

"That fat fuck was looking at you when he did that shit. I saw his eyes. I saw how he stopped you before you got to me. What the fuck going on at that damn restaurant? What the fuck he means by does he knows who you are? Is he eating your pussy or are you sucking his dick?" Popcorn said with jealousy as he approached me in my face.

"No. He was probably doing that at the girl standing beside me. She is the new girl. The one he is fucking. He told me that much today," I stated to calm him down.

"What the fuck is he doing telling you about a woman he is fucking unless y'all talking about fucking? What the hell you doing talking any damn way when your ass supposed to be working?"

"No, he said I couldn't fire her and then he said because she gives awesome head."

He looked me over, and said, "He's talking about you giving head?" Popcorn began looking for something on the ground.

"No, listen, baby" I said as I grabbed Popcorn by the collar to turn him toward me so he could hear me clearly. "I said he said the new girl gives awesome head, not me. I've never tasted him before."

He must have heard me, for he said, "Oh, don't make me put something on your ass because of that fat fuck. Your ass goes to work to work and not running your damn mouth, chopping it up with him. I'm going to split

52

your shit. Think it's a game, don't you? Try me and watch me cut the fuck up."

Popcorn walked off and left me standing there. He went over to his Zion Ridge click and began smoking and even drinking. I was almost angry, for I had not ever seen him so jealous and outraged about something that was not even happening.

Soon as I made it back to the crowd, Big Quack got back on the mic, and said, "Which one of you freaks looking for the Candy Man?" The women hollered like he was a superstar. I shook my head and did not look up, for I knew my husband was somewhere looking. Big Quack said, "I want to be somebody's Candy Man tonight."

The DJ quietly played the instrumental music of Candy Man. Out of the blue, Big Quack began rapping:
I want a pretty pussy that a woman can put in my face.
Open wide so I can see what's all on my plate.
Her pussy juice is the sweetness, I need to taste.
I'm hungry now so please girl don't make me wait.
I will take my time using my tongue not going too fast,
eating slow because the feeling I want it to last.
Don't believe me then put my tongue to work.
With every stroke and every pull your body will jerk.
Fat pussy, skinny pussy in my face not my hand.
I'm Big Quack, I eat it from the back, I'm your Candy Man."

The women yelled out at him louder. Big Quack had the DJ hold the microphone in front of him. What he did next made me gasp. He made his thumbs touch as he leaned his fingers over to cross each other, but leaving a gap for the mouth. Next, he brought his hands up to his mouth and began wiggling his pink tongue between the gaps. It was like he was licking around his hands as if they were the walls of a pussy. He made kissing and slurping sounds. It was funny because women went by what they heard, and men went by what they saw. That night, they acted up from the sight they saw.

"Your fat ass can be mine. Come eat this pussy I'll return the favor," one woman yelled out.

Between each statement he made, his massive tongue waved back and forth. Yes, you could get excited if he was your type. He gave the demonstration one final loud kiss, and said,

"I'm in the mood to eat up a good fuck, and I guarantee you would want only me tonight."

The DJ finished playing the song *Candy Man.* I wanted to go dance, but something told me not to. However, I kept my eye out for Shay and like clockwork; she was all in my husband's face. I eased over to them undetected.

"Excuse me, baby, you ready to go?" I politely said to my husband, completely ignoring her.

"We are having a conversation about seeing the baby," she spoke.

"This is not the place or time to discuss such issues. Wait until tomorrow when you both are sober."

"You need to have your own child before you can play momma to mine," Shay blurted out.

She had pulled that whore card too many times and I hated it when she did it, especially in front of my husband.

54

"I'll be one to mine when you can be one to yours. Because I know your child is looking at you like 'Damn, bitch, you going out again?' Or, better yet, 'Who's the new guy?'" I spoke with attitude.

"I got your bitch, bitch!" Shay sputtered out at me as she came toward me.

Popcorn got between us. I was ready for her shit for some odd reason. I wasn't in the mood for her, and, in fact, I was fed up with her not letting him see a child he paid for every two weeks. He couldn't buy the child anything unless she told him what to buy.

"She right as usual, Shay, that's why I love Shondia," Popcorn said.

Shay looked us over, and said, "You mixed looking bitch, you gonna get your issue. You are not perfect. I know it and you know it," she spoke as she walked back to the crowd.

"Ignore that bitch, Shondia. She just mad and I don't know why. We ain't ever been in a relationship."

"Honey, let us go back and enjoy the rest of the party before I get tempted to take you home and rape you," I teased.

"Since I am high and defenseless, you will win," Popcorn stated as he smiled that 'I'm going to fuck you good tonight' smile.

We went back to the party. I stood back in my usual spot while he went over to the ZR click. The DJ said, "This is for the niggas on Zion Ridge. We are going old school for you tonight."

Down For My Niggas, blared through the

speakers.

Zion Ridge was on the floor and in the middle was Big Quack. Of course, his goons surrounded him, even my husband. *Big Quack must be the hype man*, I thought as his big ass jammed harder than the rest of the smaller ones. He had to wipe his forehead with a towel from time to time. The next song was *Fuck the Club Up*.

I saw niggas come from everywhere. On the left, New Zion was deep with their click. They got in their own circle, although, they have many members no one out numbered Zion Ridge. On the right, Greensboro, Center Ridge, and the uptown niggas from the Quarters were in their own huddle. In smaller groups close by me were Antioch, Pleasant Grove, Ebenezer, and Spay. They all were clicked up and ready to fuck up anybody that jumped stupid with them. Then *Set It Off* rang loud as New Zion took over the floor doing their thing. The other communities did not jump stupid; they were laid back and chilling. Everyone told Big Quack they wouldn't start shit, but wouldn't take shit, either. Usually, when Zion Ridge gave their word, they tended to stick by it that much I did know.

Catching my attention was Chug. He wore all white and appeared to be high and drunk as usual. Loud as I could without causing attention to myself, I yelled out, "Chug! Chug! Over here!"

He looked up, walked over, and spoke, "What's up, cuz?"

"I thought I saw crazy girl Michelle here," I warned him.

"Yeah, her crazy ass here because I told her fat ass to come. I have to nut tonight. I know her ass want some of the young dick," he spoke as he drank some more out his cup.

"Your ass already drunk and can barely stand. What the hell can she do with drunk dick?" I spoke. In all my days, Chug always had some type of woman at his side. He had never discriminated and on some occasions, he lowered his standard just to get pleased. "Just keep that bitch from me. I still haven't forgotten what the fuck she did. She lucky I don't get any 397 girls to blitz on her big ass," I spoke as I looked at him.

"Wait, yo ass don't party like we do. Why the fuck you here, anyway? Clubs and parties furnish their own women. Popcorn should have told yo ass to stay at home. If I were..."

I cut Chug off, and said, "If you weren't so weak, that bitch would not have punk you out that night at McDonald's. That's what you were going to say, right?"

Chug smiled as he spoke the jester, "See, that shit ain't funny. I'm a small ass bastard and have you seen the big bitch. You probably told her that I bought the last fucking hamburger and fries, and her ass was hungry."

We laughed with great hilarity before I asked, "If her weight bothers you, why stay? You are always calling her a big bitch."

"She is a big bitch. I call it like I see it. She is a big bitch who has money, her own ride, she can't have a lot of my time, gives awesome head, and the pussy isn't too bad, either. Oh, did I mention the big bitches are the biggest freaks?" Chug spoke with more humor.

"You don't need to be using her," I said defensively.

"True, but women love dog ass niggas. I'm a dog ass nigga. I told her that I am young and I'm no damn good. I told her that I love pussy and getting my dick sucked. She doesn't want to listen. Guess she thinks she can change a nigga like me. But look at her. She sprung on the tongue."

"Ugh," I spoke with disgust.

Chug kept on talking like he wasn't upsetting my stomach. "She trying to be faithful to me and she has a husband. Now, that is fucked up," Chug spoke as he hollered at women passing by us with no regards to his lady friend.

"Yeah, that is fucked up," I spoke.

"She is a fuck partner to me and that is it. Bitches like her get emotionally attached, especially with a nigga like me. Michelle should know that I don't give my heart to bitches, especially married bitches. I learned that shit a long time ago," Chug said as he did a two-step.

"Bitch, you just a little over nineteen and a long time ago my ass. How old were you, twelve?" I spoke, and we laughed.

"Funny, motherfucker, very funny. Ain't no twelve-year-old hung like me," was his response. I looked toward Michelle, who was staring in our direction. He assumed like I did that she was trying to see who I was. "Let me go and warm her up for later on. I can't keep staying over here. You have your own problem."

"And what is my problem?" I asked to see if he knew what he is talking about.

In a sassy tone, he said as he pointed, "Ex-lover, baby momma."

He was absolutely right. *Dance Like a Stripper* came on and bitches started taking off clothes left and right. I kept turning my head to find Shay because it was an opportunity for her to get my husband's attention. There, in the middle, was Shay. I was turned on and grossed out at the same time by her actions. She was already half naked. When the song started, she pretended to undress what was left of her clothes as she rolled her ass. She had a way to make a motherfucker go off and I, for one, wanted to take her ass home.

I moved over a few feet to see who was behind her. It was my husband and his back was turned. He turned around just when Shay made her ass shake the dumb way. I wanted to put the ass in my face as I did earlier. Popcorn had his eyes closed. She was all on my husband, rolling her ass all around. Then, he put his hands on her hips the way he had done me many times.

The bitch knew what the fuck she was doing. When she saw me, she disappeared into the crowd. Being that her boyfriend was from uptown and had family from Pleasant Grove, they were behind him as he made a fast pace toward my husband.

"Oh, hell no," I said as I started in a trot.

Her boyfriend beat me to him. He tapped Popcorn on the shoulder and once Popcorn turned around to see who it was; her boyfriend stole on him dead in the jaw. I would have thought that High Point would be with ZR, but they didn't. I saw guys that Popcorn talks to on everyday basis against him like I said it would be, and that shit pissed me off. To my left, bitches were against each other. *I guess it doesn't matter, friends or not. It's about your town and how you represent it*, I thought as people began to yell.

The DJ got on the mic, and said, "Big Quack said…" Then, he played the chorus of, "Y'all better not fight in this bitch." He stopped the music, and said, "If you fight, you go to jail."

That did not stop people. Popcorn and Shay's boyfriend were on the ground. He was on my husband from what I could see, and then Popcorn got on top of him. I thought that Shay would try to fight, me but she was getting in the Big Quack's caddy when I finally saw her again.

Returning my focus back to the situation at hand, Popcorn swung like he was out of it. I could not tell who was who, but I did know that Ebenezer and Spay was nowhere to be seen. On the other hand, I did see was the DJ packing up his shit and cars leaving.

I heard someone call out, "They done called 5-0!"

"Popcorn, come on, let's go! Let's go!" I screamed out.

My husband acted like he did not hear me. Thankfully, some of his friends separated him and Shay's boyfriend. I ran to my car and pulled to the edge of the driveway. Popcorn and Chug got in and they were bloody as hell. I drove off toward home and when I passed Major Brown Road, the police had their lights on. It seemed to be four carloads as they turned left on Zion Ridge.

"Honey, you ok!" I questioned as I drove faster.

"Hell yeah. That motherfucker better be glad someone pulled me off him or his ass would be catered by now," my husband spoke, full of excitement.

"You glad you could have killed him?" I asked.

"Yeah, that fucker came at me. When I turned around, his bitch was all on me. What the fuck was I to do? I wasn't focused on her. I was dancing," Popcorn said.

"So, he hit you because you were dancing with your baby momma?" I questioned.

"It wasn't like that. Nobody was fighting over no stanking ass Shay. I know what you getting at. It's the principle of the matter. He came at me wrong. I wasn't going to stand for that," Popcorn said as I went around the steep curve.

"You were fighting over her," I kindly reminded him, for I didn't want to get angry.

"No, the fuck we weren't. How the hell you gonna tell me who or what the fuck I was fighting about when I am the one he swung on?" my husband said loudly.

"I didn't do anything tonight, I chilled. I was there. I know how it played out. You, on the other hand, were partying and I didn't like it. You had your back turned. When you felt her or something, you turned around and began dancing. She was all on your dick, rolling her ass all around, and then you put your hands on her hips. That is when I started walking over, but her boyfriend beat me to it. Shay took off running and he stole on your high ass. I thought she would use the chance to fight me, but she didn't. I saw her leave in the car with Big Quack."

"She left in Big Quack's caddy?" he asked in astonishment.

I gave him an evil look. I was telling him how the fight started and all he could worry about was who she left with. It made me angry to see her doing that to get back at me, but I held my own. Becoming subject to quietness, I drove to our driveway. When I stopped the car, I got out and slammed the car door. I unlocked the house door, stripped, and got in the bed. I left him and Chug alone in the car. The way he acted was uncalled for and I wondered if he really had feelings for my slutty bitch.

CHAPTER 4

The next morning, I awoke to hushed talking. It sounded like Popcorn was whispering to someone. I didn't remember Chug staying over and I could not think of anyone else other than Chug to be there. Easing up off the bed, I carefully placed my ear to the bedroom door to hear in the living room. I concluded that it was Popcorn. *Why was he talking where I cannot hear him?*

I heard him say, "Why the fuck you leave with Big Quack? He kin folk and he in the same hood I'm in. Save the damn excuses, I don't care about that shit you talking."

From the question, I knew then that he was on the phone with Shay. *But why talk secretively?* My heart began beating faster as it crumbled. I was in my own home eavesdropping on my husband. As I shook my head to halt the tears from falling, I noticed that he wasn't talking.

Finally, I heard him say, "I know I'm married. Your job is to take care of the baby you never let me see. Fuck that shit. Just don't be fucking in the same hood I'm in. Go to Center Ridge or some damn where else." He was quiet, as he spoke in a more aggressive tone, "I know you're grown and don't give a damn about that. Don't worry about my wife, that's my job. I got this. You worry about sucking." He was quiet again, and laughed before saying, "Yeah, I bet you can. Come? I can come. Remember, I had it first." He started laughing again. I opened the door, and he said, "Ok. You said your peace, goodbye." He hung up the cell, and said, "What?"

"Who are you telling to come somewhere?" I

mocked.

"Shay called to apologize about last night."

"Oh. Was that all she said, for you were laughing as I came in?" I asked to see if he would tell the truth.

"Basically, I don't want to talk about her." I felt like he was brushing me off as he tried to change the subject. No way was I going to let him lie to me like that and get away with it. He defensively said, "You got mad over bullshit last night. I wanted some pussy last night, but you were tripping on some bullshit. You also know damn well I wasn't fighting over her. It wasn't even about her."

How could you say this was bullshit? Anything that involves you or I is not bullshit, I thought as I looked at him. He smiled, and I said, "Yes, it was? Oh, you think this is bullshit?
Popcorn, I don't trip over bullshit unless it's my shit, and you are my shit," I angrily spoke.

"No, you're twisting my words and you bad about that shit. For the record, it is bullshit in a sense, but since you want to put it out there like that, yes, it's bullshit to the fullest. Fuck her and this bullshit you talking about."

"Is that what the two of you were plotting to do? Being that you told her that you had the pussy and how she doesn't need to mess around in the same hood and how..."

"So, you are eavesdropping now? You want to accuse me of plotting on pussy I have had before? Tell me, have you ever fucked Big Quack before? You want to ask questions, now answer that one."

"No, I never fucked Quack before! Stop trying to change the subject. Besides, he has never asked to fuck me

64

and what does that have to do with this?" I inquired.

"Everything! You accusing me of plotting on pussy from Shay? Shit, you around your pussy eating boss almost every day. How the fuck am I to know what that wide tongue motherfucker isn't after you?" Popcorn stated as he glared me in the eye.

"To begin with, you don't! I have never given you any reason to think otherwise. I'm not in the living room whispering to a bitch, you are. When I met and married you, any games I might have played subsided. I am in this marriage to win it, but you have me thinking that you and she have something more going on."

"How the hell is that? She always asking about you or trying to tell me how to handle you," Popcorn asked, clueless.

"Because you and her boyfriend were fighting over her," I stated.

"Shondia, yo ass need glasses. He came and stole on me, so how the hell did that make us fight over her? He hit me! His ass sucker punched me!" Popcorn screamed.

"Yes, he did hit you, but it was because she was all on you throwing her ass. Shit, I was going to come over there, too, but he beat me to it."

"She was not. She was not on me like that. Don't you think that I would know if her ass was all on me? Hell, you were there. I wouldn't pull some hoe shit like that. I value my marriage, and she is not what I want," he pointed out to me.

"So, if I wasn't there, it would have been ok for you and her to dance that way?" I asked to see what he would say.

"No. Who do I come home to, huh? Who do I love? I don't want her ass on me because one thing I know and that is she is drama. That is something we don't need."

"You say you love me, and you come home to me, to me that is irrelevant. Coming home to me and dancing the way you did has nothing to do with it and, most of all, honey, I was there. You put your hands on her hips, too," I mentioned.

"One, I do love you. Two, I come home to you. Three, no the fuck I didn't fight over her. Four, you're not just a lie, but a damn lie. I only put my hands on hips to pull ass back to me for fucking. Was I fucking?" Popcorn sparred at me.

"Maybe not then, but you another damn lie" I sparred back, for I had never spoken like that to him at all. Popcorn glared at me. He knew that I was getting fever in my mouth as I spoke to him. "If you want to fuck her, do it and watch what I do," I blurted out to him.

"What the hell did you say?" Popcorn asked.

"I said if you want to fuck her do it and watch what I do. You might be good, but I can be better and if you..."

I didn't finish the announcement before he hit me. I didn't know if he didn't know he flexed because he looked shocked. However, I cared not. I slapped him back and it was on. When I hit him, he got angry. I swung connected most of my punches on him. Seeing that I was not letting up, he pinned me down. Finally, between grasping for breaths, he spoke, "Look, baby. Look at me! Turn your damn, head to look at me!" Tears were all over me. I didn't want to face him, but I did, anyway. More tenderly than ever, Popcorn stated, "If you think I disrespected you in any way, I am sorry. Damn, baby, I am sorry. To me, I was not going to look like a pussy or a punk. Please, believe me. I would never be dancing with her and especially with my hands on her as you say. If I did, I didn't know it was her because my eyes were closed. It wasn't until he came over that made me open my eyes. By then it was too late, the punk bitch hit me. End of story. As for her on the phone, I was whispering because I did not want to wake you. I told her to worry about the baby and stop all that hoe shit, but she started throwing you up in my face. I told her that you are my wife, and I will worry about you."

To be blunt, I responded, "Let me go. Just let me go."

"Did you not hear what I just said to you?" He probed my face for an answer.

"Yes, I heard you," was all I could say.
"You going to try and fight me again if I let you up, Shondia?" he asked. I was quiet for a moment because I really had no idea what I was going to do if he let me up. He could only assume that I would not hit him again. He knew that I was thinking about what to do, therefore, he asked again in a sterner tone, "Shondia! Are you going to try and fight me again if I let you up?"

"No! Just let me go. Just let me up so we can talk like adults and not children," I cried out. Popcorn let me go and I desperately wanted to hit him again, but he and I need to resolve our marital problems better than that. If we continued to fight every time we got into it, we would forever be going through the motions. Taking my time to look at him, I said, "I know you love me, but I am a woman. As the laws of nature have it, we women look at the glass half full while; you men look at the glass half empty."

My husband surely did not understand what I was saying because given the impression of his facial features, he was lost. I smiled. He lowered his brows to squint his eyes to say as he laughed, "Huh? Speak English. I don't have that Nanih Wayia education like yours; mine comes from Louisville High School."

"In other words, we both have our own perception of looking at the situation. I see two men fighting over a woman because the two of you were dancing. You, on the other hand, say you were fighting because you have to defend your honor and if you didn't, you would appear to be a weak man? Correct?" I asked.

"Yeah, you right. Baby, let us agree to disagree. You are going to see it your way and I am going to see it mine. We will be forever at it if we don't kill it now."

He was right. I was not going to back down and neither was he. My husband used his hand to wipe away my tears. I, in my own selfishness, cried the more. Popcorn, being who he was, tried to make me smile by speaking, "How about giving me some of that pussy I didn't get a chance to get last night?"

The ball was in my court, and I kindly said with a little laughter, "Can't. Big Quack has me doing inventory today so we can order needed material for this week."

"On a motherfucking Sunday? His fat ass won't be there, but he wants you to be there," My husband squabbled.

"It's my job. He being there or not matters not, inventory has to be done. You are welcome to come and watch me as I do my job," I asked, hoping he would come for I didn't think he had ever been to the restaurant.

"Sure, why not? Big Quack may try to stop by thinking you are alone and then get his feelings hurt," my husband stated as he got up.

"Big Quack may come by. I would be surprised if he did because he usually never comes by on inventory day. I do the inventory, and he orders what I write down, and that's that."

We both stood up and he kissed me on the forehead. "We good, baby?"

Smiling, I replied, "Yeah, we good. I don't want you to be whispering on the phone anymore. If you want to talk to her, talk to her with me around, that way there won't be any room for misconceptions"

"Baby, please, stop using big words." Popcorn laughed as he looked at me with happiness.

"I can't help it, but I will try and stop," I said as we kissed.

I got up and showered. When I walked out, Popcorn was already ready. I was stunned because he was almost always the last to be ready. "Well, this is a first," I stated.

"Yeah, whatever. Damn, that waitress outfit looks fucking good on you."

"Stop it. Men have to tip me, plus, I look like this every day I go to work, you just don't pay attention."

"Shit, tip hell. I'll give them a tip."

"What will the tip be?" I asked out of curiosity.

Laughing nonstop, Popcorn said, "Don't holler at Popcorn's wife if you want to live another day."

We chuckled hard at his statement. Getting up from the chair, Popcorn placed his hands on my hips and held me passionately from behind. It was a wonderful feeling to be held by the man that loved you more than you could have ever imagined. It actually gave me great joy to be with him, and to be loved by him and only him.

Sizing me up like the prize that I was to him, Popcorn gave me that smile as he twirled me around to truthfully say, "Shondia is it just me or do you need a new uniform. Either the one you have on now is hugging your body in too many places or you are filling out before my eyes."

"It's the same one I had on yesterday."

Shaking my head as I smiled was my approving of him finally noticing my work outfit. A horn blew and put a dent in our sexual build up moment. We peeped out the living room window and saw that it was Chug. I saw that it was Michelle's truck and chances were that she was with him.

"Damn, it's Chug with that married woman," I said to Popcorn.

"She has a nice ass truck."

"Nice ass truck or not, there's something about her I don't get," I spoke, leaving Popcorn to lure out the window.

I walked out the door first and Popcorn was behind me. Michelle and Chug got out her truck. He walked closer to us while she squats at the door of the truck as if to remove something by the fender. She had on black boots, a mini skirt with her thong showing, a strapless shirt, a locket, and her usual head full of curls.

"Damn, she big, but not that bad looking from this view," Popcorn whispered to me as we steadily approached the truck. I nudged him slightly in his side as Chug walked over to us.

"Chug what the hell you doing bringing her here? I don't need any shit to jump off from her husband. This isn't a meeting house for y'all. I already told you what to do if I were you." I talked loud enough for her to hear.

In a low tone, Chug said, "Sshh, calm the fuck down, Shondia. She with me and I had her to bring me out here to chill for a few. Hell, I need some money, so I got to spend some time with her."

"You have a job. You work at the Pig for seven dollars, and some change an hour," I said in reply.

"See, even yo ass know that I don't make that much."

"As long as the bitch doesn't cross me, we good and I ain't forgotten about that night at McDonald's, either."

"Popcorn, tell your wife to calm the fuck down so I can get some money out this bitch."

"Baby, chill out. She didn't know who you were. Now, she knows you well," my husband said to me.

"Ok, only because you asked me to."

Chug waved for her to come closer, and she did. Wearing a big smile, Michelle said, "Hi. It is finally good to meet you both."

"Hi," was all I could say.

"You're handsome" Michelle said as she quickly

71

put her hands over her mouth as if it came out.

"And he's taken, like yo ass," I harshly said.

"Damn, Shondia, if she thinks Popcorn is cute, he must be cute. I personally think he looks like shit, but who am I to judge?" Chug spoke as he and Popcorn tussled for play.

"I didn't mean to offend you, but if you think it, you should speak it," she replied as her eyes never left my husband.

"Like I said, he's taken like yo ass. So, if you're going to watch a married man, watch yours," I said to put her in remembrance that she is married.

She walked off and threw her ass all over the yard. Popcorn looked at me and snickered. I left them all alone while I called Big Quack. There was no way in hell I was leaving that bitch out there with my husband. Peeping over my shoulder, I saw the two were still playing as another car pulled up across the street to Aunt Rose's brick house.

"Run your mouth," Big Quack answered.

"I will not be able to come in today."

"You know we have to do inventory."

"I know, but can't I come in and do it earlier?"

"What's wrong with today?" he questioned.

"I have company and can't leave, that's why."

"Sure, you have company. You probably in the bed and fucked all night, that is why you can't come in today," Big Quack said with humor.

"No, you probably fucked all night and can't do it. That's why you want me to come in," I responded.

"No, I got my dick sucked and ate too much

chocolate pussy pie last night. That's why I can't come in," Big Quack said as he laughed.

"Uh, you didn't have to tell me."

"Ok, come in early tomorrow morning. When I say early, I mean early. I don't mean five minutes before you start. I don't mean thirty minutes before you start, around two hours before you open. We have a lot of shit to order, been behind."

Laughing I replied, "Ok, bye."

Popcorn walked back over to me, and asked, "Baby, you ready?"

"No, I took off today."

"What?"

"Yeah, I took off today. There's a big bitch here that will fuck anybody, and she won't fuck on my watch."

Popcorn laughed, and said, "She's not going to be fucking me. I love the pussy I get at home."

"You better love the head, too."

"Damn it, boy," was his reply.

They all went across the street while I went in the house to change clothes. When I walked out, almost the entire Zion Ridge click was out there lifting weights. I usually didn't hang around them, but something about Michelle didn't sit right with me. I was going to watch her, for I didn't trust her and it was not because she was married.

When I made it to the porch, Popcorn was on the weights and the other two were spotting him. I loved the way his muscles popped up as he pushed up on those bars. Smiling, I could not help but be happy that all of him belonged to me. A few seconds later, a horn blew. It was Big Quack.

Chug said, "What the hell Quack wants with his nosy ass?"

Big Quack came over, and I said, "What? You thought I was lying about having company, so you had to ride up this way?"

"No. You're not big on lying because you love to make money. I was just coming to see what kind of company you were having," he responded.

"Big Quack, if you're not nosy," I joked.

Popcorn got up and his other friend got on the bar to do his sets. Big Quack said, "She pretty as hell. Shondia, you didn't tell me you had a beautiful woman here."

Chug spoke up, and said, "She with me, but my big bitch will do anything I tell her. Ain't that right, big bitch?"

"Fo sure, my Chug. What you want me to do?" she asked.

"Now, that's the shit I'm talking about. You tell her what you want, and she does it?" Big Quack said with amusement.

"Hell yeah, if I pull my dick out, she'll suck it and if I tell her to suck all y'all's dick, she will," Chug said.

"I know one dick she better not put in her mouth," I said as I stared her up and down.

Popcorn elbowed me to calm me down, but he didn't know that one bitch recognized another. Using a cocky tone, she raked my husband's body up and down before saying, "I love sucking dick, and the balls are a treat. I'm a bad bitch and I know that I am a bad bitch. I don't mind drinking him up and fucking him down. One night with me and I promise your fuck life won't be the same. The only way I don't put that dick in my mouth, Chug don't tell me to and he don't want me to."

The others laughed as if it were funny. Popcorn said, "Big bitch, we won't have that problem because you ain't sucking my dick."

The look she gave him said, "Really?"

With courage and readiness, I said, "When you put my husband's dick in your mouth, I promise yo ass won't be able to swallow. I will rip your throat out and put a feeding tube in."

Popcorn and the rest of ZR laughed harder, but my husband knew that I was for real. You didn't fuck with a bitch from the sticks of 397. Shit, my ancestors scalped motherfuckers for a living and peeling her wig back wouldn't be anything but a thang for me.

Popcorn knew as well as Chug that I did not play about my man and my money. Glancing around, I saw a small brick on the ground a few paces from me. It was big enough to fit in my hand because if she attempted to touch my husband I was knocking her big ass out.

"Shondia, fuck that shit you talking about. My big bitch is a freak and that is why we get along so well. She don't want Popcorn, at least because we here," Chug said as everyone laughed. He continued, "But she knows I'll eat her asshole and suck all the juice out that pussy ain't that right, big baby? Tell them I will take yo ass to another level."

Michelle laughed as if it was cute. Before I met her I

would have given her a chance to be with my cousin, but to know that she didn't have any moral sense about her, I felt he needed to dump her and go on to boot camp.

Seeing her gawking in my direction, I responded, "She can suck and fuck whoever she wants but my husband's dick, she better get her thoughts off of it."

Popcorn walked closer to me, and said, "Baby, I'm right here with you. You're all I need in a woman." I didn't reply because when I was not around there was no telling how he really was. I could only assume.

Chug laughed as he retorted, "My big bitch so bad, you can bend over, and she can suck your dick and your balls from the back at the same damn time." The men hollered like they were at a ball game. Chug went on to say, "That shit is unique. You don't learn that shit overnight; I tell you. That's why I can't leave her nut drinking, dick sucking, and any hole you want it in ass alone." The men went hysterical. They jumped around like little boys in a candy store. My own husband scratched his head and walked in a small circle as he laughed.

"My, my, oh my, a bitch after my own heart with no shame in her game," was Big Quack's humongous reply as he licked his lips.

"Shit, y'all think I'm bullshitting? That night she did me like that, my legs couldn't stay there. I was shaking and all my toes were pulling off my feet. Her suction is as powerful as a Hoover vacuum cleaner," Chug said to keep the laughter going.

"I'll give her fifty dollars to suck anybody's dick out here right now like that! I have to see this bad bitch in action. I have to see this shit live and in person," Big Quack said.

"Shit, she can suck anybody's dick she wants. She's grown, but she gonna suck mine first. There is no damn way that I go second. Hell no! I'm nobody sloppy seconds. When she demonstrates her extra curricula activity, then you give me the fifty dollars for her ass to suck dick. The catch is, can't none of their dicks be bigger than mine," Chug said.

"Man, ain't nobody gonna compare dicks. That's some gay ass shit," Big Quack spoke.

"She don't care if you have a small dick, Quack. She'll find that nut and get it out you, and if that don't work, let her teabag your ass," Chug said as everyone laughed at his words.

"You can say it's small all you want. I bet that any woman I fuck off with will let me get it again because my big ass can bang her down, then eat her up," Big Quack said as he laughed.

"Come here, baby, these motherfuckers are illiterate and need to see a show," Chug said.

Michelle got up and walked over to Chug. He wrapped his arms around her, and she smiled as if she was Beauty Queen in a pageant. "Yes, baby" she stated.

"You see that fat bastard right there?" Chug said as he pointed to Big Quack.

"Yes, why?" she asked.

"He don't think you are a bad ass bitch," Chug replied with a scheming smile.

"He don't? You didn't tell him who I am? You

didn't tell him just how naughty and how I go loco when that nut shoots out?" she replied in a coy tone.

"No, he doesn't think you that bitch. Think we need to show him and the rest of these motherfuckers how a real woman sucks a man's dick," Chug spoke as she noticeably acted hot. She smiled and looked my way. I gave her an attitude as I stared at her. Chug replied, "Big bitch, let's show them what you can do right here and right now, me and you. What the fuck you say to that shit?"

"I say let me do my thang, my Chug" Michelle spoke with a tease.

"Y'all nay sayers form a tight circle, like a football huddle, to block the road and hurry up," Chug spoke with haste.

Without warning, Chug faced the weights, pulled his pants down, spread his legs, and spread his arms out on the weight's bench bar. The excited men blocked the view as they were told as she got on her knees right under Chug's ass. I started laughing because she let all know that she wasn't about shit.

I figured she must have been doing it right, for the men were tightly fitted together. There was no way anyone could see, but by chance my husband and I were standing where we could see her back and Chug's butt cheeks. The men hyped her up as she tugged on Chug. I couldn't see his dick, thank God, but I could see her acting like an animal trying to pull the prey to its death. Looking over, I saw Popcorn looking like the rest of the men. Even Big Quack acted up as he spoke with mere joy, "Damn, she's sucking balls and all in her damn mouth. You big, mouthed bitch!

Shit, she's doing that shit! She's doing that shit! Ooh fucking wee, her ass is really doing that shit! Fuck, she making my dick hard."

I could tell that she loved the attention, for she let go of the dick. She spread his cheeks and licked up and down his small ass. At one point, she attempted to bury her face in his ass. The men went ballistic as they howled and focused in on her more. Michelle took him back in her mouth and pulled countless more times from the back. Chug moaned and encouraged her more, by saying, "My big bitch, get that nut out this dick and put my man milk on your face."

When he said that, she mumbled and slurped like she didn't know what she was doing. Seconds later, Chug spoke, "Damn, that's good! Do that shit again. Fuckers, watch me spray this bitch with homemade white frosting."

Quickly, she covered her face with his semen and then kissed the dick head. The men laughed and rubbed their dicks, for Chug did cum all over her just like he said he would. She turned around and faced me with a crafty look.

Chug moved from his picture pose and pulled up his pants. With Chug's nut still over her face, she smiled and said to Popcorn, "Whose dick next?"

Before he could say anything, I responded for him with an evil glare in my eyes, "Suck it and I'll make your ass kiss the grass."

"Shondia, she's not going to suck his dick. We not getting paid for Popcorn's married ass dick," Chug spoke raspy.

"Well, I'm letting the big bitch know ahead of time just in case she gets the urge," I said to him as I glared at her.

Popcorn pulled at my arm for us to walk off. As soon as I turned my back, I heard her say, "For her to act like that, Chug, I'll suck his dick for free."

I didn't ask her to repeat what she said because I reflexed quicker than I ever imagined. That brick was in my hand as I blitzed back through the crowd to hit her. I cold cocked her with the brick on the side of her face. Her big ass fell face first on the ground just like I told her she would.

Blood and teeth went everywhere. That did not stop me. I continued hitting her. Big Quack and the rest of the click pulled me off her big ass. Through all the commotion, I told them to let me go. I looked at her lying on the ground. My boss looked at me and shook his head with a grin on his face. I know he was stunned that I acted in such a way. "Now, wake that big bitch up, Quack. I'm on some boss bitch shit, talking about sucking my husband's dick. Let the sticky mouth bitch try it now!" Some laughed and some were flabbergasted to see me go off like that. I couldn't even believe I did that, but I had to put her in her place. I took as much as I could. Just to think she came to my hood gazing after my husband, bitch had nerves, naw bitch had balls.

I saw T. with his cell phone open, recording and talking about how she got knocked out. He saw me and I spoke, "Put that shit on U Tube under How to knock a bitch out, Zion Ridge style."

Popcorn walked behind me. He twirled me around to say, "What the fuck! What the fuck you do that shit for!"

"She won't disrespect me about sucking and fucking you. That'll teach the big bitch not to talk about my dick in my face again. That lick would be the same lick your ass would have caught if you would have whipped the dick out for her to suck. Now, let her suck that for free."

My husband did not say another word. I truly did not give him time to. I was so angry about everything; consequently, I went to bed.

CHAPTER 5 (September)

My thoughts roamed. I was in a suite that I didn't recognize. It was very bright, candles were lit all around, and a hint of sex filled the atmosphere. The room was like no other and, honestly, very intriguing. I thought *I don't know where I am, and this room does not come to mind. Is this some type of honeymoon present that Popcorn has for me because I used to tell him all the time that I should be pampered like a princess and treated like a queen.*

Smiling, I went over and peeped outside. When I moved the curtain, I noticed that I was on the top floor at the Home Gate Inn Hotel on Highway 15/25 at the bypass. No cars passed by, and the day appeared to be wonderful and bright. "I've never been here before and I don't remember the day ever looking like this," I said.

When I walked further into the room, I opened the door and saw a white sofa. I wanted to turn around, but something told me to wait, and I did. Hearing a noise, I poised myself against the wall as my eyes took in the vision. There, as if I was not there, was my husband and Michelle. I wanted to snap, but I could not move. It was as if I was forced to watch a movie I did not want to see.

Everything I tried did not help. With my eyes open wide and no voice, I watched in dismay. Popcorn, with his lean body, sat back on the sofa chair naked with his arms outstretched. His legs open as his penis stood at attention. The smile on his face was beyond phenomenal.

When I glanced in front of him, I saw Michelle in a purple, laced, two piece teddy looking like Barney. She stood before him with her hair in a bun, hands on her hips, and that cunning smirk. With all my might I tried to move, but something held my feet in place. I tried wiggling my body free from whatever was holding me, but that did not work.

I heard something soft. I couldn't understand what was playing because she started dancing in a slow grind. When she did that, I did not give a damn what was playing? I centered my eyes on that big bitch. As her hips swayed to and fro, my love began licking his lips as she moved closer to him.

How am I so close and they can't see or hear me? What is going on? What is this? I thought if it was a dream, I wanted desperately to wake up. I did not care to see him make her feel the way I felt when I was with him.

Taking her time, she eased closer to the prey on the couch. He stood up and his penis was swollen and ready, just the way I knew it to be. She eased off her teddy bit by bit. When her outfit fell to the floor, Popcorn whispered, "You are a lot of women, but I can handle it."

At that point, I yelled out, "No! Don't do it!" but they never looked my way, and it did not stop Michelle from lying back on the sofa where Popcorn once sat. She parted her legs. Although, I could not see her pussy, I knew the fat cat was revealed. I half expected him to take her, but he did not. What I saw next grieved me sore like no other. He got on his knees in front of her and began tasting her. I gasped, for I could not believe it. Tears fell from my eyes.

From my view, he tasted her like he was in love. He took his time and from observing the motion of his head, he went slow and gentle. He made her feel the way he made me feel. She would, on occasion, put her hands on his hand and smash his head deeper into her pit. Michelle wrapped her legs around his head to hold the fulfillment in place. The big bitch put all her juices on his face, and he did not let up.

With dire need, I tried hollering out again, but that was to no avail. More than I ever I tried move because I was going to break up that shit. No way would he ever touch her and still have me. I could not take it. The scene was too hard to bear. I yelled again at the top of my lungs for what it was worth, "You promised to only taste me! You son of a bitch! You promised to only taste me!"

However, they ignored me. It seemed like the more I cried out for him not to do it, the more he took pleasure in doing it. The way his head wavered between her legs brought back memories. She, with her eyes closed and her mouth opened, called out for him stop in a go-ahead manner. He moved back, and she got up and patted him on the head. Popcorn smiled like a good dog.

She put her knees on the sofa and what a sight I saw. My husband divided her ass cheeks and licked her hairy asshole. A part of me wanted to die right then and there. He and I had never performed such a gruesome act. I knew it must have been a dream because he didn't eat assholes. I tried again to move by slapping my face, but nothing would move. For some reason, I was forced to watch my husband please another and it was hell doing it. My head would not move, and my eyes would not close. Realization set in. I must watch the encounter.

With tears all over my face, I took in the vision of him still eating her big ass out. It was not only the fact that Popcorn had never eaten my ass out, but there he was doing it to a woman that was not me. He was doing to her what a man should only practice with his wife. The more he licked her cheeks, the more she cried out, "Eat my ass. Yes, eat my big ass up, you ass eating bitch. Get full on my shit." The more he moved his head, the more her irritating voice reached my ears, saying, "Her ass doesn't taste near as good as mine. Yes, lick the ass walls and put the tongue in the hole just like you doing now. Eat it up and kiss her when you get home."

She acted like an ass eating coach for my husband. But that did not stop me from yelling out, "I'll fuck you up and, Michelle, your ass is mine! Bitch, do you hear me?" I knew she didn't, but I could not just stand there and not say anything. I had to get that off my chest because I was going insane watching them in action.

My thoughts were stopped by Popcorn. He rambles words I could not understand. I didn't know what happened, but he moved back, and she got up. Michelle whispered something and he sat on the sofa as he was before. His mushroom cap was in full upright position and ready for an attack.

She began massaging the slender muscle. With a pleasurable gleam in her eyes, she wobbled back and forth on the head. She licked him up and down and kissed his penis like she loved it. The more she sucked on him, the more he moaned with desire. I knew he was in another place because he closed his eyes and laid his head back on

85

the sofa.

From time to time, he fucked her mouth like he was mad, and she took it. She took his entire dick in her mouth and down her throat, for I heard gagging sounds. When she took his dick out her mouth, it was slimy and soaked with her spit. I sat there drenched with my weeping and sorrow as I witnessed my husband and another woman pleasing each other very intimately.

Jerking up as if something let me go, I breathed heavily, and tears had soaked my face. Placing my hand over my chest, I realized that it was a dream, and I was in bed. I felt so relieved to know that it was a dream, and it never happened. My throat felt sore, which I could only assume was from all the hollering I did in my dream. Looking around, I noticed that Popcorn was not with me. Looking on the night table, I saw his phone, but not mine.

The time on the clock was almost twelve. Sitting up straight in the bed, I heard Chug's voice in the living room. I knew he is talking to my husband, and I didn't care what he had to say about me knocking that bitch out. Putting on my house coat, I opened the bedroom door, and Chug hollered out as he laughed, "Laila, Laila, Laila Ali! You a bad motherfucker!"

I chuckled and smiled when I saw my husband. Going over to him, I sat in his lap and kissed him feverishly, for he didn't know how happy I was to see him.

"Damn, baby, you kissing like that? I need to take you back to bed," Popcorn spoke with joy.

"I love you and only you. Do you hear me, Popcorn? I am the woman for you," I spoke with joy and gladness.

"Yeah, baby, I know, and I love you even the more. You my wife and I'll be damned if I fuck this up," he spoke, for he must have felt a need to reassure me that he loved me.

"I know, and I am honored to be your wife and have my entire being for you and only you. No other man or woman can take away what we have for I won't let them," I said with seriousness.

"If you don't think that I will kill for mine, then let me assure you. Shondia, I will kill you and any man you fuck as long as you are my wife, and I am your husband. You, your pussy, and all belong to me and only me. Now, is that clear?" Popcorn said as he nibbled at my ear.

"Yes, baby," I seductively spoke.

"Y'all need to get a room." Chug said.

"You need to go home, we got a room," I said as Chug laughed. "Where you been hiding at anyway? I haven't seen or heard from you in about two weeks, what gives favorite cousin?"

"I've been laying low."

"Sure you not mad at me for hitting your freaky bitch in the mouth?"

"No, you good because she should have kept her mouth shut. But instead, she taunted you about your husband. You probably made the sucking better by knocking out a few teeth. I can understand if this bitch right here," Chug said as he tilted his head toward Popcorn.

"Hell no! I ain't that bitch" Popcorn spoke with humor.

"Like I said, I can understand if this bitch right here was a boyfriend, but he is a husband, and you don't say shit like that to a woman about her husband. Not in her face, anyway. I wanted to knock the bitch out, but I needed that nut first and make fifty dollars," Chug said as he sat back on the couch.

"Chug, you full of shit," Popcorn said.

"You act like you don't know the deal," Chug said to Popcorn.

He acted like he didn't know what Chug was implying, therefore, I asked, "What is the deal?"

As if I didn't know, he responded, "We don't dick'em, we trick'em."

They both laughed as Popcorn slapped hands. It was funny and after all the chaos Chug had put me through, I should have known. Popcorn smiled at me, and I said, "Well, she started it. I can't help it if she wants what God intended for her not to have, and that is my husband. Not hers, but mine. M-I-N-E. Mine."

"No, Shondia. You wrong. She only wanted to suck your husband's dick, you could have him back after that," Chug whispered in jester.

Getting up from Popcorn's lap, I picked up the pillow on the couch and hit him. He opened his eyes, picked up one, and we were pillow fighting. Popcorn got in on it and we double teamed Chug. Somewhere along the way, they both ganged up on me. We all laughed and played for a while.

"Hold up stop. Let me catch my breath," Chug spoke.

"See, smoking is bad for you," I exclaimed.

"No, smoking cigarettes are bad for you. I smoke weed. There is a difference."

"Back to what we were saying, she had it coming. I wished I had knocked her ass out for sure."

"You did knock her out along with a fractioned jaw," Chug spoke.

"Wow, I did that?"

"Shondia, you picked up a small ass brick and cold cocked the bitch. What the fuck you think was going to happen? Let me guess. You expected to hit the bitch, and she would get up shaking your hand? That shit was all on Face Book and some damn body put it on U Tube. Hell it had over five thousand likes, mostly from this side of Winston County" Chug said.

"Naw Chug, she expected to hit her then say, 'I'm sorry, I'm not usually this aggressive," Popcorn said to get on the joke about me.

"Well, a fraction jaw was not it. We were walking off and I heard her tell you that she will suck him for free," I said.

"How the hell you assume that?" my husband asked.

"You were there, were you not listening?" I asked him.

"Shondia, that is why you can't hang out with me. We joke like that all the time, and shit, there is no telling what the hell you may hear or see. I don't think she was real. I think she was only messing around. She more likely didn't mean it," Popcorn said in her defense.

89

"You like the big bitch, ball sucking show, didn't you? Don't lie. Tell me?" I asked, for I wanted to know.

"Well, it was pretty interesting, and I have not seen anything like it. Hell, I was hoping you were taking notes," Popcorn said with laughter. He spoke again before I could flex on him, "I'm playing, baby. I'm playing. It's a joke."

"Bet it was a joke," I spoke.

"She not going to press charges," Chug said.

"Fuck her if she do. I could counter charge for indecent exposure, trespassing, and my favorite, threating to break up a marriage," I added.

They laughed at me. Popcorn said, "You watch too much *Law and Order*, *CSI*, and some more shit to come up with those crump up charges. Black people don't sue for shit unless it's a hefty penny. Not for bullshit that happens every day all day."

"Seriously, there is a law for married people. It's a well-known case about that. I tell you right now, if a woman breaks up my marriage, I, the wife, can and will sue her ass," I said.

"How the hell you gone sue for something that didn't happen, that's fucked up? Unless you know something that I don't," Chug asked.

"Well, I stopped it before a lot of money could have been spent, didn't I?" I said as we laughed.

"You work today?" Chug asked.

"No, I am off today" I spoke.

"Wonder what her husband said about her face?" Popcorn asked to redirect our conversation back to Michelle.

"From my understanding, he didn't say a word. She told him she was in a fender bender with a girl and her face hit the steering wheel."

"The bitch is a good liar, I tell ya that," I said to Chug and Popcorn.

"The good news is that I officially left her alone."

"What? You left the dick drinker, ball sucker freak alone, why?" Popcorn asked as he joked with Chug.

"Well, I'm getting ready to leave for boot camp. I don't need any leftover baggage while I am away. Anyway, I thought about what you had been telling me about leaving her alone, Shondia, and you were right. I got on your cell and told her it's time for me to get the fuck on down from her. She begged and asked me why. I told her I didn't like her like that and how she is good, but I need a younger woman, and she wasn't it." We didn't say a word but continued to listen to Chug as he looked at me to say, "Plus, you knocked the bitch teeth out. You did her wrong, but you did what you had to do. When she talk, she spits on me, damn, I can't deal with that shit." We laughed at Chug because we knew he was exaggerating, but he continued to put on the show for us by saying, "Anyway, she cried on the phone and asked me where I was at. I told her meeting my main woman in the country. She said she wasn't going to let me go easy and I will pay for breaking my heart. I told her she knew damn well that I didn't have a heart in my chest and how I was only in it to get on my feet. She said she wants her phone back and everything else she gave me because I listen to other people and not her. I told her she could have the phone back and I didn't listen to my cousin. Then she asked me if you told me to do this because she wanted to suck Popcorn's dick? She asked if you were scared that he would enjoy her head job more than hers."

"I know she didn't. Chug, she better know that you will lie to me" Chug did not answer.

He continued. "I told her you didn't give a damn about how she wanted to suck her husband's dick. He faithful to her and she isn't concerned about your damn dick sucking tactics, and as for her not wanting us together, you can't blame her for what the fuck I do. She cried and cried, and I told her to dry that shit up because if she going to cry, I was going to hang up on her red eyed ass." Along with a smile, Chug shook his head, and said, "What I say that for? She began to cry harder. Finally, I said big bitch, you will always be my big bitch, but you knew like I knew that we were just fucking around. Then, she yelled out, 'For two years? I was not just fucking around with you. I fell in love you. I can't function without you in my life. Tell me what you want me to do it, and I will. No matter what it is, I will do it. Let me prove my love to you." I told her she wasn't supposed to get emotionally attached because that was the worst thing she could do. I told her I couldn't afford to get attached like that because she married and not many people leave their damn home for some outside nookie. And we both knew I couldn't take her home to momma. She would cut the fuck up on me for bringing a married woman to her house. She said she would divorce him to be with me, but I cut her off quick and told her she better stay with someone who will take care of her because I can't, won't and I

92

refuse too. Honestly, I can barely take care of myself and to add another mouth, shit I can't let that go down. Her ass better realize that the grass is greener with him and if she thinks it's green here, she is sadly mistaken. The grass is brown and dying fast. Anyway, she continued begging and finally I hung up on her, plus, I need to grow up some."

"Some, just some and not a lot?" I mentioned.

"Ok. I need to grow up a little" Chug spoke with humor.

"A little? And give me my damn phone."

"Shondia, I admit I need to grow up, let me finish talking," Chug spoke as he gave me my phone. A few seconds later, he said, "I had to let her go. She is not the type I would want for a woman. She will fuck who I tell her and damn, that is not what I want."

"You should have thought about that when you started fucking off with her," Popcorn said

"Right, you should have thought about that beforehand," I added.

"She too out there for me, not caring if someone saw us together or if her husband found out about mc."

"Really! She too far out there for me. I can't have my woman that damn gullible and letting other men see her get down. I'll whip the hell out of Shondia if she was a bitch like that."

"You saying that shit because I am here," I added to his sentence.

"Wouldn't mind if you could try that move, she did on Chug, though. How the hell she put all that in her mouth at one time is beyond me," Popcorn stated with a sexual smile.

"Keep on minding is all I can tell you. Shit, the way she swallowing all that at one time, I don't see how she does it, either. So, get your damn mind off it," I spoke.

We all laughed. Popcorn asked Chug, "When do you supposed to leave again?"

"Actually, it is today."

"Get the fuck out! Yo ass leave today! When? What time?" I exclaimed.

"Well, I need one of you to take me to the bus station in Meridian so I can get on down," Chug said as he looked at my husband and me.

Popcorn turned his head, and I knew that it was on me. Taking a deep breath, I spoke, "Fine, I will take you, but you better have my gas money."

"Damn, Shondia, a nigga leaving town to go learn how to fight like the white man, so you scared niggas won't have to, and you still asking for gas money?"

"I didn't tell your ass to go. As for me not going to fight, fuck that."

"Shit, they can try all they want, I will go missing," Popcorn said as he sat back further on the couch. Popcorn's phone rang. I already knew who the caller was because of the ringtone.

"Give it to me let me talk to her." My husband gave me the phone and I stepped outside.

"Hello, Shay. Why are you calling Popcorn?"

"Hey, bae. You forgot that you choose that dick over coming back to me, so if you want to play, fuck it, we will play," Shay said.

"Why won't you let him see the baby? He really wants to see her."

"Shit, you know like I know that I don't know who her daddy is. He is the only naïve one to take the fall."

"What do you want, Shay? What the fuck do you want?" I asked.

"I want you back with me. I hear about you trying to give Chug advice about his love life, but you can't do shit about your own."

"He is fucking off with a married woman, there is a difference."

"So, am I, Shondia, or you don't include what we do as fucking off?"

"No one knows that we have never stopped fucking, but we have to."

"Say what you want, you love me just the same."

"If it takes me tasting your good pussy again, fine, I will. I just want to please Popcorn, and he wants to see the Kenosha," I spoke to her.

"I tell you what, let me think about letting him see my baby Moochie," Shay said as she hung up.

That bitch was up to something. I went back inside and moments later, we heard a car outside. Popcorn and Chug didn't move. I got up, peeped out the door window, and noticed that it was the florist shop from uptown Louisville. "Why the hell is the florist shop out here?"

Chug and Popcorn both raised up to see what I was talking about. Seeing the van, Popcorn said, "Big Quack might be sending you something. Let him do it so I can make that yellow duck a bloody duck."

95

"That will be a lot of damn blood, Pop," Chug added as they both laughed.

I went to the door and the young, white lady asked, "Does Popcorn reside here?"

"Hey, girl, I'm Mr. Popcorn," Chug said.

She smiled and I nudged him out of the way to say, "Hi, I am his wife, and this is my cousin. Why do you wish to know of his residency?"

"This is for him." She handed me a huge snack bowl of candy corn, chips, juice, and a card that read, *same time, same place. P. S. The dick is damn good.*

Chug walked the girl back to the van as I still stood in the same place. I was furious and dazed. I believed I almost blanked out. When I turned around, Popcorn was standing in the door.

"What? I know damn well Quack didn't send that shit to you."

To ignore him, I walked past him. Once the door was closed, I yelled, "No, motherfucker! The shit's for you. What the hell is going on and you better not lie!"

"What the hell you talking about! Ain't shit going on, on my end. You better bring your voice back down."

Without saying a word, I handed him the card. He read it and smiled. I tried to knock his head off before I realized it. Popcorn grabbed my wrist before I could make a good connection to his body. He twisted my arm back and I gave all I had to strike him.

It was no use. My husband was too strong to be skinny as he was. We broke the lamp as we rolled back and forth on the couch. Each time I got an opening I hit him, but he did not hit me back. When we fell on the coffee table that did not stop us.

Suddenly, I heard the door open, and Chug yelled out, "What the hell!" Chug got between us and broke up our fight. We struggled for breath as we stood with Chug in the middle.

"Shondia! I don't know who the hell sent this. The shit is funny. Where have I been? Huh? Just where the hell have, I been? I'm always where you can find me! Either at work or at home."

"As for you, this card says you been fucking," I hurled out the accusation.

"Someone is playing a joke on me, and I find it funny because I know who I am fucking, and I know where all the hell I'm at all times. How can you believe what a fucking card says over me, your husband?" Popcorn said.

"I know where the hell you claim to be, but I'm not in your pocket all the time, am I? See, yo ass is the last one I would expect to fuck up! Yo ass! How the hell will someone send a good dick card, and you don't know, tell me that?" I asked.

"Shondia, are you serious? You really think I am fucking up on you? You done lost your rabbit ass mind to think that I would mess up our marriage for some outside pussy. Especially pussy I didn't know I was getting."

"I really don't think so, but who would send you shit like this if it weren't true? Who else would know how good your dick is since I am the only one you've had since we met?" I questioned.

"Shondia, I haven't had anyone but you and before

97

you I wasn't a damn saint. I fucked on a regular basis and pussy was not an issue to me. So, tell me why would I hurt you? I made you my wife, not those bitches," Popcorn said with much sincerity in his tone.

Tears were in my eyes as well as on my hand as I wiped them back. So much flowed through my mind and the last thing I needed was for him to see me cry. Making sure my face was turned, the tears flowed more freely. I made the mistake when I sniffled.

"Baby don't cry. Shondia baby, please, don't cry. You know it hurts me to hear you cry. That shit rips at my heart when you are sad," Popcorn said as he walked around Chug to wipe my tears like he did on our wedding day.

"May I say something?" Chug said as we both looked at him. "Y'all better than this bullshit. Breaking up ya furniture and scrapping like you don't love each other. What the hell is really going on? But I think that this could be Shay. I'm sure she has heard about you hitting Michelle. What a perfect opportunity to bring bullshit in your solid marriage. Didn't she call right before the stuff came? Y'all, know she loves drama."

"True. Yeah, she does." I added.

"You two can stand here and think what the fuck you want. I know who I'm fucking and that's you, Shondia. Don't give anymore thought to that bullshit. I love you and I am faithful to you and only you," Popcorn said as he threw the entire bowl in the garbage.

"Who the hell would send you something like that if you weren't doing anything that is all I am saying. Just look at it from my viewpoint," I demanded.

"Lower your damn tone, Shondia, and fuck how you are looking at it. Its bullshit and you feeding it like whoever wants you to. Just put this shit in the back of your mind and keep it there. Better yet, leave it off and don't think about it," Popcorn said angrily.

"I will lower my tone when you tell me what the hell is going on and stop trying to play me weak," I spoke back.

Popcorn dropped his head and got upset. He then said, "I'm not fucking up, but if you accuse me long enough, I will fuck you and anyone I choose. So, stop the shit right now. Kill it and be done. I don't have any intentions to fuck up but push me and I'll fuck. Just like that."

"Just like that?" I asked him to make sure I heard him correctly.

"Yeah, just like that. I haven't had any other pussy since you have me on lock. But I don't want to do that. I'm just saying that I will," Popcorn continued to explain.

"Go ahead and try it. I bet you will cry before I will," I said in a rational tone.

CHAPTER 6

Quicker than a blink of an eye, Popcorn grabbed me by my throat, and said, "No damn body will ever know how you are. Don't push me and don't play about fucking up. You belong to me and I spas out when I think about you and another motherfucker fucking. I'll be damn if that shit goes down."

I could not breathe. Fear gripped me from every angle and my husband was not letting up. The more he talked, the more he squeezed on my throat. I bucked like a bull trying to throw a rider.

Before I felt like I was going to pass out, I heard my cousin say, "Hell no! Fuck that shit. Let her go, man. Popcorn, man let her go. You love her, man. You love her. Let her go before you kill her." He tried to pull his hands from around my neck.

When my eyes opened back up, my husband had tears in his eyes. The only other time I had seen him cry was on our wedding day. Those were tears of joy, but the tears he had now confused me. Popcorn loosened his grip and moved off me a little. I coughed and tried to catch my breath.

He helped me up and, in a raspy tone, he said, "Don't you see someone wants to break us up? It could be that fat ass boss of yours for all I know. Damn, it could be anybody that wants you or me. These streets don't give a fuck who they fuck. All they want to do is fuck. Believe this; I will kill the hell out of you if I ever thought you to be unfaithful to me. I love your trick ass. Girl, I love the shit out of you. I'll give my life for you and to know that you don't believe me, that you don't believe me." I could hear the sincerity in his voice. He cried uncontrollably. My husband appeared to be extremely hurt about what someone had done. "I got to get away, fuck this shit. I got to leave. You don't trust me. What the fuck is going on? I have to leave, Shondia."

Popcorn slammed the door before he left the house to get in his vehicle. The way he backed out scared me because he fish tailed as he drove on the pavement and left. Chug and I stood alone, staring as Popcorn left. I wanted to cry all the more.

We had never parted ways angry at each other. I had no idea what was really going on and to know that someone would do such a thing was really upsetting. Chug did not want to say anything, for he witnessed his friend, my husband, on the verge of killing me. Thankfully, Chug was there because he saved me from Popcorn's wrath. "Well, there goes my ride to the bus station," Chug blurted out as we continued to stare after Popcorn. I did not answer.

Oddly enough, cars passed and blew more than usual. I did not feel like being hospitable to anyone because my life was in an uproar. Chug and I waited a few minutes longer before he said, "You and Popcorn will be alright. You know jealous ass motherfuckers are everywhere, and they see that he is faithful to you and you to him. Seeing that what y'all have is real, what they do? They hate and hide behind some candy and pretend that shit is going down, and nothing is actually happening. It is not like him to be angry with you, so take that into consideration that he is mad and is going to get to the bottom of this. Shondia, you yourself know he's not fucking up on you. All that nigga does is work, lift damn weights across the street, and hang out down Big Quack's. Now me, I'm the type of nigga that will fuck up your world, his world, and every other bitch world up. I'm not trustworthy and faithful is just a word with two syllables. I'm not worth a damn. Shit, so aren't you glad you never met a fucker like me?" I laughed hysterically. "See, I made you laugh. You and Popcorn going to be ok, it's just bullshit and the dumb shit."

"It's not dumbed to me. You understand what I'm saying?"

"Yeah, I do, but you should know your husband better than that. You are his world, and I don't think he would risk what he has with you for somebody else; even though Michelle is a bad ass, big ass freak. She good now and if he ever fucked off with her before you, then you might have to worry, but Shay. Ha! That ghetto bitch, you win hands down," Chug spoke as he giggled.

"You know your momma has always told us where there is smoke, there is fire. The smoke is the flowers showing up and the fire is yet to be seen."

"Hell no. I do believe that momma is wrong this time," Chug said as he moved out my way.

He knew that I was about to hit him because I always talked with my hands. That did make me laugh. In all honesty, it felt great to laugh but my mind was on my spouse. I knew he had to cool off, but I was worried about him.

"Popcorn is going to be ok." I glanced up at Chug and it was like he knew what I was thinking. "He is not with any woman. He is probably at Big Quack's house relaxing." I frowned at Chug, and he spoke, "Cruz, you know I know you too well. We have been close ever since I was born. What, you thought I was going to say since we were born? Shit, your ass old."

I laughed again. Smiling, my response was, "That's why you my favorite cousin."

"Yeah, you my favorite cousin because nobody else in the fam will take me where I need to go. Shit, I have to help keep you happy because if I don't, I'm screwed," Chug responded with humor.

"You are dirty and selfish sometimes, but I love you. Thanks for trying to make me feel better about what has happened."

"Since you feeling better, do I still have to throw out a hint?" Chug said.

When those words reached my ears, my first thought was, *what does he want me to do for him now?*

"Yeah, I do want something from you. Being that you didn't believe my ride, he has stormed off and left me. You are now elected to take me to the bus station."

"You know I will take you since my better half acts like he is too busy by running off somewhere."

"Well, I thought I didn't have to come out and ask, but you act like you couldn't take a hint," Chug suggested with the funny side of him.

"What hint?" We laughed even more as I cleared my face and my voice.

"Now that is out in the open, don't ask for a lot of gas. You broke that shit up by using that brick," Chug spoke as he ran off toward my car.

I followed behind him and noticed that he already had his bags at the car. "When we go down 397, you need to say goodbye to auntie?"

"Momma was the one to drop me off, grandma cashed her check in years ago, so there is no one else I need to say goodbye to," Chug spoke with humor.

Hearing the term "cashed her check in" was always funny because not many people that were raised around older people knew that it meant to have passed away. In many ways, my cousin was an old man in a young man's body, and then at a lot of times he was young and whorish at heart. I looked across the street as if I saw my husband lifting weights.

"Bitch, stop daydreaming and come on. He's not lifting weights today," Chug spoke as he put his bags in the trunk of my car.

Lifting my finger as to quiet him, I called my husband. Like I thought, it went to voicemail. It sounded great to hear his voice. Leaving a message, I spoke as softly as I could, "Hey, I'm worried about you. Hope you are ok. Call me and let me know where you are. In case you came, and I wasn't here, it's because I've gone to take Chug to the bus station in Meridian. I will be back soon as possible. Hope you will be home so we can talk. Well, I am about to go. Love you so much."

Hanging up the phone, I felt happier, but seeing him would make my day go even better. Locking the front door,

I got in the car and backed out. The first thing Chug did was turn on the radio. Me, with a lot on my mind, advised him to turn it off.

"I guess so because I don't have shit on gas" I hit the brakes so fast that I didn't even get on Shellie Brown. In fact, I pulled over at the center and looked at him. Being my cousin, he read my mind, and said, "Man, come on, Shondia. I have a little, but not much. Damn, I do have to survive."

"That does not have anything to do with me. Yo ass volunteered to go and was not drafted. So, save the sad story for one of ya weak minded women," I said as I drove off.

"See, Shondia, you always talk shit and if I know one thing, if I can listen to your sermon, I can get about anything you have, but the hardest thing is to listen to you talk about bullshit," Chug spoke as he looked out the window.

"You know to look out the window and not at me." We laughed.

I turned right on Highway 15. Chug broke the silence by saying, "I think that getting out of Winston County will be good for me."

"You mean invade new territory and up your game on some new, helpless woman," I said as I drove to the intersection of Highway 14 and 15/25. I asked, "You need to stop by Mickie D's or what?"

"No, no money and, plus, I am ready to get on down highway" Chug spoke as he began texting.

My phone rang but it was not Popcorn, it was Big

Quack. Out loud, I said, "What he want?"

"What who want?" Chug asked, being nosy.

"Big Quack. I know I don't have to work today," I spoke out of curiosity.

"Well, answer the motherfucker. Shit, you getting out of town now. Fuck that," Chug said with all seriousness.

"Don't worry cuz, you getting to the bus station no matter what," I said as I let the phone continue to ring.

"I know damn well I am. Shit, I gave you gas money, too." As soon as those words left his mouth, he laughed, and I cut my eye at him. He spoke, "Just flow with it."

Laughing, I replied, "I know you want me to just flow with it because you and I both know that you did not put a damn thing in gas."

"It did sound good, though, didn't it?" Chug said as he got a text.

I could only laugh as turned left by Shot Eubanks onto Highway 397. We continued to ride in silence. Soon as we passed Nanih Waiya, our old school, it brought back memories. I looked over at Chug, and told him, "I had some great memories there. Didn't you?"

"I enjoyed the dumb blonds. Shit, those snow bunnies were crazy about a half Choc like me."

"You know what? I hate I asked," I spoke as Chug shook his head. We passed the day care, and I asked, "We just right here, you don't want to drop by the hood?"

"Keep this motherfucker in drive." We laughed.

So many memories on that side of Winston County

made me miss home in a way. It was so peaceful and tranquil. Many a day my cousins and I walked the road feeling carefree and content. We did not have community drama or drama from bitches. *Those days are long over*, I thought as I drove on down the highway. Once we made it to Preston.

The old general store still looked the same, I thought of so many times we went to the store. The memories flooded my mind even though I had only been gone a little while. I wouldn't change my life with my husband for anything. The thought of Popcorn reoccurred, and I felt sad all over again. *Why hasn't he called me?*

"Your husband is thinking of you, I am sure," Chug said.

"Thanks, but he hasn't called me."

"You accused him of fucking up. What you think he is going to do, run your ass down?" Chug point blankly spoke.

"No, but I am his wife."

"A wife that accused him of doing something he isn't doing," Chug added to the rest of my statement.

"You right, so tell me why are you a whore?"

He laughed, and said, "That is a good question but to sum it up, I love pussy. The freakier the bitch is the better." It was funny, but kind of true coming from my cousin. "Real talk. Oh my, oh my what fun you can have with a big bitch like her. You see women like her will do anything she is told. That includes assholes and all."

"Uh," I butted in.

"Well, I'm telling you. Men love dykes, freaks,

church girls, and all outdoors whores."

"I get freaks, but what do dykes, church girls, and all outdoors whores have to do with it?" I just had to know.

"To start off, dykes, if they are not true, will take a man every so often. In my book, that means not many men have been there, maybe two or three, but not that many more, so the pudding will be tight, hot, and good, like Shay. Your ex- girl doesn't mind showing love to any man or woman. You know she is a community helper." I scanned Chug and noticed that he was all in the conversation and telling me from his point of view about the women. I couldn't help but cry laughing as I drove. "Yo ass laughing, but I am serious. Anyway, church girls are often sheltered and haven't been out there. That tells me that they are almost willing to try anything. Party for me because when they rebel, I am there to help them out. Most men won't waste time with them; then again, I am not most men."

After I passed Brown's church on the hill, I pulled over. He was being too ridiculous, and I couldn't drive right. Tears clouded my eyes. I had to get out and fall on the ground. "I'm serious. Get your ass up and come on. I have a bus to catch." Moments later, I got up and got back in the car. "You ready to finish hearing my side?"

Taking a deep breath, I sighed out, "Ok, I believe I am ready to hear your side."

"Where I stop at?" Chug asked. "Yeah, church girls' parents want a guy to go to their church and play like they all in it, but honestly, I'm a wolf waiting to pounce on their lambs when they are away."

"Please, stop it, you are too much."

108

"Let me finish. All outdoors whores are the worse because you and all your friends can run a train, and I guarantee one of the dumb fucks will try to make her his wife."

I laughed and swerved a little. "Cut that swerving out, I do want to make it but let me finish. With a woman like that, men only want their nut and if the pussy or head job is off the chain, so will his dumb ass be running after her, off the chain, jealous and protecting a bitch that can't wait to get the drops on his dumb, whipped ass."

"You stupid," I spoke with happiness.

"No, those motherfuckers stupid for falling for a trick ass bitch."

"Like Michelle?" I suggested.

"Oh, hell yeah. Her own husband can't leave her because he's crippled and old, so a younger woman on his team works for him. She said all he can do is eat pussy and that gets old."

"Wow. You serious?"

"Hell yeah, he knows of her infidelities, he doesn't want to be alone."

"I guess the term an old truck and a good dog doesn't apply to him."

The comedy show my cousin put on had died down and the silence was back on. I saw him scoot over and slump his head, but I thought he was looking at himself I the mirror. I said to Chug as I noticed that he had fallen asleep, "My auntie's whore is sleep, poor thing."

Without skipping a beat, Chug said, "You should know what whores need, bitch." I busted out laughing, and

I reached over and hit him with my right hand. "Ouch don't get mad at the truth," Chug spoke as he let the seat back to further relax.

We made it to Highway 16 in De Kalb, it still looked the same. Chug and I traveled that road a many a day going to the club in Meridian, and when I went to Meridian Community College. However, it was different from when I attended the Math and Science school in Starkville. On the other hand, it was neat, but I didn't see a future dealing with those two areas.

I only went because I wanted to see what the world was like, and auntie was against it. Anyway, all that stopped when I got a full ride to University of Mississippi. I decided to take up Hotel and Restaurant Management, which was unusual. My family never knew that working at the Luigi's for a few summers turned me on to the restaurant industry. Then, my life changed when I met Popcorn.

I couldn't lie; he had my nose wide open like a six-lane freeway going one way. All I could do was eat, drink, and breathe Popcorn. After all my obstacles, I began working for Big Quack. Thinking of Big Quack reminded me that he had called over an hour ago. Reaching for my phone, I saw my husband had texted. I swerved and Chug work up scared.

"What the hell! You on drugs!"

Not able to control my laughter, I spoke, "Popcorn texted me and I was trying to see what he said, but I dropped the phone."

"Fuck that, let me see what the hell he said. Shit,

you trying to endanger my life. A nigga can't even take a nap," Chug said as he picked up the phone. He opened it up, and said, "What the hell! You swerved just for him to write the letter K." It was funny and it made me happy because he would be home when I got there. "Shondia, let me get this straight, you swerving just for him to text a fucking letter? He could have written you a damn text worth seeing." Shaking my head and crying out in amusement was all I could do. "Shit, I'm woke now. Your ass spoiled the rest of my sleep," Chug added.

"We on Highway 19 now and will be in downtown Meridian in a few," I told my cousin as he searched his own phone for missed texts.

My phone rang again, and it was my boss. "Answer your phone. Fat bastard keeps calling you, see what he wants," Chug said as he handed me the phone from the console.

"Run ya mouth," I spared off at my boss with fun.

"You been around me too long," he said.

"Ok, what's up? You blowing me up and everything."

"You are not on schedule to come in for tomorrow, why?"

"You told me to switch days with your trick and I obliged," was my response.

"Well, she gonna be busy tonight and I need you to come in."

"What if I have plans like she does?" I questioned back.

"You and I both know that you don't have shit to do

but run behind your husband," he spoke as he laughed.

"Sounds like you don't have shit to do but run behind trick ass free women."

"Ooh, that was a good one. Come on, Shondia, I need you to come in. Do me this favor." He sounded like he was begging.

"What I get?" I asked.

"Just like a nigga, always want something when they call."

"Well, I've learned from the best and like I said, what is in it for me?" I asked again.

"If you change your plans and come in for me tomorrow, I will give you an extra day off, but not to be used during a peak week, a holiday, or anything like that. It will be with my discretion."

I was going to do it, anyway, but I was going to make him sweat for it first. "I don't know. We have a lot of peak days, no more real holidays, unless you include far away days like Christmas and Thanksgiving. You giving me a day would be close to never."

"Come on, Shondia. I will add that I have to give it to you sometime in the upcoming month. So, do we have a deal?" he wanted to know.

"First, tell me what she has to do so important that she can't come in?"

"She has to go to the welfare department in Philly and check on getting her an apartment at Frog Level."

"Why can't you come in and take her place?" I asked as I laughed.

"Shondia, you being nosy now," was his response.

"Yeah, I will come in. I'll be there early to do inspections," I added.

"You see, that is why I made you the manager."

"Ok, bye, see ya in the morning," I said as I hung up.

"That fat bastard knows she only wants his damn money. Even I know that from sitting right here," Chug said as he began talking on the phone.

We finally made it to the bus station, and it was almost empty. Chug went inside to get his ticket while I stayed outside. I saw him coming and got out. Soon as we went in the trunk and closed it, that red truck pulled up beside us. Instantly, I knew it was her. Turning to Chug, I asked, "You have company to see you off?"

He glanced up as he closed my trunk to reply, "No and hell no. Her big ass came on her own. I didn't tell her to come."

"Well, you better keep her in her place because I have a Louisville Slugger on my back seat."

When I mentioned a bat, she got out the truck. Her face was slightly swollen with a small print in her face. She really looked fucked up. It wasn't all my fault. We stood by the car as she came closer, and said, "I want to talk to you, Chug baby, please, give me a minute to talk before you get on that bus and I am never to touch you again."

"Big bitch, didn't I tell you that I was leaving, and we have nothing to talk about? Take a damn hint. Look, I'm wrong for you and you should know by now," Chug said to her.

"We have a history, and you are not wrong for me,"

113

she said with tears in her eyes.

"You call letting other motherfuckers fuck you while I watch a history?" Chug said.

"I did all those things for you. I did it just to please you. Why else would I do it? Tell me?" she told him to defend her actions. She turned toward me, and spoke, "Tell Chug to talk to me since you tell him everything else."

"Hold ya damn horse. He is grown and does what he wants. Now, it's not my fault if you weak to his game," I spoke to her.

"We'll talk later, but as for right now I plan to talk to Chug," Michelle spoke with tears in her eyes.

"You can talk to your damn self," I spoke, but she did not reply.

I almost felt sorry for her, but I remembered how she was openly flirting with my husband as if I was shit. That thought brought back anger.

Chug said, "Cruz, don't leave until I am on the bus because I don't want to come up missing. This big bitch would try anything to keep a motherfucker like me." Focusing his attention back to her, Chug raised his voice some. It was a tactic he usually used to act like he was mad, but I knew better.

From the look on her face, I could tell that she was eating it up and wanted a napkin. "Damn, girl, you don't have a mind of your own. The shit you do is degrading. Sucking my dick from the back, which is good, but in front of motherfuckers you don't know. What kind of bitch does that shit?" Chug asked her.

"Your type does. I am your type. All these things

114

are for you and not for me," Michelle pleaded as Chug shook his head.

CHAPTER 7

We walked toward the bus station from the parking lot. I walked through the building to the back and sat on a bench. It was rather nice and quiet to be a bus station. Moments later, Chug brought his guest in tow. He stood by the pole, and she stood close by. He turned to her, and said, "Look, Michelle, you a great girl, but I am not about shit, and you don't need shit in your life. You have lost a few teeth, which worked in your favor but..."

She cut him off. "Please, just think about it while you are away."

"What is there to think about?"

"We have two years and that is the longest that I have been involved with just one man."

"That is, you and your business. I told you not to get emotionally involved. You fell for this king ding a ling, didn't you?" Chug said with a taunt.

"I love everything. I haven't had anyone like you. Can't no one eat my big ass like you can and you know how I love it when you put one in my mouth and one in my asshole," Michelle said to entice Chug. She was making me sick.

"Big baby, be quiet, don't you see you making my cousin sick," Chug said with a smirk.

"When I am with you, I don't care who is around and who is listening. You bring that out me," Michelle said as she got closer to Chug.

"And what is that that I bring out you, girl?" Chug spoke as he winked at her.

"You bring this bad bitch out that is down for whatever and whoever."

"Is that right, my big bitch?"

"You know that I am your bitch and only yours."

"You know that I know bitches like you can't keep your mouth and your pussy to yourself while I am gone," Chug spoke as he looked at her.

"True, but when you get back, I'm all yours again and whoever I am fucking off, with they would have to get the fuck on down."

By listening, he sounded like their relationship was a friend with benefits thing. However, the way she pleaded, you would think that she was truly into my cousin. It made me look at things differently. She turned her back to Chug and placed her palms flat on the concrete as to give his dick a stand-up dance in public.

"Shit, quit that, girl, before I have to delay leaving and go AWOL before I make it to the damn camp."

"What's wrong? Don't think you can handle it?" She taunted as she moved her big ass up and down.

To me, she pretended that Chug was a pole, and she was the stripper. What a sight it was. He put on a show by hitting her ass. I was appalled by their public display of fucking. He glanced back at me, and he heard his bus number being called. I grinned at him because if I knew my cousin, he was thinking of plan for her. Chug saw that she was willing to do anything for him and he loved that shit. Giving her that smile, he gave her a hug.

I stood up and he walked off from her, gave me a hug, and whispered, "I need to stop, don't I?"

"Stop is not the word," I replied.

"Keep ya head up. Pop going to be alright when you get home."

"Thanks," I whispered to my cousin.

Leaving her to say her goodbye to him, I walked off and left them. When I made it back to my car, I saw her walking up behind me. I opened the door and got my bat out the back seat. She stopped by the rear of her truck. I faced her and used a rough tone. "Bitch, not today. You don't want this issue. I promise you don't."

"No, bitch, you are going to wish you hadn't made me your issue."

"How is that?"

"First of all, you should have minded your own business. Who Chug fucks is his business. Your world is going down. You should have stayed quiet, but now everything is going to talk."

"If that is true, what does that have to do with me?" I wanted to know.

"You told him to leave me alone, why?" she questioned.

"Dude, you're married, and you don't honor your vows. I told him if I were him, I would leave you alone, but you know like I do that he has a mind of his own. He is young and has his entire life ahead of him. He doesn't need an already married woman following behind him."

"Shouldn't it be my business who runs after who? Isn't your business who runs after you?"

"My business is my business. We don't have a problem with me and mine. It's about him asking me for my opinion and…"

Cutting me off, Michelle spoke, "Which I see he varies, other than your husband who is stupid, of course. He listens to you."

"Let me get this straight. You mad at me because he asked for my opinion about you and I told him that you are married, which you are, and for him to find other single women, which he needs to. Yeah, bitch, if I was him, I would cut you the fuck a loose."

"Yes, and because you wrecked my life by giving him ideas about leaving me alone, watch and see what happens. Bitch, you gonna learn to mind your own damn business and if you have something to hide, watch that shit come forth," Michelle spoke to me.

"I don't have shit to hide. My cousin, on the other hand, is my business. If he asks for my advice, I will give him my advice. Fuck what you think," I told her.

She touched her swollen face, and said, "Second of all, the hit you gave me was true. I may have been out of line, but your so-called husband didn't stop me when he was behind me. He enjoyed more than the view and I can tell he did, didn't you?"

"You stay the hell away from my husband before I really fuck your ass up," I spoke to get my point across.

"You slow bitch, your husband or ya so called friend? I can't do any more to him than he allows, and you know he is a nice, gullible guy. He won't know what hit him until he is doing it."

"You're a big ass big bitch and Winston County isn't big enough to keep me off yo ass."

"Well, as friendly as he is, he and I will always be friends," she spoke with assurance.

"What makes you so sure you will trick my husband? Shay tried and failed, you're no different."

"I'm not that fake ass Shay. I'm Michelle. If you haven't heard by now, who am I, you need to make a trip uptown and go farther to find out. There's not a dick in town that I can't go back to."

"I don't give two damn what you are. Know what the fuck you are doing when you cross me and mine," I spoke, staring into her face.

"True and honestly, your husband is just a pawn to play with. He always want to help people and all I have to do let him be that captain save a hoe and watch how quickly he'll be caught up. Young bitch, you don't know enough for me. That little amateur dick sucking I know you do is for kids. If I ever get that dick in my mouth and when I twerk it, listen to me, I didn't say if, I said when I get that dick in my mouth and I twerk it, I plan to take it to the head. Truthfully, you ruined my life, and I see you love Pop like I love Chug. Watch the fuck out."

Before I could respond, the security officer drove by and saw my bat. He stopped, and asked, "Is everything alright, ladies?"

We both responded, "Yes."

I went on to say, "I was just telling big b that a brick to the face isn't anything like what a Louisville Slugger can do to legs, head, back and hands."

I got in the car and he watched until I drove off. When I made it back to Louisville, I decided to go by the house.

In the yard was Popcorn. He saw me and went in the house. I felt nervous and excited all at once. Getting out the car, I went in the house. Using love, he said, "Hey, baby."

"Hey, baby, I'm glad to see you," I mustered.

"We need to talk," Popcorn said as he pats the seat next to him.

Walking toward him, I stopped near him hoping he would kiss me, but he didn't. My first instinct was to touch his face, so I did. He turned his head and kissed my palm. That told me that he was happy and had time to think about the day's event.

"Shondia, I love you to death. I take my vows seriously. I would never do anything to hurt you. You are my wife and nothing and no one can take the place of that. Do you understand me? I make mistakes, but I love you." Tears flowed from my eyes with ease. "Baby, don't. If you cry, I won't be able to finish talking," he said as he wiped my tears away, which he had done often. "Don't ever doubt my love for you. You are the one I have in my heart," Popcorn said as he placed my hand on his chest to feel his heartbeat. "You don't want me to jump stupid. My love for you is crazy as a motherfucker. I have never been sprung and to be sprung in love is some deep shit. No woman has ever made me mad and happy at the same time."

I could not say a word, for tears were streaming down my face all the more. "Baby, it hurt me today to know that I was telling you the truth and you ignored me. It was like you didn't believe me and God knows, since the day I met you there has not been anyone but you. I don't want anyone but you. Trust me; there is no one but you.

Please, don't doubt me again," Popcorn said as he leaned closer to kiss me.

On my own, I wiped my tears to say, "I am so sorry, but I got very jealous. I have never experienced so much anger as I did today."

"Oh, hitting Michelle with that brick was nothing, huh?" Popcorn said to make me laugh.

It was a great laugh, for my husband always made me laugh. He always knew what to say to me. Women couldn't help but fall for him. He was considerate, gentle, and someone you could talk to whenever you felt angry or just a needed a word of encouragement. Women always felt closer to him and that was something I had learned to deal with. Facing my husband, I said, "See that is what I am talking about. I have never had that feeling to come over me and God only knows what might have happened if I was really angry."

"I'm yours. You don't have to act like the rest of these bitches around here. You are unique, that is why I married you, Shondia. You are everything in the sky to me and then some."

"Speaking of Michelle, she came to the bus station while I was dropping off Chug."

"What she doing there?" my husband wanted to know.

"To see him off and tell me about how she wants to fuck and suck you like a Hoover vacuum cleaner."

"Damn. What the fuck!" Popcorn yelled out with jester.

"Yes, she didn't say the Hoover, but from her

gestures she wants to mess up my marriage because I told Chug to leave her alone."

"Whoa, one thing at a time, you told him to leave her alone?"

"Yes, he asked for my opinion, and I told him she is married and married vows are sacred, and for them that commit adultery or break up a home, God was going to get them."

"You know he probably told her that shit just to get the stuff off him. He's your cousin and my boy, but he will lie on you as well as me just to get what he needs. Damn, what happened to us, or anyone else, for that matter."

"True, but he asked for my opinion. I can't make him do anything, just like I told her."

"What she say?"

"You are a pawn, in other words, a toy she will play with and to top it off, when she gets your dick in her mouth she is going to twerk it. She said when and not if because you are a captain save a whore. You are too nice, and you see her as a friend, and the little stuff I do to you is for kids."

My husband stopped me in my sentence to say, "All she is a friend. Michelle started coming around with Chug. Since he been gone, she hangs out and kicks it with the ZR click at Big Quack's. I think they have something going. Besides, I don't see anything going any further than that. I am nice to everyone, and I know that woman can't help but to fall for me, but fuck them, I have a wife."

"Baby, I did have a dream that you fucked her, and you enjoyed it," I said to see what he would say.

123

"No, the hell you did not. I fuck you and only you. I'll have to be drunk and high on something to ever fuck her. She is not decent. In case you don't know, I have standards, and she does not meet any of them. She's bigger than you. Why the hell would I want her? She is just a friend and that is all. That's Chug's woman and some other man's wife."

"She seems to be hell bent on fucking you and to be honest; she is right in one aspect."

"What is that?" he asked, for he seemed like he wanted to know.

"You are too eager to help people and now days, women will use anything just to get a man. They will always say as she did, 'I can't make him do no more than he doesn't want to.' They don't look at the idea that it is two people that are married and not three. I don't care what lies you may tell a woman; they will be thoughtless for listening to a man with a wife."

"You right baby, but in this day and time they not on that honest shit. Besides, you know you women can get attached to a man that will treat you like somebody and before y'all know it, ya fucking maybe a time or two, but fucking is fucking. A man will tell a woman lies just to have his cake and eat it, too."

My husband spoke it like he had been in that position before. It sounded like it was coming from his heart and not his head. To ease the air, I said, "True, but you have to love someone to stay with them, no questions asked. I don't see why women want a part time man than one that will be there for them? Too many diseases going on and I love

124

me."

"You do know that men see things not as women. They will see a woman as a plaything when the wife is on bullshit and vice versa," Popcorn said.

"Yes, I know men are green and unaware to a conniving woman. Men usually don't see it when a woman is up to no good. Before ya wake up, it is too late and out of control," I added.

"True, but I know who I love, and I know what woman I intend to be with," Popcorn said to me.

"Baby, just be careful. I heard Chug tell her that he knows that she is not going to keep her mouth, pussy, or asshole to herself while he is gone. They talked like it was ok for them."

"She is married and yes it matters not to them. When you are in a relationship with a married person, you only want what you can get. It can come to the point where the wife or husband is disrespected by the outside man or woman. When that shit happens, somebody has gotten emotionally attached and needs to wake the fuck up."

"She made me feel like there was something she knew that I did not know. Does she know something that I do not know? Because I think she is going to try and fuck you just because she is not happy. Is there anything you need to tell me? If so, tell me. I would rather hear it from the man I love than the streets that don't love me."

"Shondia, she is a friend, and she means nothing to me. As for her knowing something, hell, if she tells me I'll tell you and we both will know. She is not worth my marriage, never have been and never will be. She always has things going on and when Chug first told me about her, she was on the verge of trying to kill her husband. Could you imagine? She wanted to kill him because he got in an accident and was injured. Instead of her being happy that he was still alive, she grew hatred. It doesn't make it right. Chug had me to talk some sense into her. He said he couldn't have that on his conscious. So, I chopped it up with her."

"When did all this take place?" I asked because it was new to me.

"About four or five months ago."

"What? Why am I just now finding out about it?" I questioned in a suspect way.

"It was nothing. We all would meet up down at Big Quack's."

"Big Quack, know?" I asked.

"Yeah, there was nothing going on. I mean; besides her public manner, she is cool as hell. She reminds me of you," he said as I gave him a look of hate.

"No, the fuck she doesn't!" I blurted out at him.

"Not like that. I'm talking about going through stuff and some of the same shit she says, you say it to. She tells me all the shit she has done, and I give her the best advice I can."

"So, what, I remind you of her? You sure you not fucking her?" I had to ask.

"No. I am not fucking her. Didn't I tell you she is a friend and that is it? She is with Chug, remember," Popcorn said to me.

"You also saw how she was willing to suck

anybody with him there, remember?" I pointed out to him.

Laughing, he said, "You don't have to worry about me and her. I know who I love and how you make me happy. Your sex is the best and I don't mean because we are married. The shit will make a man like me show his ass. Now, there has been a time in my life that I was unsure of my love for you, but I remembered the vows I took with you and how that night we almost broke up. I rededicated myself to you with all my heart."

"I remember that. It was almost as special as the first time we pledged our vows," I spoke as I began to tear up.

"You don't have to worry about me and her. She is a friend and that is it."

"Well, I am telling you what she told me."

"What you tell her?" he asked in amusement.

"When the security guard came over because he saw my bat I said, I was just telling big b that a brick to the face isn't anything like what a Louisville Slugger can do to legs, head, back and hands."

"No, you didn't."

"Yes, I did, and if you ever fuck her, I can't tell you what I would do, just don't you do it," was all that came out my mouth.

"You don't have to worry about that, I love the little stuff you do to me. I don't need an experienced prostitute to do a damn thing to me but stay out my way."

"So, we good?" I asked.

"Yeah, but I have to tell you something."

"Oh, ok, what?"

127

"It came to my attention that Big Quack is in love with you."

I laughed, not intentionally, but it was too funny. To hear those words were odd and unreal. Watching my spouse after a few times, I had to shake my head at him each time because the words he said held no truth. "Honey, that is not true. In fact, I began working for him before I met you. Ever since I met you, he has not said anything to me. Before I met you, he…"

Popcorn stopped me mid-sentence. "Whatever he said or did was before us, and I can't get mad. Now, if that fat bastard said something to you once he found out about us, then that is another story."

"Well, no need. Since he found out about us, he never came at me at any way. He has been a dear friend."

"That is how it always starts out. I have been in a position before. I confused at what was going on when I had just a friend. I don't want to see you get in a mess like I did before," Popcorn stated.

Touching his face ever so gently, I said, "He has not ever come on to me. He doesn't talk about you, and I don't bring my marriage to my job. Now, he will talk of his latest conquest to gloat, but that is about it. He knows who my allegiance is with. You can keep that lie."

"That is the same thing he said. You sure he didn't call you and y'all plot the same line to tell?" Popcorn said in a serious tone.

"He called asking me to come in tomorrow in the newbie's place because she has to go to the Philly to do some stuff. He said he will give me a paid day off of his

128

choice within the next month. That is all he said."

"I know because I was there when he called you. In fact, when I heard about it, I went to him. You see, Quack is kin folk, but he is dirty. He will fuck you and laugh in my face like nothing ever happened. You see, shit like that will get his fat ass killed," Popcorn said to me as he glared at me.

"Wow, I can imagine how it is going to be when I go to work tomorrow."

"I want you to quit sooner because thoughts are going through my head about you and him."

"What the hell!" I yelled out.

"Yes, since I heard it, it's like I remember him at the party."

"I also told you that it was not to me. I am not his type."

"Yeah, but I remember how he comes by the house, and you are the main person he talks to."

"We work together. I am his leader at work and that is it. Suddenly, you get flowers and now you don't trust me on my job?" I questioned him.

"I see the way he hungers for you and if he or you mess up, I'm killing for mine."

"Popcorn, seriously?" I questioned.

"Hell yes. You are mine. How many times do I need to make it clear to you?"

"Well, what am I to say?" I asked.

"About what?"

"About what Michelle said about you? Don't you think that is speculation enough? Don't you think that by chance I might be stepping back, and taking a look at you and your friendship with her?" I spoke.

"I get it, but it is different."

"How?" I needed to know.

"You don't know Quack and how he does his women. You don't know how a woman is just fun and games for him. He doesn't mind breaking up a home or going to Murder Lane and causing shit to go down."

"You are implying that my friendship is different because I am a woman and Quack is a man?"

"Yes."

"Well, you are a man, and Michelle is a woman that threatened me about fucking you. Tell me the difference? For this sounds good. Do tell?"

"You don't understand."

"If we are going to argue over Quack or Michelle, then it is a problem. If it is just friends, there is nothing to argue about. The problem comes when someone has feelings and if someone is lying."

"Well, I am not lying. Michelle is a friend," my husband persisted.

"Quack is a friend, and I am not lying. I know where my love is at. If you were treating me wrongly, I would not be unfaithful because I love, you enough to be yours and only yours. Now, if we are divorced, that is a different story."

"Well, you won't have that problem. No matter what we go through, I am not divorcing you. I don't give a damn what we go through. We can overcome and weather any storm."

"You mean that, Chadwick?" I asked with love in my tone.

"Yes, Shondia. I mean it. I know you had a life before me, and I have a child before you. You know that I was not a saint when we met and so far, no secrets are between us. Let me rephrase that, I mean, since we have been married there is not anything that needs addressing," Popcorn said.

"Do you want to know what ever happened between Big Quack and me?" I asked.

"Hell, no because it was before me and if it is too bad, I'll be going to his house to kick his ass tonight before I go to work."

"Shit, you do have to go to work, and you haven't had any sleep, and I haven't had my make-up sex," I teased.

"Tomorrow, we have to start back making time for each other. You are always at work and so am I. What you want to do?" Smiling, I shrugged my shoulders. "Come here, girl, let me give you a little something to hold up until I get home to finish taking care of you." I lay back on the sofa that we fought on earlier and allowed my husband to pull my sweatpants off to reveal my thong. He licked his lips, and I giggled, for I knew what he was going to do. With a strong tug, he tore off my thong and in his view was my bald pussy. "You know what I want. Kick those legs up and keep them up," was his demand to me.

Obeying him, I did. His first taste of me was like a nervous child. Thankfully, I was still clean and fresh. He then became more engrossed into my body that I began to

131

yell out and grab the deep pillows. My husband knew how to make me feel and for that, he did it better than Shay. I couldn't help but to lay there for as long as I could to take the pleasure he gave me.

"Please, I can't take it," I faintly spoke.

He continued to put his face deeper into me as if he was trying to find his way out my ass. Every flick of his lean tongue muscle caused me to be on the brink of releasing an experimental orgasm that was long overdue. He tasted me like never before. To me, he was apologizing for something and at that moment, I didn't care, for his loving was like no other.

Out the blue, he stopped, and said, "Tonight before I go to work, I need you to release all over my face. Just tonight, I will drink you up and keep your scent around my nose. I need to smell you all night to be driven wild by you and only you."

He did not give me a chance to reply. However, I could not reply because sexual tension was all over me. Popcorn began the teasing and with each tease, my body raged with fire from within. The feeling I had with my husband was not been like any other. My spouse pleased me to satisfaction every time we made love.

Popcorn drank me slow with intense passion. He seemed to know when my body was about to quake and shiver because his head motions changed with me. My toes began to lock. Parched was my voice from the pleading to let me go, for the pleasure was very fulfilling. His extreme way of tasting me was too much. Trying to get away from his vengeful mouth, I scooted to the floor. It proved to be a big mistake. My butt was on the floor, but my legs were still on the couch and he, with his head still in position, used his hands to lock me in. I am trapped, came to mind as I gripped whatever I could.

The carpet became embedded in my finger nails I believed I hit him in the back with my foot, for he bulked a little, but that did not stop my sticky vitamins rushing out of me. It was everywhere, all down the crest of my hips, his mouth, and the carpet beneath me. It was always explosive, but that time was better than before. He even used his face in my thigh crest not to waste any of me.

Out of the blue, he entered me, and the passion was explosive. My mind was blown. Each time he took me, it was much needed and long overdue. I guess tasting me opened his mind up for fucking. I did not remember him getting up after he buried himself deep within my vagina walls. However, for a second, I saw his feet by my head as he placed cover on me. I heard the door close and that was all I recalled.

CHAPTER 8

I woke up with a smile on my face and my husband by my side. It was joy and I knew it. I ruffled the cover a little and saw my husband still sleeping. I was weak, but I got up. I felt so fortunate to have his love and to know that he loves me so much, made me feel wonderful. I leaned to kiss him, but he, in good humor, spoke with his eyes semi-closed, "Don't kiss my mouth, it's nasty, remember?" We both laughed. I left out the door and went to work.

When I got to work, Big Quack was the only one there. Glancing at the time on my cell, I saw that it was not time for the others to come in. I parked out back and went in through the employee entrance. Once I made it in the kitchen, I could smell food had been cooked. I continued to look around. Making my way to the front of the house, I saw Big Quack sitting at his favorite table. I saw that he was deep in thought, so I attempted to close the door.

He saw me, and said, "Come on in."

"You sure, look like you were deep in thought?" "I was. There is a lot going on with me, and sometimes I just have to think." Big Quack did not talk like himself. His head seemed to be in the clouds or somewhere. I stood up at his table, and he said, "You can sit, I don't bite."

"If you bite, I have a pit bull that will wear you out," I spoke to make him laugh, but he gave a faint grin. "You ok, Big Quack? You don't seem like yourself," I spoke as I still stood up.

"I know you want to know why I've asked you to come in earlier, don't you."

"Yes, what is the urgency of me coming here? You claim that the newbie had business to take care of and you wouldn't be here, either," I mentioned.

"She does have business to take care of. I wasn't going to be here, but I just had to."

The way he said that puzzled me deeply. He hadn't, on any occasion, acted the way he was now. It is almost scary to see him bothered about something. On the outside he was a cool character, but on the inside, he was just like anyone else, but on another level. He had the persona of trying to fit in and like he had to prove a point for some reason.

He was not his hyped self. Something was on his mind heavily. I didn't want to pry, but if he, like the rest of them, brought their problems to the job then I had a problem. Remembering that, I spoke, "You know as well as I do that if you are bothered by something, you will not be a productive employee. You will be agitated by the slightest thing. I can't have that on my shift."

"That is why you are a leader, Shondia. You bring joy to this place. All shit aside, you have something that I don't have." He stared out the window.

"Ok, now you are scaring me for real. I don't know who you are, but bring the real Big Quack back," I yelled out.

He smiled, and said politely, "Don't you want to sit down first? You know how the end of the day you will complain about your feet and how tired you are. I say if you stop eating, your feet won't hurt. Look at me. I know what I am talking about. I see you gaining a little weight in your hips."

It surprised me to know that he listened to me, that was almost a month or so ago. I thought he ignored me because he never said anything to me. Now to know that he really listened to me stunned me like crazy. I decided to tell him, "You actually listen to me complain to you about my feet and you know I am always eating. I thought you ignored me like you usually do."

"I listen and I see. I just use selective hearing and seeing," he said with a small smile.

"Thanks for passing on the truth, boss man." Feeling strange, a blank look was on my face.

Big Quack jumped up and came to me, speaking, "Girl, you, ok?"

"Ah, yeah, I am ok. Something smells funny."

Easing me down in the chair, he prompted my feet up in another chair and fanned me. "You sure you, ok? I can't have a liability on my premises," he said with more bass in his usual tone.

"Yeah, I'll be good, just have to sit here for a few minutes."

He went back to his seat and looked more earnest at me as I sat across from him. "Eat some of this. I made it this morning while I was thinking."

"Sure, this is white cheese dip. It takes a minute to cook and cool. You must have been here a while this morning?" I spoke with a smile as I sat down.

"You know it. Have things on my mind. You know what it is like you finally realize something, but you don't know how to handle it?" he responded.

"Ok. What's up? I'm here and I am listening," I spoke as I ate a bite of the dip.

"You always listen. That is one of the things I like best about you. You listen and not because I have money and everything. You treat me the same and I am grateful for that, for your friendship only."

"I know it is friendship only. How can you suggest otherwise when I am married and you are a…" Clearing my voice, I did not finish the sentence. He knew what I was implying, so he smiled harder.

"Your husband thinks we are having an affair," Big Quack spoke kindly.

"How is that?" I said with laughter because was funny to me.

"Why is this funny to you?" Big Quack asked.

"Me and you? Get for real. Now I know why the conversation last night. What is going on?" I said as I ate more and more of the dip.

"Yeah, we chopped it up like fam, but he knows where I am coming from, and he understands."

"But I don't know where you coming from, fam."

"Popcorn and I talked about his speculations. I assured him that I love you as a friend and if I thought you would have had me, I would come after you but the day you came in professing your love for him, I backed down. Since then, I only have a friendship love for you. People like you don't come around every day. You are special and one of a kind," Big Quack said seriously.

"We spoke a few seconds more, and he said he would talk to you and be honest."

Quack had me nervous. "Honest about what?" I stood up as I asked him the question.

Slowly, Big Quack placed his hand on mine. It was sexual for him to touch my hand while having my full attention. Seeing my boss for the first time as a great guy, he said, "You know that you are a great worker, and I wouldn't trust anyone else with my business. You are smart, sexy, and a great person to be around."

I cut him off to say, "What's this really about? You are confusing me like hell. I mean, you giving me the old he ho speech. Am I being fired or what?"

"Firing you? Never," he said as he sat back in his chair.

"Ok, why the mushy speech?" I asked.

He did not say anything at first. Then, he said, "It's nothing. Don't worry about it. Just know that I am internally thankful for you working here and not just that, but you listen to me, and I can have a conversation with you, and it won't go any further than us. I like that. It proves to me that you are a real friend and that is rare. I hope Popcorn knows how blessed he is to have you."

"Well, boss, I hope he does. For I love my husband. He has a piece of my heart and there is no one else for me."

My boss got up, and said, "Damn, hearing that it makes it harder to say. Shit! How I got in this predicament is beyond me."

"What are you talking about? What predicament?"

"I can't tell you how to react, but I hope you don't be mad at me or anything."

Plainly, he said the words any woman dreaded to hear.

"Your husband has fucked this woman, and someone sent the proof to my cell today."

I turned my head to face him and blinked my eyes numerously. I got up and faced my boss. Faintly, I replied, "Popcorn fucked someone while being with me? You lying, Big Quack. If this is some ploy to get you to eat my pussy again, it won't work."

"No, I am not lying."

Cutting him off, I said, "Let me see it! I want to see it now!"

"I am debating because it is a marriage, not a couple dating. I told him that if he didn't tell you, I would. We almost got to fighting because he said he will deal it his way, but I see you here today and I know he lied. He probably didn't think I would tell you, but you are my friend."

He took out his phone and handed it to me. It was the night of his party, for I remembered seeing the Zion Ridge click wearing those outfits and there in the middle appeared to be Michelle. Studying the girl's face closely, I knew it was, indeed, her. I looked up at Quack and he would not look at me, he kept his face toward the window. Paying attention to the cell, it was there by the door I saw my husband.

He appeared to be enjoying himself. Anyway, she was naked and acted like a worm on her back. To me, it was a hot mess, and then my husband got on his knees and tasted her. The way he moved his head was all too familiar to me. All his friends were there cheering him on to eat her pussy up as he became more engrossed in his sexual act with her. I heard a familiar voice; the angle went upwards to Chug. He was there watching like the rest while Shay, my bitch, was sucking his dick as he sat on the couch like a pimp rubbing her head. I literally wanted to pass out but couldn't. Tears covered me like never before.

Seconds later, Michelle said, "Eat that nut out me, motherfucker."

He continued until she came on his face. He got up with her pussy juice all around his nose and mouth. He acted like a champ. Next, he said, "Bring that ass to me. I need to make you pay."

She replied, "Pay for what?"

He said as he laughed, "For being my fucking friend."

They all giggled as he got on top. She miraculously wrapped her fat ass ankles around him as he scoots her big ass all over the place; almost like I saw in my dream. I threw the phone back at Big Quack as I screamed. He caught the phone, walked over to me, and held me in a friendly manner. I could not help it. I cried like a newborn baby.

There I was witnessing my husband fucking his so-called friend. The very woman I did not like without a cause, but now had one. It was just yesterday that she acted like she knew something that I did not, and she actually did.

The lying face of my husband appeared before me, and how I asked him about her and the way he lied to me. I felt like a fucking fool to know that he did not love me enough to stay faithful. I cried. It was so unlike me, but the pain was unbearable.

"If there is any consolation, he got high and was dared to do it. Someone from New Zion, Greensboro or some damn where videoed the act. I don't believe he intended for you to ever see it. I'm sure he loves you."

"Liar! How can you love someone and fuck someone else?" I screamed between tears.

"It is just the way it is," Big Quack spoke with compassion.

"How can a man say he loves you and come home to you knowing what he did with another woman, probably on more than one occasion?" I asked as I cried.

"Shondia, men can do stuff like that and most of the time they do not get emotionally attached. You mean the world to him. He told me such." I kept shaking my head, for I didn't know who to believe anymore. "I know you are hurt and believe me; he tried to say that I was only going to tell you because I wanted you. I told him there may be some truth, but you know what you want and so far, it has been him. You are married to him. I may be a lot of things, but I really do try to do what is right."

His words were not heard. I continued to cry like a baby born into the world. He handed me a napkin, and said, "Y'all can work this out. The hardest part is over. It is now up to you if you want to stay with him or my favorite one, get her ass."

I laughed, but I knew that would not solve anything, at least not now. My own blood cousin was there and through the whole process tried to make me believe that my cheating husband was faithful. He, too, was in on the whole shenanigan.

"Go home, Shondia, and rest. Take you a vacation, a paid vacation."

"No, I must stay busy, but I have to leave because he is at home, and I am going to handle him."

"Shondia, do things the right way."

"Tell my heart to do things the right way and maybe we will listen."

Images of him and her plagued my mind. How could he shove my love around like that and make me feel stupid? They both would have to pay for the ache I felt. I left and began driving. Before I could make it home, I pulled over at the next exit to throw up. It was literally making me sick and the more I thought about them, the more I vomited. I sat there for at least thirty minutes feeling sick on the stomach. Quack must have told Popcorn because he called me. I pushed the button, but did not speak.

He was frantic in his tone. "Baby, where you at? Please, talk to me. Quack told me he told you and I'm going to kick his fat ass for what he did."

I yelled, "What he did! Don't ever talk to me again." I hung up and sat there sick as hell.

All I could see was him and the rest of the Zion Ridge bastards having fun with a fat ass whore who didn't give a damn about her own marriage, but helped fuck up mine. I hope all those sons of bitches rotted in hell.

Gathering my thoughts and trying to dry my face, I continued on to Highway 25, crossed over, and got back on Highway 15. After a few minutes of driving, I turned left on Shellie Brown and stopped on the train tracks, partially wishing a train was coming to kill me. Nothing came, so I drove off and took the left on Zion Ridge Road. After driving for many seconds, I turned in our driveway. Popcorn stood in the door, not saying a word. I sat there, unsure of what to do.

Finally, I got out the car. He walked toward me and tried to place his arms around me as I tried to walk by. He was dumbfounded when I hit his fake ass in the face. I tried to kill him with my arms, but he crushed my body beneath him. We were on the ground wrestling, and I didn't care anymore what my fate with him was.

"Calm the fuck down, Shondia, and let me explain." All I could do was cry. I felt myself about to throw up. Popcorn got up and let me move, and then vomit went everywhere. "What the hell! Shondia, please, hear me out," were his words to me.

"Get your shit and get the fuck on down!" I yelled at him.

"Shondia, it was not what it looked like. I was high and was fucking off. Shit, I was just trying to do something that I had never done since I met you."

I charged him. "Just fucking off! I go to work just to fuck off! I fuck with a woman just to fuck off! I pay bills at this bitch ass house just to fuck off! I did everything and you did nothing before you started working just to fuck off! So, don't tell me you were just fucking off! I fuck off!" I spoke with retaliation.

"Baby, it meant nothing to me. You my everything and that fat ass fucker have fucked my world up all because he wants you. Yeah, that's it! He wants you, so he fucks up my world for your ass."

"You can't switch this around on me. You fucked Michelle stanking ass, ate her worn out ass pussy and, evidently, you don't love me."

"That's not true! I have always loved you!" Popcorn yelled to me.

"A fucker like you doesn't know the meaning of the word love. You throw it around lightly, just like your tongue and dick in that low grade, home wrecking, no good bitch."

"Don't say that" Popcorn spoke softly as he shook his head no.

"So, you loved me when you were fucking?" I yelled.

"Yes, hell yes, I loved you, even when I did it. It was just that one time!" he screamed at me.

"So, the bitch was right. I saw it. You had plenty of time to tell me and you didn't. You didn't tell me. You chose to let me catch hints from her, and then you let someone else show me. You had plenty of time to tell me and when I confronted you, you still choose not to tell me. Instead, you would change the subject or get angry with me. You didn't see it when you did that, your attitude toward me changed. Everything I did wasn't good enough. You complained to me about every fucking thing that was nothing. You no good excuse of a man. Fuck you and that bitch. I trusted you. At least if you ask me anything, I would have told you. The problem is you have never asked me anything!" I hurled at him.

"How about the fat bastard loves you and how he wanted you before you met me?" Popcorn said.

"The magic word was before. You hear it? Before means before, not after we met. You illiterate son of a bitch, you will pay. You wrecked me and put my heart in my hand!" I yelled again.

"How the fuck you talking? You were with him, and you act like it is ok."

I yelled out to him, "Since you are so hell bent about thinking that I fucked around on you, let me tell you what happened before you stop me again, that's if you really want to know."

"Say what the hell you want; I know what the fuck I see. I know the fat fuck is in love with you and would do almost anything you ask of him."

"Fine, since we talking about Big Quack and no other things. Do you recall the night before we made love for the first time and how we had a truth night? I told you I had done a few things that I didn't want to do and how it was one of the worst things that I had ever done in my life. I told you that there are things about me you may not want to know, but you may need to know."

He thought about my question, and then responded, "Yeah, I remember the truth night, why?"

"Right before I met and married you, Big Quack did say something out of the way to me. In fact, he did more than say something out the way to me."

"What the hell did that fat motherfucker do?" Popcorn questioned.

"He asked to eat my pussy. Not to stick it, but for

145

me to cum on his face because he said I looked stressed and that was his way of helping me. At first, I didn't want to because I was involved, then I found out that my love was fucking off with dick. Anyway, after it was over he gave money to help me out. I turned it down, but he gave it to me, anyway. He was right, I was stressed out and it was never about money. He and I became the best of friends, and he has never come at me again. We actually never talked again about it."

Popcorn was silent for a moment, and then he asked, "He did what?"

"You fucked after you met and married me, so why you look like that? This was not on camera. I didn't have to tell you, but I wanted to tell you because I did not want anything to come between what I am trying to have with you." He was lost in thought as I looked at him puzzled. I had just told him what I had been trying to tell him since we met and all he could ask a silly question.

"That fucker sucked on your pretty ass pink pussy lips. He muzzled his pie ass face in your pussy. The same pussy I love to taste whenever I can?" I did not reply. "That fat bastard drank your pussy juice because I know how wet you can get when I ready." I was still unresponsive to his questions. Finally, Popcorn said, "All those times I talked to him thinking maybe, just maybe, I was wrong about him wanting you. And, how maybe, just maybe, he is just a friend and that I was reading more into it than I should. You telling me that you let him taste the only pie in town that I thought no one else had ever tasted. You mean to tell me that my pie been sliced by a pie eating motherfucker like Big Quack?"

Immediately, I knew I messed up. Before I could retract the confession, he yanked me by my collar and threw me against the car. Without hesitation, Popcorn was all on me. With tears in his eyes, he said, "I trusted you. I would never imagine in this life that you would stoop so low for a few dollars."

"You trusted me! You make me laugh. I trusted you. This happened before you and you actually fucked and ate pussy. He only tasted it, not fucked it."

He released me and kicked the fender beside me as he started crying like never before. I had never seen my husband so distraught, and it tore at me. Trying to make sense in what was going on, I spoke with honestly, "It was before you and on numerous occasions I tried to tell you, but remember, you would not hear it. When I would bring it up, you would say no, it was before me."

"Hell, I wasn't there. You could have made a river in your bed," he spoke with anger.

"What the hell are you talking about?"

"You getting wet as hell in his bed."

"We weren't in a bed," I defended.

"Where the fuck did all this take place?" he questioned me.

"It doesn't matter, it was before you"

"What the fuck you mean it doesn't matter!" Popcorn demanded.

"Like I said, what I went through happened before you, not after like yours," I said in truth.

"You dirty half breed bitch; you have turned that

Down Low Diva book into a reality, huh?"

"It wasn't like that. I know who I love, and it was all before you. I don't understand why the rage. You were caught on tape fucking and eating pussy that any and everybody have probably tasted, remember? Here you stand in my damn face mad about something that happened before you. Nigga get fucking real."

"I feel like a motherfucking fool. I'm running around here thinking I'm the only one that has tasted your nectar, and, in fact, you have let that big ass oversized hummingbird taste your sweetness. Why did you really let him taste you?" Popcorn asked with more pain in his tone.

"I was trying to get back at my friend at that time and my car was in the shop. I let him do to me what he does," I said as I glanced over at him.

"Bitch, you get the hell away from me."

"Honestly, I blocked it from my memory. When I met you and found out that you were cousins and you told me how you don't like to fool with him because of how he is, I tried to tell you who it was then that I did that regretful thing with. Other than that, you must believe me, Popcorn. However, I told you that I had never had sex with him. I did not lie. He has never entered me. I told you about it when we started dating and we had that confessional moment, but you didn't want to listen. I told you that I had done something, in fact, one of the worse things I have ever done, but you stopped me."

"That was then. I had no idea that you got your pussy ate by his fat ass," Popcorn said as he muffled back from crying.

"You ate another woman's pussy on tape with a lot of men around. How you going to talk about me and what happened before you? You had her juice all over you as you fucked her with no condom. You probably came home and were glad that I was asleep."

"It doesn't matter," were his only words.

"So, because you did it, it doesn't matter? Think about it. All the times he came around me when you were there, did I ever disrespect you? No, but you put my heart in my hands all because you were drunk, horny, and for a dare? You have messed up our lives over pussy everybody getting, you the stupid motherfucker. Should have used clear wrapping paper while you stand there looking like you are innocent. You put my life in danger as well as yours," I mentioned.

"She don't have a disease."

I laughed at the naïve bastard. "You can't tell if a bitch is sick just by looking at her," I wanted to scream, but was hesitant. I only shouted, "Where your white coat at? You damn doctor! How the hell you know? Unless you were the only one, she was fucking, which we both know the bitch gets down wherever with who ever."

"She is just a friend," he continued to say to me.

"Friends don't fuck friends, you thoughtless, irresponsible bastard. There is a line they don't cross and once you crossed it, it is no more a friend!" I yelled to him.

"How you talking? You work for the bastard."

"That was the main thing about Big Quack that I have never told you, even though I tried. Since it happened before you, why does it matter now?" I stated

149

Popcorn looked up at me, and said, "Bitch, please. You kept the friendship that is why it matters. I can understand if it went in this form, it happened, we met, and you never contacted him again. But it went like this, he ate the good pussy, you met me, and you continued to talk to him. Not just talk to him but work for him. What the fuck! I understand it was right before we met, but you kept working for the bastard. To me, you kept the door open for him to want you more by taunting him and knowing how he felt. Don't tell me you think he was feeling you as a fucking friend, and you didn't know that as long as he could talk to you, he didn't care about you or your thoughts of love. I have always done right by you. Women come at me a lot, but I turned them down, except that once, because of my love for you, and to find out that you let that fat ass bastard taste your pussy, tasted my sweet tasting pussy. The one person on the Zion Ridge that I detest, the one person that doesn't really talk to me like he does T. nem, but when you come up, he is always in your face, that fat motherfucker!"

He could not speak anymore, for he was crying. I desperately desired to touch him, just to let him know that I was his and his alone. Most of all, he seemed to forget what he actually did to me a few months ago. Moments continued to pass by. I thought all the questioning was over, but his tear bank dried up as he spoke, "Was it good? Did the fat fucker eat your pussy good? I need to know the answer."

"When you were with Michelle was it good?" I questioned back.

150

"No. I was just being a man, and I am street like that. You are not. You are my wife, my fucking wife!"

"Popcorn, I refuse to answer. I only want to remember my sex life with you," I protested.

"Answer the damn question. He calls himself the damn international pussy eating king. Did the fat fucker please the pussy? How many times did you cum in his mouth? Tell me! How many times did he drink your juice while he buried his face in you? Did you ride his face or were you in your favorite position, on your back?" Popcorn demanded again.

"I did not cum in his mouth like you think. He did not get the full benefit of tasting me like you think. That is the entire truth. Please, stop all these questions because you are not answering mine. And, as for keeping the friendship, you made me believe that you had never talked to her and I find out that you stopped her from wanting to kill her husband?" I replied.

"I see. What kind of friendship did you have after that? How nice was the motherfucker after he tasted you? Bitch, tell me! I swear to God you better not lie!" he yelled at me.

"Have you forgotten that you actually fucked a woman in Big Quack's house while I was at home angry at you? I need to be questioning you and what you have been doing. Maybe you need to tell me of your friendship with that bitch! You put all parts of you in her bare backed and all I did was get my pussy ate before my marriage."

"You better answer me before I put a hole in your damn head," Popcorn said as to dared me to make a move.

151

"I don't know exactly how he felt. I avoided him. He offered to eat it again and pay any decent amount. I told him no. All he wanted to do was taste it. He told me that he wants someone like me to have on the side and how no one would think of me with him. I told him that I am looking for more in my life than a fuck partner or a pussy eater. I am looking for stability and someone to have a family with. He has no interest in any of those. We talked no more about it, but that was it. Since then, it has been a friendship thing. We talk about the business, his friend girls, and what I think of this and that, but never about him and me. What occurred between us was history, you are my future. Not him and not my job."

Out of the blue, he stared into my face for a reaction after he asked silently, "Did you suck his dick?"

"What? I just answered your questions."

He began to rock as he spoke, "I know how you are when I taste your pink lips, I know how squirmy you get as I suck on your pussy lips, and I know how you enjoy tasting me, so tell me before I draw my own fucking conclusions. Did the dick taste good?"

"No! I've never tasted anyone but you. Everything I went through with him was before you. In fact, you are guilty, that is why you only want to talk about what I did before you and not what you did after me. You are the one who is ashamed. You are the one who feels guilty, so you try to spin this all on me to cover up how you feel!" I yelled.

Popcorn stood there not looking at me. I continued to speak, "Again, I had never tasted anyone but you. There has been no other man in my life. No, I have not tasted him or any other man for that matter. I lived a sheltered life and if you know your facts, then you know that he loves eating pussy, which I didn't know then."

As if that was not good enough, he asked, "Why didn't you suck that fat fucker's dick? Was it too short or did it smell like sweat and shit?"

"Why all the damn questions? I've confessed to what I did before I met you and since it was before you, why does it matter? I'm hurt, God knows I am hurt. You won't even discuss what you were caught doing. Were you ever going to tell me?" I suggested.

"On my own time. He put me in a damn corner, but I did that. I man up to it."

"If you man up, why are you very angry about me and him, and not what you were caught doing?"

With a straight face, he spoke, "It matters because number one, what you did back then is hurting us now and, number two, you kept the fucking friendship. It would have been better if you did it and you departed ways, but you kept it. I'm a man. I know how the fuck men think. I know he wanted more, but he knew that you didn't, so he just kept it friendly. Just waiting on a chance to fuck you again, yeah, and oral sex is still sex, bitch," my husband announced boldly.

Tears paraded down his face more connectively than before. I understood what he was saying. Big Quack and I had been just friends in my eyesight and to me that was all we were. It didn't make it right, but he was right. I cried harder than he did because something had my heart in a

153

grip lock. The pain was excruciating. I had never felt any like it before. Reaching up, I went to caress his brow, but he snatched my hand.

"Don't you dare touch me! You bitch. If I didn't love you, I would kill you and him, but fuck y'all and, most importantly, fuck you."

"Popcorn, that happened before we even met, and since then we have been only friends. He and I have a friendship, nothing more. What about what you did, huh? Justify what you did in his house in front of your boys while I was asleep at home. When you came in did you wash off? Did you fuck me after you had fucked her? Did you compare the pussy?" I claimed.

"Bitch, she wasn't family, and you have done enough." Without any more talking, he walked a few paces, and said, "Since you want to talk about things that happened before you, let me drop this on you. Before I met you, the boys and I used to run trains on bitches from 397 and your home girl the Snow Queen was one of them. She used to suck me sore and when I didn't think I could nut, she would go deep and find that nut. I only quit fucking off with her because I fell in love with you. When I found out that she was your home girl, I let that part go because I believed in breaking all communication, unlike you, I didn't keep my thang going. You kept your friendship with that fat fuck. Keep it, but you won't keep me. When I get home, have your ass out my shit and maybe now I will be able to see my daughter. Been kept from her because I married yo ass. Goodbye."

The only thing I could blunder was, "You should have

said something before I paid all your bills here."

"Money? Here, take every damn dime in my pocket. Get the hell stepping, you Zion Ridge community, click fucker."

After he threw the few hundred dollars toward me, he walked out to his truck. Close in tow I was, not letting him go as I fell on the ground by the force of his hand. Each time I got up I ran to him, but he slung me off him and kept going. Popcorn got in his truck and sped off. I only sat on the ground and cried, not caring who saw me.

The love of my life had left me, and it was all because I kept a friendship, although, he was not looking at what he had done to me. If I had known it would have had those consequences, I would have quit working for him and saved my marriage. I recollected my friendship was not in question; it was his loss of love for me.

CHAPTER 9 (October)

Still dazed about everything, I slowly began to pack my things. I had nowhere to go and no family to go to. Auntie would take me in, but I couldn't have her in my business, either. The more I thought about leaving, the sadder I became. *Where is there to go?* I continued to ponder on the question. I couldn't go to Shay, for I wasn't in the mood to hear her talk shit.

I sat beside the bed and wondered *how the hell did I get in the situation?* Michelle was the only answer I came up with. "That big, fat, dick sucker has not only changed but rearranged the only stable life I have had in a long time." Trembling and frantic, I slowly felt dead toward love and the possibilities.

There was not much for me to pack, but my car was packed enough. I checked my bank account, and the amount was not good enough; even the money he threw on the ground was not a substantial amount. Suddenly, I felt ill and didn't feel like driving. I made my way down the road to my boss' house, not to stay but to borrow on my check.

When I pulled up in his yard, Popcorn's truck was there but he didn't come out and I didn't beckon for him. Instead, I called my boss on the phone. He picked it up after the second ring, and spoke, "Get your ass out and come in."

"No, he is in there and after our argument I can't stomach him, literally."

"Aight," was all he said before he hung up.

His car porch door swung open, and he walked out in

Superman pajamas. It was a funny sight. I spoke out to him in regard to his PJs, "I hope you are not the final chapter."

"If I am, a lot of people will be shit out of luck," he spoke as he squats at my car door. "It's after hours, so it must be important."

"How can he show his ass about what you did and then come to your house? That's fucked up."

"That is just the way men are. If it's any help to you, he is in the house about drunk and miserable. Come in and get your husband."

"Look in my car. He snapped about you eating my pussy before I met him."

Big Quack was quiet. He stammered the words, "That shit was before him and not since him. We only have a business arrangement. It is always business before pleasure. Yo ass keeps money in my pocket. I can't fuck that up for nothing."

"I know, but he says it is because I kept our friendship."

"That shit was before him and I understand where he coming from, although, it is over. He is jealous and thinks negative. You are beautiful and a great person, so he is right."

A few minutes went by, and we both were quiet. Breaking the silence, I asked, "May I borrow against my work check?"

"For what? Your ass may not pay me back." I gave him my "You silly" look, and he asked, "What are your plans if I loan you the money?"

"I believe I am preg..." was all I could get out.

"It ain't mine!" he shouted as he cut me off.

"Shush. I haven't said anything to anyone. I've been vomiting and everything."

"Why you leave for, you may have a kid? If I were you, I would not go anywhere."

"Well, because he told me to get the fuck out and be gone when he gets back."

"What the hell that means? Y'all married and he can't keep you out unless you move out, which you are doing now."

"He kicked me out and now that I am out, he can see his daughter little Moochie that Shay keeps from him, and he said things I won't repeat."

"He is just being a man that is hurt."

"Fuck that! He actually fucked and it wasn't that long ago. My thing occurred before him."

"That shit doesn't matter. We are men. It's getting late and I have a hot piece in the bed, what you need?"

"About three hundred."

"Oh, hell no. You just got paid."

"I also paid the bills while I was there."

"What you need the money for?" he asked me in his usual tone.

"I am going to stay in a hotel, the Home Gate Inn, to be honest with you."

"Then what? You can't afford to stay there long because that shit will add up for real."

"I guess back to 397. Go back to where I came from. There is nowhere else for me to go, Big Quack, I have nowhere else to go," I spoke with slight sobs.

"When you do, your ass going to dip on me. I can see it," Big Quack said with humor.

"You going to give it to me or not?"

"Yeah, let me go in here and get it."

Sitting in the car was not what I wanted, but I had to. Popcorn came out and saw me. He went ballistic. He ran toward my car and kicked the front end. "What, you thought I was not here to catch your ass! Come to see your lover! Your ass couldn't wait until I wasn't here! Bitch, get out the car so I can whip your ass right!"

His Zion Ridge boys tried to keep him off my car and they had a hard time. They kept screaming at him to leave me alone, but he was like a mad man on steroids. Big Quack came out the door trying to see what was going on. When he saw that it was my husband, he ran to my defense.

I heard, "Man, leave her alone. Your drunk ass can't see that you have a wonderful woman that loves your stupid ass."

"She loves me so much that she likes getting her pussy ate by another motherfucker," Popcorn said.

"You out of line, Pop. Control your tone. You kicked her out and she needs to borrow money. I am her boss and if she needs doe, I'll give it to her. What the fuck you going to do? Whip my ass for helping out my friend?"

They were squared toe to toe, and I never knew Big Quack would act the way he did, but my boss stood up for me. Everyone was quiet as Popcorn said before going back in Big Quack's house, "I don't have anything on me to hit your big ass with. Tell your friend I said to stay the fuck away from me."

The scene was over, and I could only cry. Very politely and with much comfort, Big Quack said, "Here, take it. You don't have to pay me back. Consider it a gift and take care of yourself, and I hope you can still come back to work. I will have a talk with that husband of yours. You go somewhere safe."

"Thank you. It means a lot to me that you're helping me," I spoke as I backed the car out.

I opened my hand and saw five hundred dollars. I was happy. Instead of going to the hotel, I just drove, not knowing where I was going. It mattered not. When I crossed Highway 14, I felt alone for the first time in years. Taking the Philadelphia exit, I kept going. I could not go home because my husband did not want me there. I could not go to my auntie's; she was too nosey. I continued to drive as I passed the new apartments on my left.

Once I did that, it was obvious that my destination was Philly. The ride seemed longer from that way than it did from Nanih Waiya. Seeing that traffic was not as heavy, I decided to go to the Silver Star. I had only been there once, that was where I met Big Quack. He was nice, but full of himself. I grinned because he had my lover Shay with him, and that was how I found out about Zion Ridge.

I continued to think as I drove about how Shay was beautiful as ever. I knew she said she was going to be fucking more than me; I just didn't think that it would be a man. However, the night I ever heard a Zion Ridge was the night I met my boss. My girl was with him. She introduced us and the entire time Big Quack, and I talked, Shay was quiet. I wanted her to say something so I could fuck her ass up for letting me catch her with one of her new lovers. I found out he owned a business and told him that I just graduated in Hotel and Restaurant Management.

It was the perfect opportunity for me to find out about this new community that Shay was fucking. He gave me his card and the rest were history. Funny enough, Popcorn stated to me that he was there, but we did not meet until I took Chug to Spay. I finally met the infamous Popcorn that Shay always talked about. I had no intentions of falling for him and giving up pussy, but shit happened.

Shay got pissed when she found out that I was fucking Popcorn. Since then, she and I had a love behind closed doors and hate in public relationship. How I missed her ass. Clearing my mind, I parked the car and went inside. The same bar was still there, and the same stools were there. I sat there and watched TV, not knowing what was on, just looking at the pictures. I didn't sip and, besides, drinking and driving doesn't mix.

The longer I stared at the TV; I felt easiness come over me a little. Men approached me and I told each that I was married, and happy at that. *Too bad I'm faithful*, I thought as my mind was cloudy again from my life. I began to feel sleepy, and the cigarette smoke was unpleasant. I could spend some money and get a room, but that would be a waste. Deciding to leave, I went back outside and left. I drove to the Philadelphia Wal-Mart and parked in the middle row that was further at the back. Locking my doors, sleep came quickly.

Time must have sped by, for I awoke to a lighted area and with no warning. Tears fell for no apparent reason.

161

Everything came down on me. I sat there not knowing what to do. I wondered what my husband was doing and hoped he thought about me. I drove to Waffle House for some grub because after all the crying my appetite had come back.

The first thing I did was run to the bathroom because when I opened the door, the smell of the food hit me. I felt as if I were suffocating. "What the hell is wrong?" I remembered the fact that I might be pregnant. The realization of that statement made me pause. Taking a sigh, my stomach growled, but I went back to my car for the smell made me sick. Sitting in my car for few minutes, I drove back to Louisville to the Health Department.

It was empty, that was good for me. I signed in, told them what I wanted, paid, and moments later I was in the back pissing in a cup. She directed me to go back out front. Still, no one was in the lobby. I was happy for that; however, I did see a girl working there that looked familiar to me but brushed it off. I didn't feel like running into people I saw often at Big Boy's BBQ, at least not right then.

The nurse called me in her office, and said, "Congrats, you are pregnant."

"What?"

"Yes, Mrs. Collier, you are having a baby according to your positive test. I am sending you to Winston General for an ultrasound to make sure all is well with the baby and get a more in depth on how far along you are. The technician there can see more."

Thinking to myself, *how I thought it was stress from Shay*

and everything else. In a surprising tone, I said, "I'm not even showing. I didn't have any symptoms until a few weeks ago, and that was only being tired and aching feet. My sense of smell has increased but do you really mean a baby, baby?"

"Yes. Every pregnancy is different. Some women don't gain weight until the end or eating doesn't change at all. It depends on the baby and the mother. Like I said, every pregnancy is different" the nurse stated.

"I've had some odd colored period, but I bled every month like clockwork. I have felt my nerves move. I have felt constipated and dizzy sometimes, which I reasoned by thinking I got up too fast or if I skipped eating."

"You had symptoms all the time, you just never realized it. Like your period being abnormal. Some women see some type of bleeding around the time they are to have a period and that is why it is assumed to be a period. They mistake the light color with stress and or weight gain. Here is your estimated due date paper. You must give this to the welfare department to apply for your Medicaid. Before you leave, stop at the front desk on your way out to get your next appointment. They should give your WIC paper, also. Go by there and get your nutritious food. Once you leave there, go to Winston General for the ultrasound today. Again, congrats, Mrs. Collier."

I took the paper, walked out the door, and it hit me at once. I remembered when things made me sick, but we never assume it was a baby. I went and applied for my Medicaid, got my WIC, and then it was off to Winston General.

When I got there, I gave them the papers. Moments later, they called me to the back and put a jelly lubricant on my stomach. On the screen there it was, a big baby. When it moved, I felt it. Honestly, it gave me a fright. All that time I thought it was my nerves. I cried because of all the times, there I was with a baby, no husband, nor home.

"Would you like to know what it is?" the technician asked.

I waited for a few, and then decided with excitement, "Yes."
Pointing at the screen he said, "It is a boy. See here and here, those are features of a boy."

"Can you tell me how far along am I?"

"According to this sonogram, you are about seven months."

I waited before screaming out loud, "Seven months!"

"Yes, ma'am. Your baby should be here no later than December seventh, if not around Thanksgiving, or take a few days."

He gave me the printout of the pictures. I headed straight to my home with my husband. When I pulled in the driveway, I saw Shay walking out the house. *What the hell she doing here? She has never been here while Popcorn was here*, I thought. In my husband's arms was the little girl. He seemed happy. I could not think. I didn't know if they stayed the night or what. I began to feel angry, but why?

Shay saw me and with evil and fast actions, she ripped little Moochie out of his arms. Popcorn looked as if

164

he didn't understand what was happening. Kenosha began reaching for him. It tore at my heart, for the child was innocent. Finally glancing up, he saw me and stopped short. In that instant, our eyes locked. My thoughts were clustered. It was as if I was an intruder.

Popcorn seemed extremely happy, and I didn't want to ruin it for him, although, we continued to stare. My eyes then went back to Kenoshia, who did not look like my husband at all. Tears fell and I was, again, sad. My instinct was to leave, but Shay said something to Popcorn, and she waved for me to stop. Not thinking clearly, I did.

She walked over, and said, "So your ass wants to fight dirty?"

"How is that when you know I love the shit out you, girl?" I spoke.

"No, bitch, you can't love my pussy and that dick. You couldn't choose, so I will help you."

"Don't do this, Shay. I want to be with him more and you know it," I said in a begging state.

"Your ass should have stayed with fucking just me, but no, you had to explore. Not only did you explore, but yo ass fell in love with my dick. The same dick I told you about."

"Shay, I'm going to leave, and we will pretend this conversation never took place."

Once I headed down the road, I vowed not to cry again for the man and woman that broke my heart. I turned on Major Brown Road and went to the end of the street. I took a right and came out by the Fly Trap. Taking the left, I was on Highway 14 and my job was the first right. *A full crowd*, I thought as cars were ever all over the place.

Parking in the employee spot, I went in through the back door. When I opened the door, Big Quack was rolling. I had never seen him sweat, for his ass was always out-front pretending that he was making it happen. But that evening he was making it happen.

"Shondia, get your ass clocked in and come on so I can rest," Big Quack yelled out to me.

"You got it," I teased. He did not respond, so I knew then that he was strung out and was ready for me to work.

Even the newbie was working. As soon as I clocked in, I began working equally hard. Big Boy's was on. My first thought was that people had the taste for BBQ. As crazy as it seemed, the smell of that food did not make me sick and soon as I found out about the baby, it was like I saw the signs that I missed all along.

We worked like natural dogs. Never had I ever worked so hard at the job until that day. One thing for sure was the place made money, and it was because we all came together as a team. When the place cleared out, we cleaned up. I was in no hurry to go because I had nowhere to go. One by one the crew left. The place was different empty. I went to lock the front door, and Big Quack was sitting out front.

Out the blue, he asked, "You, ok? I saw you didn't look well a few times."

"If you call homeless and pregnant ok, guess I am," I replied.

"What? You pregnant?" he asked as he got up and

encouraged me to come sit in the chair, he pulled out for me.

"Thanks, my feet do ache," I spoke as I sat in one chair and put my feet in the other.

"Yes, I just found out that I am pregnant."

"What Popcorn say?"

"You are the only one I've told, and I didn't come here to work tonight, but glad I did."

"Why haven't you told your husband?"

"When I came back Shay and the baby was coming out our house, so I left," I spoke, feeling sad all over again.

"What? Shay coming out ya house with little Moochie with her. You serious?" he questioned.

"Same thing I said when I saw them. Popcorn's persona was of joy. He finally got what he wants."

"Shondia, are you going to tell him?"

"I don't know. Right now, he finding out me being pregnant is my least worry."

"You going back home tonight? I mean, you are pregnant. Isn't that what you and he both wanted?"

"Yes, it was, and no, I'm not going back. Was kind of hoping you have something I could rent." His expression was unreadable. Big Quack was quiet, as he was focused on the words I spoke. "Well, either you have something, or you don't?" I demanded.

"To begin with, I don't want any shit from that husband of yours because I gave you a place to rent."

"How is that? He kicked me out. I just didn't leave."

"Look at how he acted that night. He is jealous as

hell of you, and I can't blame him."

"Well, Big Quack, what he thinks is not my concern nor should it be yours."

"It doesn't matter what he thinks, it is how he reacts, and to know that you are renting from me will make him furious."

"He won't be. Shay is there to take my place. Besides that, he can see little Kenosha but not his son, who's due this November or the first week of December."

"You having a boy in November or December?" Big Quack exclaimed.

"Yeah, found that out today as well."

"I have been noticing your spread. I just thought it was because you are always eating my shit up at the restaurant," he said with too much humor.

"Ha, ha, very funny. I do be eating, though. The funny thing is I never suspected a baby. I had no real symptoms, and I still look the same."

"On the real, the house down the street won't be available until the first of the year, the mobile home park is full, and, honestly, the only thing I have is my man cave."

"I'll take it," I blurted out, not letting him finish.

"Wait," he said as he laughed, "Let me finish." He paused, then continued, "You can use it until Super Bowl, but if Popcorn doesn't wake up you may need it longer, by then something else may open up. I'll help you as much as I can, Shondia."

"Ok, how much rent? You know I do work for you and the pay isn't too good."

"Cute. Since it is you and you are pregnant with a

168

new Zion Ridge member…"

"Whoa, I didn't say that. He could be a 397 boy," I spoke with laughter.

"His dad is not a 397 boy, and he won't be, either. Shit, I'll whip your ass for him if you try to bring that boy up in those sticks running through the woods barefoot, having bows and arrows on his back" Big Quack laughed as he said that to me.

"Remind you, his father does not know yet and I may not tell him."

"That is why you should tell him. Let him make that decision."

"What you say sounds right, but how do I know that he is not with Shay and child playing the happy family?"

"Shondia, you won't know until you tell him. Don't you decide for him, let him do that on his own."

"Ok. I might just tell him. You go home just in case I have to come over and get in my new place. Speaking of new place, how much is rent again? I can't give you an arm and a leg."

"How about the leg because I need you to continue to work as long as you can, but if you get to the point that you are hurting or something you got to let me know," Big Quack spoke with compassion.

"I will. This is all new to me, too, ya know."

"Rent, uh, can you pay two a month?" he asked.

"I have no choice, and two is cheap."

He cut me off to say, "Dirt cheap, you mean."

"Ok, dirt cheap. I will take it."

"I will have the agreement drawn up, but if you

need it before then you can move on in."

"Thanks so much, Big Quack."

"It is not to be a whore house unless I am invited."

"You stupid," I exclaimed to my boss, my friend.

"Yeah, and I don't want any trouble with your husband because don't you know that he will cut the fuck up when he knows that you will be staying here?"

"Excuse me, I am grown, and I have to do what I have to do. Wish me luck."

"Aight go on and let me know."

CHAPTER 10

When I got to the house, it was different to me. I parked the car and assumed that I could stay because I forgot that he would be at work. When I tried to open the door, it would not open. I went around to the back door and that, too, was locked. Then, I heard a familiar voice.

"Is that you, Popcorn? You home early."

My mouth dropped. It was Shay. I got angry. "Bitch, what you doing in my damn house!"

"No, bitch, Popcorn's the bitch for fucking up my house. It also doesn't matter why I'm here; you just need to take care of your bastard baby with Big Quack." Hearing her say that stunned me. No one knew but me and Big Quack. For that hoe to know was beyond me. She noticed that I was quiet, therefore, she said, "Yeah, bitch. Popcorn knows you are pregnant by Big Quack. I told you your ass gonna get caught."

"Shay open up and let me talk to you." She opened the door and looked good. I walked in and the place did have a different appeal to it. "So, yo ass want my world?" I asked her.

"Hell no. I was fucking him first and since you act like you don't want to fuck me, I decided to play on his weakness," she spoke with laughter.

"You and I both know that your daughter Kenosha is more likely not his."

"I know, but he doesn't. He is so desperate to do anything for her, and shit, you can't beat that."

"You know I am not pregnant by Big Quack."

"I know that, but he doesn't know that."

"Why are you doing this? It's wrong."

"Why am I doing this? We had a good thing going until you started fucking my dick. Now, what's wrong is that you know, and you didn't tell him, and it's wrong that you won't let me taste that pregnant pussy."

"I didn't say you couldn't taste it, but where is the little Moochie?"

"She asleep."

I pulled off my sweatpants and she sat on the floor between the couch and the ottoman. I already knew my position. Sitting on the ottoman, I lay back and placed my legs on each side of her shoulders. "Bring that pussy to me and let me see if it's any different."

Doing as she asked, I closed my eyes and let her taste me. Shay flicked her tongue back and forth on me, the way that only she could do. I wanted to pull her head to me, but I couldn't. It was much needed, so I laid there and let her have her way with me. I screamed with joy like never before. Shay knew how to make me crave her and knew how to take me higher than Popcorn. *Damn, I love this girl. Why can't I have my cake and eat it, too?* I mused over how ironic it was to live a double life. Once she sucked all the juice out me, I had to taste her.

"The pussy tasted sweeter to me," Shay said.

"Really?" I asked with a glow on my face.

"Hell yeah, and to think you and I have been lovers for a long time just to let a piece of good dick break this up. Let us live here together with Popcorn? I don't give a fuck about him, I just want to be with you, Shondia, and when I can't have you, I get pissed off" Shay said.

"Less talk and more play." She already knew what was on my mind. She scooted the ottoman next to the couch. Shay climbed on top of the ottoman and placed her elbows on the couch with her beautiful ass perched out on the ottoman. "Bend your back some."

She did. I got on my knees, spread her ass cheeks, and tasted her. The fragrance was of cucumber melon and lilies. I dug my tongue deep into her wide ranged hole. It fit me perfectly as I licked the cheeks and watched her ass become wet from excitement.

"Look under the couch cushion," Shay spoke as she trembled.

I looked as she suggested and saw our old friends, Vaseline and Mr. Dildo. The sight of the two made me ready to plunge into her soft, luscious ass. "You must have known I was coming?"

"I had hoped you were coming back to tell Popcorn, and I was right."

Strapping on Mr. Dildo, I couldn't resist. I licked her ass again, making it wetter than before. Standing behind her light brown ass, I greased up Mr. Dildo and anxiously introduced him to the best asshole I had ever had.

She said, "Oh! Work me slow, baby. Show me this is your ass."

With Mr. Dildo buried deep into her I grabbed her small waist and began pumping her vigorously. The thought of my husband enjoying that good ass made me mad. I couldn't stop; I had to punish that bitch. She needed to know that she was mine and Popcorn was mine. The more I worked her ass, the more she threw it to me. I saw that she was delighted in the ass fucking, so I slowed the pace.

"What you doing? You know how I like it," Shay spoke as she tilted her head back to me.

"I know, but I'm letting you know that you don't run shit, I do."

"Well, punish me. I've been a naughty girl laying up with your husband and enjoying his dick."

She said too much, for I forgot about making her beg for more. I bounced her ass up and down on Mr. Dildo. She took all of it, and she began to cry out. I took Mr. Dildo out of her and drank her from the back. When all of her was spilled, she leaned over on the couch from exhaustion.

"Put Mr. Dildo up," I said.

"See, you may want your marriage, but you can't stop fucking me and I can't stop fucking you. Let us give this another try. I know we broke up because I fucked up, but that is in the past."

What she said was right. When I was with her, I only wanted her, fuck Popcorn and his dick, but when I was with him, I only wanted him, and fuck Shay and her good pussy. The two toiled in my mind and now that I was pregnant, I had to get with the dad and leave Shay alone.

"I hope you are thinking about moving back in here and the three of us live together until one gets greedy," Shay said.

"Shay, you and I have been together for a long time and I love you, girl, but I'm married now."

"Oh, here we go with this married shit again. You

married, but I'm in the house with your dick. What the fuck is wrong with this picture, Shondia?"

"Yes, this married shit again. I love Popcorn and you know I do," I spoke with love to her.

"You love him enough to tell him that you prefer to eat as much pussy as he does or you like digging into my wetness just like any man would? Which is it because I am confused?"

"I will tell him, but for now I have to leave you the fuck alone."

She jumped off the couch and kissed me fervently. I was overpowered by her tongue as I indulged her taste. She lifted up my shirt and rummaged her tongue in every spot. Twitching away from her gasp, I breathed heavily as she said, "He can't make you feel like I can. Admit it."

"No, he can't. You satisfied now!" I hissed at her.

"No, I'll be satisfied when you come back to me. Come back to where you belong."

"Shay, I won't, and something tells me that someone is out to get me. Someone is trying to break my once happy home up."

"Well, if it were I, wouldn't I have told him about me and you, and how you know that the baby is more likely not his?"

She had a point, but I played it on, "Then who?"

"Keep fucking me and I will find out," Shay spoke as she licked her juicy lips.

"I have to go. I have to plead to my husband that I am not carrying another man's baby."

"Girl, plead all yo ass want. I will believe you

quicker than he would. He is stubborn."

Dismissing her, I quickly put on my clothes and was on my way to Wal-Mart. I had to see my husband myself to see if what she said had truth.

I arrived and called his phone. It went to voicemail. I kept calling and finally left a message. "If you don't come out, I'm coming in and everybody is going to see me acting up."

A few minutes later, he called me. "Hurry up and talk, I am at work."

"I am not pregnant by Big Quack, it's yours. We finally have our own child."

"You calling me about this bullshit? Hell, this shit could wait, I am busy."

"Bullshit? Telling you about us having our own baby is not bullshit," I spoke to him.

"No, rewind, you have your own child and you trying to pass it off as mine. That's sad, Shondia. I expect better from you, then again, you are fucking someone in my hood."

"I am not fucking anyone but you. What happened to innocent until proven guilty? Remember again, you were found guilty, not me."

"You moved, where he at? Bitch, you could have gone anywhere but there."

"If you haven't kicked me out, I would have been there with you."

"Like I said, you just proved me right by being down there with him, so take your baby to the real daddy."

"Popcorn, it is yours. You know I am telling the

truth."

"Why didn't you tell me? I had to hear it from the streets," he spoke furiously.

"I came by to tell you, but that tiger pouncing ass trick Shay was there with her baby."

"Don't call Shay that, so shut the fuck up talking about her."

"I haven't been gone and now y'all a damn couple?" I asked between tears.

"No, her new apartment in Ivy isn't ready."

"What about me? I am homeless. Your baby homeless and we had nowhere else to go. And, so what, Big Quack was the only one that reached out to help your family. You turned your back on us, so you need to shut the fuck up talking about the very one that is trying to help me."

"You don't tell me to do a damn thing. Shit, if you can handle it, you can come over and we can all have fun, like you don't know what I mean," Popcorn said to me.

I hung up, for words could not explain how I felt. I wondered if he knew that I was a dyke before I met him and to some degree, still was. Between the tears, I drove to the job and sat in the parking lot. A few hours past and a big red caddy pulled up. I already knew who it was.

He pulled up next to me, and said, "Why I get a phone call that a car was at my business sitting?" He looked at me again, and said, "What the fuck did he say?" Shaking my head, I cried the harder. "Damn. Come on to the house, Shondia."

He pulled off and I drove behind him. When we

arrived at his house it was quiet, but I recognized Michelle's truck. Now my mind raced, but it is none of my business. I parked my car in front of the man cave, which was on the far side of his house off to itself.

I got out and so did he. I smiled, and he spoke, "Hell no, it's not what you think."

"What I think is irrelevant. How about he says I'm having your baby?"

"No, the fuck he didn't. I wish it was mine, at least you wouldn't be homeless and wouldn't have to work," Big Quack said with surprise.

"How did Shay know? Most importantly, how did he know if you are the only person I told?"

"I don't know. I didn't tell anyone. You do know you live on Zion Ridge, and everybody knows everybody's business. Life here is an open ass book."

"How come I didn't know that Shay moved in with the baby?"

If looks could kill, my boss might have been dead because he started laughing and jumping around. "Damn, Pop could have played it off. Then again, he wants to look at the bright side of shit. Come on, let me show you in."

He unlocked the door and turned on the light. The place was nice. There was a big screen TV, a wrap-around couch, to my left, a nice kitchen area, and straight ahead I knew must the bedroom. "This is nice, boss."

"It's nothing," was all he said.

"Shondia, you are very special to me, and I am glad to help you any way I can."

"Thanks, but all I need is for you make sure that no

lies are told. I am a renter, and I pay in cash, not ass." Big Quack laughed, and that made me laugh. "I'm serious."

"Shondia, I have a guest, I have to go. You funny because people here going to think no matter if it is true or not."

"You right."

He gave me the key and left. I sat on the couch and cried. So, it was true that he was fucking his baby's momma. There was no telling how long that had been going on. I had to call him, and he didn't answer. I kept calling and he finally answered to say, "Shondia, get back to Big Quack and leave me the fuck alone."

"Popcorn, it is a lie. It is your baby, and I need to talk to you. Please, talk to me. We have to work this out. I will tell you everything if you just listen and ask me."

"We don't have shit to talk about and I need to get off the phone before I let the devil use me for about ten minutes on your ass, then his ass."

"You are making a mistake. I am faithful to you" I hysterically cried.

"How the hell is that? Instead of going to your peeps, you run to Quack, that fat motherfucker and his money. You keep screaming I will tell you everything if I ask. What else are you hiding? You know what, fuck it. I don't care what you have to say. You've told me enough. Huh, you know what? You fooled me. I give it to you. Your ass was good but now fuck you and your baby."

He hung up and left me hanging. I was alone and wondered what to do. What I did know for sure was that my husband did not care for me like he used to. He did not believe me and on top of that, I tried telling him about me and Shay, plus, she had moved in our house.

Curling up on the couch, I cried and fell asleep. When I awoke the next morning, I bathed and got ready. I took a full tour of the man cave, and it was actually a nice place. It was almost like it was designed just for me. Opening the fridge, I saw some things I liked, but that morning I was not hungry nor was I sick. Closing the door, I looked out the window and saw Michelle's truck still there.

I didn't give her another thought because I couldn't be mad at her for what he did. Now, Chug was another story because he was my cousin and my dearest friend. I, in a way, didn't want to talk to him because I was still in denial. Ever since then, I questioned my existence by trying to find some type of reasons to go on.

Comparing things that went on was all I could do. I kept thinking that my husband didn't want me and no one else had come on to me. He had a daughter, and I was having his son. He kicked me out and moved another baby momma in, he used to believe me and now he didn't.

Refusing to concentrate on my life, I felt my baby move and I jumped. It surprised me. As if a light went on in my head, a reason to live and go on without Popcorn was made known. If he wanted to play, fuck it, we would play. I was tired of being the innocent one because it seemed like I always got my ass hurt. Hearing voices, I looked out the window again and it was Big Quack walking Michelle to her truck. His eyes went in my direction, and I moved back, thinking he could see me. She got in the truck and left.

"Shit, here he comes," came out my mouth as I saw

my boss walking my way. Thinking quickly, I sat on the couch and calmed my heart as he knocked on the door. Slightly, I said, "Who is it?"

"Yo ass not sleep. I saw you peeping out the window."

Amused, I said, "Come in, it's open."

He walked through the door and stood there. "What is it?" I asked.

"You don't have to fake sleep."

"I wasn't asleep. I happened to look out the window and there you go. You with the woman that fucked my husband."

"Well, looks like he is fucking somebody else now," he said, as he put his hand on his mouth as if he didn't mean to say that. Words could not come out my mouth, turning my head was all that could be done. Seeing my pain, Big Quack spoke, "I'm sorry."

"Sure," I replied as if I did not care.

"No, serious. I don't know if he getting good ass, head or not." When he said that, I grinned, and he laughed. "I was just playing. You know he knows you are here. So, he may not come down here."

"Hope he don't. I don't' care if I don't ever see him."

"That's on you. I came out here to tell you that I am not coming in today."

"You don't ever come in after you work hard. I thought you were going to tell me something else that I did not know."

"You think you know me, don't you?"

It was the way he said that question that took me by surprise and made me not respond. "Well, apparently I don't know anything, so tell me."

"You on a need-to-know basis," was all he said before he laughed.

"A sense of humor, I see. We getting one now, huh?"

"Anyway, can you close today?"

"You are my boss and now my lease owner. Yeah, I can stay. I don't have anything else to do."

"Good, I'll get at you when you come in, that's if I don't come by the place."

"Ok. Let's go before you make me late for work."

He and I walked out the door and when I heard my name, I saw Popcorn. Without knowing what he was thinking, I could feel it. I would have thought the same thing, which I did when I saw Shay coming out the house that day.

"What do you want?"

He and Big Quack shook hands, and then Quack left us alone to walk on to his ride. I looked pass Popcorn, and I could see my boss making faces behind my husband's back. A smirk escaped my lips, and Popcorn turned around and Quack pretended to be walking.

"What the fuck is going on!"

"I should be asking you the same thing. I am gone for one day and that bitch ass Shay is coming out our house. Are you fucking her now?"

"Shondia, you really are stupid. To have book sense, your street sense isn't worth a damn. You are simple and easily tricked."

"You come down here to tell me what? How you don't want me because you have your daughter in your life?"

"Fuck it. I never should have come," he spoke as he began to walk off from me. Quick thinking, I snatched his arm, and he jolted it back. It caused him to stop, but he was harsh. "Keep your cheating hands off me. I know they been on that bastard all night."

"You wrong! You the one with a bitch in your house!" I yelled.

"You reckon?"

"I have been having a pity party and it's all because of you. Tell me that she can love you like me. Tell me that you don't believe me when I tell you that I love you and how this is your child."

"Lately, I don't know what or who to believe."

"You are one to talk. I find out you screwed a ball sucker, nut drinking bitch. I feel like shit when I saw it and to think, I had remorse for hitting her. I wished I would have done more damage."

"I come out here to talk to you and I see your fat ass, pussy eating boss coming out your love hut and you behind him smiling. I should wipe that smile off your face with my fucking fist."

"He came by to ask me to close because he wasn't coming in today. Nothing else. Don't you want to know what we are having?" I threw in.

"You and he can have what the hell you want."
"Well, you will have you a son to go along with your

daughter."

I could tell that he wanted to smile, but for some reason he did not. Popcorn continued to play hard. "It is yours regardless of what people tell you. I know who made this baby with me. From this day forward, if you want people to come between us, fine, that is you, but as for me, I am going on. I have a son that will be born in a couple months."

His reply did not come soon as I would have liked, but he did say, "A son, a couple months?"

"Yeah," I spoke.

As if a possibility of a son being born crossed his mind, he said, "I'm confused and maybe it's good you not with me, but if I catch you and that fat bastard again coming out his man cave, I'm getting that ass. Bitch, you my wife and these games you playing are going to stop. You can't handle the ass kicking I will put on you."

"You forgot, I'm pregnant and this is his place. He can come and go as he like." Popcorn squeezed my arm. "Stop, you're hurting me."

"I'll show your ass how Popcorn pops, baby."

"Is everything alright over there," we heard the neighbor from across the street say.

"It is ok. Thank you."

My husband did not say anything else to me. He got in his truck and stared at me as he drove off. I went back to the parking area where my car was and stood there. The back glass was intact, however, when I walked to the driver side, I saw that it was keyed with huge dents in the door. The windshield was caved in on the driver side. Whoever it was, they wanted to make sure that I could not drive my car.

Tears fell unstoppable. I had no idea why anyone would want to break up my home with my husband or mess up my car. Reaching for my cell, I called Big Quack. "What's up? And, why you not at work?"

"Someone has messed up my car on your premises."

"What you mean, messed up your car?"

"Just what I said. I'm going to take pics and send them to you."

"Damn, now this is pissing me off. What, you have a bounty on your head?"

"Big Quack, it's not funny. Somebody came here while I was inside and did damage to my shit."

"Oh yeah, no homeowner's insurance," he spoke quickly and hung up.

"Fat bastard," I spoke as it came to mind that I had full coverage. I called Progressive and they shocked me by saying that Chadwick dropped the car in question.

I called Popcorn, and he answered the phone by saying, "What is it now, Shondia?"
"Someone came to Big Quack's and damaged my car. When I tried to make a claim, they told me I was no longer on the car insurance. How you do that when I must sign papers to make it legal? I've only been gone a day, and this is what I get? Am I off your work insurance, too, or what? You act like I am not coming back home."
"It's not what you know but who you know. As for you coming back here, that has not crossed my mind and the

truth be told; I don't give a fuck. I have other shit going on."

Listening to him tell me that me coming back had not crossed his mind broke my heart. As calm as I could, I said, "You are telling me that you do not want me anymore because you have moved Shay and your daughter in. Is this correct?"

"It's not that I don't want you, but you are pregnant, and it may not be mine."

"It is yours, dammit! I have not had any man since we met, but it looks like you have been with her the entire time because you don't move another woman in the next day you kick your wife out."

"Be thou as it may. I will always have love for you, just not right now. You have thrown a lot on a nigga and who the hell I talk to or move in my shit is my business, not yours."

"Me? Put a lot on you when you are the one that was caught on a cell phone having sex! For the record, everything you do is my business."

"That was not sex; I was just fucking a freak."

"You intentionally screwed her then?" I needed to know.

"Yeah. I heard the boys talk about how she will let you stick any hole without limitations. You were pissed over some bullshit, so Chug and I went back down the road and it all went down. I was releasing pressure. Just like that."

"Was it good?" He only laughed.

Popcorn let my imagination to run wild because he

would not straight out answer me. After paying attention to the laughter, I firmly replied, "I see. I guess there is nothing left for me to do but to get out your life."

"Shondia, it's like this. Fuck what I do or don't do. If I get wind of you and that fat ass pussy eating bastard fucking or doing anything out of context, your ass will be mine," Popcorn threatened.

"Oh, but you can move a well-known community bitch in our home and expect me to think that you won't be fucking her no less in our bed? I know how you love your dick sucked before you stick it."

"Are you deaf? I don't give a damn what you think. I'm telling you what will happen if I hear anything between you and Big Quack."

"Popcorn, I have loved you since the day we met and to know that you have thrown me to the wolves is a pain I will not forget."

"You did this shit on your own."

Deciding that enough was enough, I cut him off to say, "You know what? You threw me and our baby out. You have listened to lies and you refuse to believe me, so hear this. I am not fucking Big Quack, but if your baby needs to be fed, who knows whose nut will feed him."

I hung up quickly because I knew that he would be cursing, and God knows what else. After I hung up with him, Big Quack called. "Your ride messed up for real?"

"Hell, yes and it happened on your property, Mr. Boss man."

"Shondia, I don't know who could have done such a

thing, but I will get to the bottom of this. Nobody going to come to my place and fuck up unless it is me." The line was silent, and he broke it by saying, "Don't you have insurance?"

"I did have insurance. Popcorn took me and my car off."

"What the hell he do that shit for? He just kicked your ass out."

"Big Quack, I can't worry about him anymore. I have a baby that needs me to be strong and as of right now, he doesn't have a daddy."

"Shondia, I am not the daddy, but I can be the godfather, if that will help."

Smiling, I replied, "Thanks, but now I need to get this car in the shop, get to work, and make a budget. I'm already in a hole before I come out."

"I'll give you a break. I already told you that you don't have to pay me back the money. Now, I won't charge you rent for now and I will let you drive my bucket."

Tears were in my eyes as I spoke to Big Quack, "Thanks so much, Big Quack. You have turned out to be a great friend to me, more than you know."

"Well, the keys are in the Honda's glove compartment, so get your ass on to work."

"Aight" I said.

"Problem solved, now take your ass to work."

We hung up and I felt really happier. My boss was letting me use his little gray, two door, hatchback Honda with rims. *I wonder how his big ass fit in this car.* Changing my thoughts, I opened the door and got the key out the glove compartment. The car was full of gas, and it looked like a new car on the inside.

Deciding to show off the Honda, I drove the long way to work instead of taking the short cut down Highway 14. Soon as I signaled to turn on Major Brown, there looking in my face was Popcorn and in his truck with him was Shay. I wanted to be angry, but I didn't. I lifted my chin up to say hello and from the look on my husband's face; I could tell he wanted to drag my ass out that car.

Giving him I don't give a fuck smile; I cruised in front of them. When we got to Highway 15, I turned right, and they were behind me. He was on my bumper as I continued to drive in the slow lane. I acted like I did not care he was behind me. That was not enough for him because he got on the side of me. Shay's face was of pleasure and that made me feel even better. Again, I smiled and gave them the head nod.

From the look of their body language, it was like Popcorn was not into her as I once thought. Giving him a final smile, I drove off, leaving them far behind.

CHAPTER 11

My stomach growled, so I bought three bacon, egg, and cheese biscuits from McDonald's. I devoured the first one without hesitation. When I made it to work, no one was there. *'Bout like black people, always late and want to leave early*, I thought as I parked the car in my usual spot. Locking the doors, I unlocked the back door and locked it back behind me. Turning on the lights, I clocked in and turned on the steamers as I put food in it. Taking out the ingredients to make white cheese dip, I then began to do some prep work with the vegetables. Moments later, others began to come in.

People packed the place. Luckily, everyone pulled their weight. I was caught off guard when the front house waitress came in, and said, "Shondia, someone wants to see you at the fifth table."

"Me?" I asked.

"Yeah you," she said.

Pulling off my apron, I hung it up and went out front. I glanced and saw that it was Michelle. I had to be calm because this was my livelihood and had to be nice. It was smart of her to ask to see me in front of people. As nice as I could, I asked, "What do you want?"

"Please, sit down," she asked loudly and nicely.

"I would rather sit in a pit full of vipers; at least I know their intentions."

She laughed at what I said, and sparred at me, "Oh, you think you know, but you are just beginning to know."

Not understanding what she was talking about, I asked,

"Why you call me out here for, anyway?" I leaned closer, and said, "You've already fucked my husband, what the hell do you want by talking to me?"

Looking me square in my face, she deceitfully spoke, "The dick from the back was good as hell. I know why you cut the fuck up, but he is going to know what you hide."

At those words, I came unglued and started strangling the bitch. Families hollered as my coworkers pulled me off her. She was red and gasping for air. When they got me away from her, I spoke harshly, "The bitch should not have said what she said."

Families stood in huddles as my coworkers were all over Michelle as if she were the victim. The atmosphere was clinched with fear. Children cried and I literally tried to kill the big bitch.

I can't believe that I snapped like that. When I heard her say, "All I did was asked if her boss was coming in and she turned on me. I don't want her man, if that is the case."

"Bitch, you lying! I should come over there…"

The sentence did not come out my mouth good because I heard, "Mommy, she scares me."

It was like a light switched on. There I was in a family-oriented environment going ham on a woman that wasn't about shit. I couldn't believe that I reacted in such a manner. My lead line cook took me to the back and when I got back there, I started hurting.

"What is wrong with you, Shondia?" Words could not form because I was hurting very bad as the baby was in a knot. I began breathing slowly like the doctor told me and the pain went away. "You, ok?" he asked again.

"Yeah, I'm ok."

"Shondia, Big Quack wants you."

"What he want?" I said out loud.

He responded by saying, "You know the shit done hit the fan, that's why he calling."

Closing the door to the office, I said, "Let me explain."

"First of all, is the baby, ok?"

I didn't think about my baby when I acted a fool. Damage could have been done to him and there I was showing my damn ass. Slowly, I responded, "He is fine so far, but I had a pain right before you called."

"The baby ok now?" he asked again.

"Yes, thank you for being concerned."

"Ok, go ahead. I need to hear from my top employee why she is fighting at my establishment."

"She called me out front and I asked her what she wanted." I told him what happened after that.

"Why you say that shit? You know she was going to say some shit to piss you the fuck off."

"I wasn't thinking about that. I just feel like she doesn't have anything to say to me."

"I understand ya, but you should have kept your mouth shut." I told him everything else up to the physical part. Big Quack was quiet, and I did not understand.

"I believe you, but you know that you will be on suspension. I won't fire you because you are very important to me, and you make money."

"Ok. I'm leaving now."

"Oh yeah, how the car drive?"

"It drove ok, kind of hard to stop."

"I will get it checked out for you tomorrow. Right now, you go on home and rest."

"Ok, thanks. Let me get out of here"

"You know that it is going to be all over the hood about you fighting over dick."

"Maybe. I don't care anymore what these fuckers think."

"Well, I believe you."

"That means a lot. Let me leave."

Hanging up the phone, I clocked out and left. When I pulled off, I went to the Chevron on the hill by McDonald's. I got out and put ten in gas. Before I could drive off, my husband called. I sarcastically answered by saying, "You are calling me, what do I owe the privilege?"

"Why the hell are people calling me and telling me that my wife showing her ass by fighting a bitch over Big Quack?"

It was hilarious to hear that when I knew that was nowhere the truth. As not to entertain his statement, I replied, "Why is a so-called husband calling a woman that he does not want to be his wife? I tell you what, whoever told you that bullshit; tell them to tell you the truth because they are feeding you lies, and to quit talking out their ass."

"Don't fucking play with me! Ain't yo ass pregnant? You don't have any business trying to fight," he said in an angry voice.

"Remember, you kicked your wife and unborn child out. So, don't come at me wanting to know my business." Popcorn was quiet as I heard Shay say something in the background. At the top of my voice, I yelled, "Don't you ever fucking call me! You have made your choice clear. So, tell that bitch and all the other bitches to stay the fuck away from me. They win. They have us separated, so now it's over. And, oh yeah, fuck you and the bitches you fuck!"

I hung up before he could say anything else to me. I wanted to eat, but I felt like crap after the conversation with Popcorn. Instead of taking Highway 14 and turning left, I forgot and began driving up Highway 15 toward Greensboro. When I started to get in the turning lane in front of the hotel, the car wouldn't stop. I had to quickly turn back onto the highway and go on up.

My heart began beating out of my chest. The brakes were not catching. I tried pumping them in hope something would happen, but nothing. The Starkville exit was coming up. I did not know if I wanted to take that exit or keep going toward Ackerman and turn off on Shellie Brown. I had to think quickly. Making a rapid decision, I took the Starkville exit, for it has more highway room. Picking up the cell phone, I called Big Quack. Soon as he answered, I yelled out, "Your car won't stop! It won't stop! Please, help me! Help me!"

"What you mean? What you mean it won't stop?"

"It won't stop, and I am on the highway heading toward Starkville. Please, come get me!" I said as I cried.

"Hold on, I'm on my way," was all he said as he hung up.

I continued driving and before I knew it, I saw his truck in my rear view. When I spotted him, he called to say, "I have T. with me and we're behind you. What is the car doing now?"

"Nothing it drives great, but it won't stop. Please, help me, Big Quack, the car won't stop. I'm so sorry this is happening."

"Calm down, Shondia, getting hysterical is not good for the baby, ok?"

"Ok. Ok. Ok."

"You calm? Do you hear me?"

"Yes, I think I am."

"Listen, have you tried the emergency brakes?"

"Huh? The brakes?"

"I said have you tried the emergency brakes?"

"No. You know I haven't thought about that. Let me try."

"Before you do, pull it up easy as if to ease the car into a stopping position."

"Ok."

"I'm serious, go easy."

"Ok."

I did as he suggested, and the car began to slowly pull over soon as I passed the Old Highway 25 Road. When the car did stop, I got out crying. Big Quack and T walked over to me. To my astonishment, Big Quack placed his arms around me and consoled me. It felt wonderful to have a friend. T. did not say anything, just looked. Even though he was friends with Big Quack, he and Popcorn were closer.

T. went over to the car and jacked it up. He glanced back at Big Quack, and said,
"Man, look at this shit. You won't believe it."

Big Quack left me, went over to him, and said, "You

got to be fucking kidding me."

"Hell no, you see it for yourself, don't you?" T. spoke as he got up and put the jack back in the trunk.

"What? What's wrong?" I asked.

"Who the hell have you pissed off, Shondia? I mean, seriously. Whose toes have you stepped on?" Big Quack asked.

"No one. I've been accused of things, and it has all been lies. I am the one being hurt here."

"Well, someone has come on my property and damaged your car, and now the brakes have been cut on the Honda. What the hell is up with someone after your ass?" Big Quack stated with his distinguished grin.

"Ouch!" I yelled out.

Big Quack was at my side with his hands on my stomach because he knew that it was the baby acting up. "You feel that!" he screamed out with excitement.

"Ah, yeah, that is why I cried out."

"T., man, this is amazing. Wow, the baby kicked, and I felt it."

"You act like it is your baby," I said as I laughed.

"The child needs a dad before he gets here and if the real dad does not want to do it, then I will. That's what friends are for," Big Quack said.

T. did not say anything, only looked. I knew he was only there to report back to Popcorn what he saw. When Big Quack moved his truck in front of the Honda, I said, "I love my husband, and this is his child. You have never known me to lie or be a cheater. Talk some sense into him for me."

He looked at me and humped his shoulders. Disappointment overwhelmed me and I began to cry. Big Quack got out the truck. He saw me crying and asked T., "What the hell you do to her?"

"I didn't do or say anything to her. Shit she's pregnant and emotional," T. said, and was more than likely right.

They loaded the car on the trailer, and I got in the back. "Hell no. T., get yo ass in the back. Shondia needs the room to stretch her legs."

With no hesitation, he helped me out the back and took my place. The front did feel better as T got in the back behind Big Quack. "We right here in Starkville, y'all hungry?" Big Quack asked.

"You buying, I'm eating," I said.

"It doesn't matter to me, man," T. said.

"What you feel like eating?"

"Chicken," I blurted out.

"Some damn bird? Are you serious? We can have anything, and you choose bird? What the hell? You can get that at the job."

"Since you are buying, I will eat it as long as it's not Chinese or anything in that line," I said as we got on back on Highway 25 and took the downtown Starkville exit.

I glanced at Wal-Mart and rolled the window down further, for the fresh air was wonderful. We got to the second red light. I laid back and started rubbing my stomach, for the baby acted up more and more. With my eyes closed, I imagined that Popcorn was being so concerned with the baby and me, but he wasn't. That thought brought sadness to my face.

Big Quack must have seen my look, so he said, "Stop thinking about your situation and look on the bright side."

"And what is the bright side, may I ask? Because where I stand it's dark and lonely here."

"You have a little man being born soon and you have a true friend in me."

"Thanks, it means a lot to me," I spoke dryly.

From the corner of my eye, I saw T. He listened and took everything in. I just hoped he reported back to Popcorn the right way. I looked again, and we were pulling into Zax's and a smile approached my face. We parked in the back the long way because we had the car on the back.

Before we could get out, Big Quack said, "We are not going to dine in. I have a lot to do tomorrow"

"Who has a lot to do?" I reminded him.

"Ok, you have a lot to do tomorrow," Big Quack said.

Soon as we got in line and placed our order, Big Quack's phone rang. He walked off a few paces. T. and I got the order while Big Quack looked dazed.

"What's wrong?" I asked.

"How about my man cave just burned down."

I, too, became speechless. He walked quickly back to the truck as we followed behind him. I didn't feel like eating because I was numb. Everything was going haywire for me, and I didn't understand. Big Quack turned the ignition on and drove frantically. Once we were through the red lights and back on Highway 25, he drove wildly back to Louisville.

We rode in silence, but when we got to the Ackerman exit, I said with tears, "I am sorry, but I don't know how this could be."

"Did you leave anything on?" he asked.

"No, I didn't touch anything. I hadn't had time to do any looking around of such. You have got to believe me. I would not burn down your cave."

The way he spoke next sent chills down my spine, although, for some reason it sounded odd coming from him. "I believe you, but I think you need to move in with me so I can keep you and the baby safe. If anyone wants to hurt you both, they are going to go through me first."

From the corner of my eye, I saw the way T. looked. His words were more like a lover protecting his love than that of a friend. I did not want to read more into it; therefore, I spoke before I knew it, "If only Popcorn could be this caring."

"Fuck that nigga. He doesn't give a damn about you. If he did, he would believe you and do right by y'all, but he stuck on stupid and only thinking about dyke pussy."

"Dyke pussy?" I questioned. "Who's a dyke?" I said as if I didn't know. However, I had to know just how much he knew. If he knew about Shay, then it wouldn't be long before I was found out.

Thankfully, he said, "Never mind that, you wouldn't know. Let's get here and see the damage."

My mind was puzzling and all over the place. I was sure that he knew something that I did not but would not tell. Releasing that thought was the community and fire department in sight. They were putting out the man cave as everyone on looked. My heart plunged. His man cave meant a lot to him and all because of me it was ruined.

He parked the truck and trailer across the street and got out rapidly. I left the food inside and got out behind him. I saw the look of despair in his eyes as he stood there and watched what was left of it. Taking a sigh, Big Quack walked over to the Fire Chief, and they began talking. My boss walked over after speaking with the Fire Chief to say, "It is reported that you left the iron plugged up and it had fallen over on some paper."

"Huh? I did not have the iron on at all. I distinctively did not use an iron or was near any papers. They are lying on me."

"It doesn't matter. I have insurance and I do believe you."

"What am I to do? I am homeless again and everything around me is crumbling," I questioned with many tears.

"It is ok. Like I said, you can stay with me."

Jerking back, I looked at him and he smiled.

"No funny business. You need a place to stay, and I want to be the one to help you. Besides, where are you to go?"

He was right. I had nowhere to go. "Ok, but I must…"

"Just be quiet, Shondia. It's going to all work out, you'll see."

I went under the car porch and sat in the white rocker. My phone rang, and I looked at it and saw that it was

Popcorn. "Hello."

"What you doing?"

"Why?" I spoke.

"I just want to know if you and the baby are okay. I heard about the brakes going out on the car," my husband said as he went silent.

"Thanks for asking, but I have to go."

Before he could respond, I heard Shay say, "Are you ready for bed? I'm ready."

"What the hell?" I screamed at him.

He said to her, "Shut up and get back, I'm on the phone."

"You about to go fuck Shay, tell me?" I plainly asked.

"Shondia."

I cut him off and spoke as nicely as I could before hanging up, "Go get your nut, your baby hungry, anyway."

CHAPTER 12

"Is everything ok?" Big Quack asked.

"It was Popcorn, enough said."

"What did he want? What the hell he want because you seemed spaced out?"

"Nothing, to be honest. I don't want to talk about him. If you have time, can you show me where I will be sleeping?" I asked, for I was tired.

"Yeah, let me take you in the house because a lot of people will still be here kicking it," Big Quack said as he held my back as we walked into the house. The house was different than when I saw it that night. However, the floor was the same where my husband fucked Michelle on the floor. I got pissed off all over again.

Sensing my anger, Big Quack asked, "You had a flashback, didn't you?"

Without denying it, I replied, "Yeah, it just hurts to know that I have been faithful to a man that could not be faithful to me."

"It's going to take time maybe a lot of time, but it can be done. You want me to change the carpet or something?"

"No, this is your house, and I just have to deal with it."

"Ok, well come on this way."

He took me down the hall. On the right was a bathroom, which was spacious. The room next to the bathroom was his and I smiled when he showed it to me. Frankly, it was really nice. He had glass closet doors, a

202

king-sized bed, and a nightstand on each side. The room was inviting and warm. He closed the door and showed me the spare room. He said it could be the baby room if I hadn't found another place to go. I smiled again and thanked him. Finally, he showed me my room.

I gasped. The room was exactly the way I would have my bedroom. I faced him and gave him an enormous beam, and he smiled back. "Oh my, it's perfect. How could you have known?" I asked as I took my time and raked the room.

"Let's just say I know what a woman likes, and I know what she needs."

"Yeah, but I have never told anyone that I want my room like this," I spoke, still in a daze.

"You didn't have to tell anyone. I know you and I know what you like."

"Again, I can't thank you enough."

"You will," he stated as he closed the door.

Leaving me alone in the room, I laid across the bed staring at the ceiling where the mirrors were. It was like a dream come true. Never had I imagined anything like this could come to life. Then, the baby kicked. Rubbing my stomach, I fell asleep.

The next morning, I was refreshed, and the smell of oatmeal crossed my nose. I stepped in the hall and saw Michelle. "What you doing here?"

"It doesn't matter what I am doing here, I'm grown," I replied.

"You might as well wait your turn because I was here first."

"Ball licker, nut drinker, I don't care who was where. It's who's here now, bitch."

"Quit calling me the name you wish you had, bitch."

"I don't want the name. You can have it."

"If you had it, Shay wouldn't be getting your good dick right now or Popcorn wouldn't be kissing that pussy," she said as if she knew about Shay and me.

I ran up on her, but Big Quack was there. I had no idea where he came from. He was our mediator. She yelled and I couldn't say a word because my baby began to kick nonstop.

"Michelle get your ass down the hall to my room now!"

She left quickly. He turned to me and asked, "You, ok?"

"Yeah, the baby knows I got upset from what she said."

"Sit down, maybe that will help you some."

I sat down, but the baby was still kicking. Big Quack rubbed my baby in a circular motion, and he was responding to his touch. He even talked to my baby, and it was relaxing because the pain eased off.

"See, the baby knows I am here for you both."

"Thanks, I really need a friend, but does she have to be here?" I asked.

"Yeah, she my fuck partner, why?"

"Nothing."

"I will try to keep you two separated."

"Let me know when she is coming over so I can

stay in my room or do something."

"You don't have to be limited to the room. Fuck her. You and the baby are important, and she knows that you both mean a lot to me."

"Why do we mean so much to you?"

"You are pregnant, and the baby needs a father figure. I don't have kids and you just happen to be pregnant," he spoke with hilarity.

"What I am going to do for a ride?" I asked.

"Well, your car should be ready today, but for now you can take the Honda. I had the Goss boys stay late and fix the brakes."

"I owe you so much, Big Quack, and I can't repay you."

"Take care of the baby that is how you can repay me."

"Thanks, boss man, but I have to get ready for work."

"You not going to eat?" he asked, looking shocked.

"Hell no, she is not going to kill me and my baby," I said with a smile.

"I know it must be hard knowing that she has had your husband, but that was then."

"It doesn't mean I have to put up seeing her. I already have a lot on my mind."

After I said that, I went to my room, got my clothes, and took a shower. When I walked out the bathroom door, I heard her screaming like she was being tortured. Then, I remembered she knew that I was there, so she was putting on a show. Shaking my head, I went to the

Honda.

I decided to take Highway 14 to Big Boys BBQ. I did not want to see Popcorn or Shay together being the family he and I were supposed to be. When I got to work, Popcorn was there. My heart began beating. Trying to contain myself, I pretended that I was not interested. It was not Popcorn, but Shay in his truck. *These whores trying me back-to-back today.* I stopped, and spoke, "What do you want?"

"For you to stop confusing our man," Shay said.

"You mean my husband? I know you're not fronting me about my husband?" I asked with my eyes beaming at her.

"Hell ya. He might be your husband, but I had him first. You found out that I was fucking someone, and you had to find out. When your ass did, you started pretending to be so damn innocent and shit. You know dick is not your specialty."

"Look, he is with you and not me. My baby is on my mind. I don't have time to argue with you or the next bitch in his bed or jacking his nuts."

"Leave him alone because I'm placing my mark all over the house so he will think of me even if you come back. You and I have already started that, haven't we? The longer you are away from me, the longer I will keep him from you," Shay spoke, as she knew I was getting angry.

"Bitch, I will forget I am pregnant and stomp your weave wearing, ghetto ass, bitch. And, to think you come here to my job threating me about my husband."

"You know it has been a while since you and I got

into a real fight."

"If you want to see me set this bitch off, keep running your mouth. In fact, fuck it. I'm tired of the shit you putting me through, anyway. I'm going to count to two and your ass better get to stepping."

I skipped one and said two. She was unprepared for the hit my hand connected to her mouth. I tried to knock her damn teeth out. Shay fell to the ground, and I began stomping her. I was always peaceful, but that day I had been pushed to the limit.

All the anger I felt from Michelle was taken out Shay's ass. I stomped her and all she did was roll up in a fetal position. I didn't even give her a chance to retaliate. She happened to cross me at the wrong time. The more I thought about the bullshit, the more I stomped her. With each stomp, I yelled, "Yo ass gonna leave me the fuck alone. I need my husband, not you. You coming here threatening me about mine. You bitch, you stupid bitch!"

Spectators slowed down to watch the stomping, but I did not care. Suddenly, I felt hands pulling me away. My feet were still swinging in the air as I was lifted up. A strong voice said, "Stop before the police come!"

I saw that it was Popcorn. I did not heed to his tone, I still tried to get to her. The more he kept me away from her, the more I tried to get to her. Who cared if she was hurt? I didn't. All I knew was that I was tired of her and Michelle. Ever since they came into my life, it had been one turn from another. When he took me to the back, I saw Big Quack's red caddy pull up.

I read his lips from a distance. "What the hell?"

"Stay here and let me check on Shay," Popcorn said.

"Fuck her and fuck you. That's right, go check on the bitch you fucking and if you come at me; I'm putting these eights on your ass, too."

Popcorn ignored me as he walked off. Big Quack said, "I leave your ass alone for a little while and when I do, your ass fighting. Shit, the dick that good, he needs to tell me the secret."

"No, the bitch came to me, on my job, fronting about my fucking husband. I told her to leave and when she didn't, I swung on her. When she hit the ground, I started stomping her ass like dog shit on my shoe."

Big Quack laughed, and then he said, "Go home. I'm giving you the day off."

"How the hell am I going to work and get on my feet if you keep sending me home?"

"What am I to do? You are hype and the baby will start acting up, too. I can't have you on the job hurting and shit. Hell no. Fuck that. Go home and rest. It's that paid day, I owe you from way back when," Big Quack spoke to me in a manner unlike him.

"I forgot about that."

"Go before I decide not to pay you."

"A lie, I need all of me."

When walked off, a pain hit me, then another one, then another one. The last pain caused me to almost fall as my hand went to protect my baby. Popcorn hit the brakes, for I saw the red taillights flash. However, like a pocket on a shirt, Big Quack was at my side.

"See this is the shit I was talking about, Shondia. You, ok?"

Taking short, deep breaths, I said, "No, I'm really hurting."

As if I were light weight, he swoops me up and toted me to his car. Popcorn drove off like he was going to put a fire out. Before I closed my eyes, I thought I saw Big Quack smirk at the sight of Popcorn speeding off. Hurting too bad to care, I closed my eyes.

"You can wake up, Mrs. Collier," a tender voice said to me. When I opened my eyes, a young, white lady was there with a smile. I kind of smiled back, for her appearance made me feel happy. She said, "You passed out from the pain. How do you feel?"

My voice was squeaky, and my throat felt parched, but I conjured up the words, "My baby."

She gave me that warm smile as she replied, "Your baby is fine. You, on the other hand, are not as well. Your blood pressure is too far up, and it must come down before you can go home."

"Why did I pass out?"
"The baby, of course. Little one is ready to get out and, also, you have dilated one centimeter."

"What does that mean?" I asked as my heart thumped in my chest.

"Just means that your baby's birth is getting near."

"So, she doesn't need to work, but stay off her feet?" Big Quack asked. We both turned toward the door, and Big Quack was there speaking to us.

"Yes, Sir. If possible, your wife needs to be off her feet, for her time is at hand to deliver."

"He's not my husband," I said as Big Quack walked over to us.

"I'm sorry."

"It's ok; he's been there like the real father, anyway."

She had a nurse to recheck my blood pressure, and it was fine. The doctor said, "Well, your blood pressure is fine. Let me get the nurse to bring your discharge papers and you will be all set."

"Thank you," I spoke.

"Damn, your ass on maternity leave and I don't have that in insurance, either" Big Quack said with a smile.

"Well, I can try to work."

"Yo ass coming to work invites fights, and now I have to promote another, which is hard. Have you seen the staff? Who would you recommend?" Big Quack wanted to know.

"Me, the others are not qualified, and you know it," I pointed out.

"True, but you can't work. How about if I fire you for missing too many days, that way you can draw unemployment?"

"Hell no, I'm not going to jail for fraud."

"Here are some comfortable clothes for you to put on."

He left out for me to get dressed as I placed my other clothes in the bag. The top had my breast revealing as the rest of it clung to my mid-sized body. I put the house coat on to cover me and the house shoes. Soon as I did, Big Quack came in and so did the nurse for me to sign the release papers.

They put me in a wheelchair as Big Quack pushed me out. I thought he would have been in the caddy, but he knew it was too small for me. He opened the door, and I got in his truck as he went to put the wheelchair up and grabbed my bag of clothes. Being nosy, I picked up his phone and saw that Popcorn texted. It read; *Let her know I want to talk to her and if she needs me to holler at me*. Big Quack's respond was, okay.

Nervously, I put the phone down in time, for I didn't see Big Quack coming. He got in, drove off, and he said, "You hungry?"

"No, just tired."

"Well, I'm taking you home so you can rest, but tell me this, why yo ass been fighting lately?"

"To begin with, it was not my fault when I hit Michelle. She came at me telling me how good my husband's dick is, that was some whore shit. Second of all, Shay came at me wanting me to leave Popcorn alone, is the bitch blind? Does she need glasses? She must be all of the above because according to the Justice of the Peace, he is my husband and not hers."

"Well, bitches will do that. They will front on the wife, and they act like they don't know the facts," he spoke as we drove further down Highway 14 toward the first light by the post office.

The light turned red, and we drove through the last two lights. Once we crossed the train tracks, Big Quack said, "I'm glad that you are allowing me to be there for you."

"Honestly, I'm glad that you want to be there for me. I've never really had friends. The girls were jealous of me, the boys only wanted to fuck me, so I rode solo, other than Chug, of course.

"Where he at anyway? Have you heard from him?" Big Quack asked as we yield onto Highway 15/25 toward home.

"I don't know if I want to hear from him because he was all in my ear telling me how I know my husband is not messing around on me and the entire time he knew. He knew and was there getting his dick sucked by Shay bitch ass while Popcorn was with Michelle."

"Hold on, Popcorn did not mess around on you."

"Yes, he did. I saw the video."

"There is the difference."

"What is the difference?" I just had to know.

"Men consider an affair if it happens over and over or over a period of time, but women don't see it that way."

"And, what fucked up way do you all see it?"

"To us, what Popcorn did was just a fucking. It happened and that was it. He did not pursue it or anything like that. Got the pussy and left."

"In other words, a man can sleep with a woman and to him it is like an exercise, something he does and that's it?"

"Yeah, it's something we did and that's it. We think no more about it."

Slightly bumping Big Quack on the arm, I spoke, "Just shut the hell up with that nonsense of a theory."

We laughed more and it actually felt good to have

someone to laugh with, even if it is my pussy eating boss. He glanced over at me, and said, "You never did tell me where Chug at?"

"Oh yeah, he is in boot camp. As for my cousin, I just don't think I want to see him again."

"You say that shit because he can't write home yet, right?"

"Well yeah, but he was there."

"He can't make your so-called husband do no more than he didn't want to do. Opportunities are placed at our feet every day, all day, but that does not mean that we take them. Popcorn made a decision, and he alone acted on it."

"True, but I'm sure Chug would not like the fact you messing off with his big bitch."

"Shit, the bitch is crazy. I see why he was leaving her the fuck alone."

We turned right onto Major Brown and left onto Zion Ridge Road heading home. The silence was unusual. Breaking the peace was Big Quack's voice. "Shondia, whenever you are alone at the house let me or someone know. With the baby coming soon, you don't need to be by yourself."

"It does have a heart," I spoke as we burst into heavy laughter.

"Ha, ha, funny."

We drove past the small, white trailer. I had to see if Big Quack would be honest with me. I said, "It really means a lot to me that you are helping me, but you want me to ask Popcorn for anything, so I won't have to ask you for so much?"

"Fuck, he did text wanting to talk to you and if you need him, for you to get back at him."

"Oh, he is confusing me. Sometimes, he acts like he still loves me, then sometimes he acts like he doesn't want me."

"I have told you one time, that's just a man's way. We are often immature and do things unorthodox, but that does not mean we do not feel. We don't do what you have for us to do, but we do on our own time. We, at often times, do things for love and to the woman it is bizarre, but it is what it is. It's our nature."

"You sound like a man who has been there at a crossroad like Popcorn."

"Shorty, you have no idea."

He pulled up at his house and it was already packed. Popcorn walked out the door first. I was shocked by his presence, but the look on Big Quack's face was readable and displeased. He looked like he did not want to see my husband there. Popcorn opened the door and helped me out. Big Quack spoke to Popcorn, slammed the driver door, and went in the house.

"You, ok?"

"Yeah, I'm good. Listen, she came on my job telling me to leave you alone. I told her to leave and when she didn't, I swung. Fuck, you are my husband, and she is checking me about you. How the hell can she come to my job telling me about leaving *my fucking husband alone*?"

"What has gotten into you? You have never acted like this before."

"I have never acted like this before?" I spoke as I

mocked in sincerity. "How about you? You are not the same you. You have changed and what doesn't kill us should make us stronger, but that is a lie. You and the baby have gotten into me. The baby because I had no idea, I was pregnant and you because you don't believe me, and on top of that you move your other baby momma in our house and fucking in our bed."

"No, I haven't fucked her like you think," he spoke as he dropped his head.

"What, you wishing you have?" I questioned.

"If I wanted Shay's pussy, I can get it. If I want my dick sucked, I could get it and if I wanted to do anything I chose to, I can get it. So, what the fuck are you bumping your gums about?" he asked. The baby kicked and I squeezed Popcorn's hand. "Is it the baby?"

"Yes, he is on a roll today."

"He?" Popcorn repeated.

"Yes, he is on a roll today. We are having a boy. I mean, I am having a boy. I already told you that."

The screen door opening disturbed us. It was Big Quack, and he said, "Man, can you bring my house guest on. She needs to get off her feet. Y'all can go in her room and talk, but for now she needs to be seen after."

"Yeah, come on. Watch your step, Shondia," Popcorn said as if he was sincere.

We made it to the door, and Big Quack said, "You can put her in my bed since it has a bathroom in it, and I will sleep in her bed across from the bathroom."

Everyone went silent as they all listened to Big Quack make that statement. Half of me wanted my husband

215

to say something. The way Big Quack spoke would have made an average man's head turn, but it did nothing to Popcorn. I could tell that he didn't like it, but he kept his cool. He took me down the hall to Big Quack's room.

When he turned on the lights, it was far more beautiful than I imagined. I glanced at it the other day, but given a second look, it was breathtakingly magnificent. Seeing my expression must have made my husband angry.

"You act like you have never been in this room before."

"No, I haven't been in here. Big Quack and I are friends, and he has not approached me in nothing less than friendship." The way he looked at me, I knew he believed me. The baby kicked again, but harder.
"Ouch!" I spoke for I was surprised the baby moved the way he did.

"You, ok? Here, sit on the bed," Popcorn said as he helped me sit on the corner of the bed. I took in the short, quick breaths. My husband's face was one of compassion, something I hadn't seen in a while. He was being there for me, but I couldn't let go of the fact that another woman was in our house.

From the door, Big Quack said, "You ok, Shondia?"

"Yeah, just had a pain, that's all."

Coming closer to my husband and I, Big Quack sat on the bed beside me, began rubbing my stomach, and talked to the baby like he had done before, but that time it was uncalled for. He acted like he was the father, and my husband was an innocent bystander. I looked up at Popcorn, and his eyes were watery as he turned his head.

"There, he's calm now. I haven't talked to him in a while, and he hasn't heard my voice. I think he is hungry, and it has been a minute since he was fed. You need me to feed him?"

"Goodbye, Big Quack. I'll get the baby fed later; don't you see we trying to talk?"

Big Quack was leaving out, then he turned back to say, "Oh yeah, Shondia, that's why I came back here, your car is ready. I picked it up today and have it parked behind the house. I also had insurance placed back on it. Now you can get out my shit."

The way he said it was unrealistic. It sounded like he was my man as my husband listened. Remembering it was Halloween, I said, "Now you need to go get the candy out for the kids."

"Shit, they don't ever come to this house, and for that I don't buy candy. One year I bought so much candy, and the kids never came. So, this year I said fuck it. Fuck handing out candy to grown ass fuckers," my boss said with jester.

My usual grin was on my face, and Popcorn got on my eye level as he spoke with massive tone, "What the fuck does he mean it's been a while since the baby was fed?"

"I haven't eaten today. The baby lets me eat when he wants me to eat, and if that is not good enough, you should have asked him while he was in here."

"Woman don't be playing games with me. I told you if I find out anything, I'm fucking you and him up."

"Why all the accusations? Yo ass have the country

217

renowned bitch living in the home that I helped you get, and you have the audacity to come in here and tell me what the fuck you will do? Have you forgotten, you kicked us out and he gladly took us in?"

"You were not pregnant then and what you mean gladly took y'all in?" he candidly mentioned.

"Wrong, we didn't know I was pregnant and, anyway, if he took us in, he took us in. You weren't there and you haven't tried to, so what is the point in this conversation?"

"Since it looks like you have fucking moved on, let me tell you this. Yeah, the first night you left, I did fuck Shay, but it wasn't anywhere near good as yours."

"You fucked her? You fucked the bitch after me?" I said as my heart raced and my thoughts ran crazy.

"Calm the fuck down, you done fucked Big Quack."

Yelling out, I said, "Hell no! He only ate my pussy before I met you and that was it. Since I met you, there has not been anyone and to know that you didn't love me enough to be faithful, fuck you, Popcorn!"

"I was confused and lonely," was his only explanation.

"Lonely! How the hell you were lonely, your ass got rid of me?"

"I wasn't thinking clearly," Popcorn said with an honest face. I slapped his face, and he grabbed my hands, and said, "I thought you had fucked Big Quack and did not want to tell me the truth."

Tears were everywhere. My voice was cracked, and my nerves shook deep within my muscle skeleton. I looked him in his eyes and spoke with all truthfulness, "Me fucked Quack? Let me go. Let me ing go. Besides, I wasn't gone a day, and you moved her in our home. On top of that, you don't believe me. I tell you it's your baby and you act like you don't give a shit. You know what? Get the fuck out! I don't even want to hear you breathe right about now."

"You can't tell me what to do."

"No, I can't, but my boss can. Would you like for me to call him and tell him that you are making the baby agitated and me sick? And for the record, when I stop crying over you, we're done."

Nodding his head, Popcorn got up and left me alone as usual. I wanted to die. The man I loved had an affair with one of the two bitches that had grieved me immensely. Since the season came in, Michelle and Shay had done nothing but fuck my husband and fuck up my world. A part of me wanted to cause them harm, but me being pregnant could not. I had to get my thoughts on my baby. He did not need his mother locked up while his dad was on the ground still fucking new bitches.

A knock was heard. I already knew who it was, and my cries were louder. "You going to be alright? I heard you screaming at Popcorn."

I could only cry. Words could not form in my mind or mouth, for the pain was too great. *How could he do this to me? Why would he do this to me? Why me?* My thoughts continued to plague me.

"It's going to be ok. I am here," Big Quack said as he sat on the bed and held me. It felt good to have a friend console me as I cried. He rocked me and rubbed the baby

219

as he moved up and down in my stomach. Everyone had left and we were in his house alone. The more he mumbled in my ear, "Everything's going to be ok, just hang in there," the more my life flashed before me. I cried and cried. No manner of words could help me. I was sad and felt hopeless.

Big Quack kissed the base of my neck, and it was wonderful. His kisses were tender and so gentle. I began to moan as kisses trailed of my neck. Slightly turning my face toward him, we kissed. The way he held my head was that of a lover. In all honesty, his kiss was obsessive. He let go of me and stood up in front of me. I removed the house coat and gown to expose my huge breasts before his eyes. "They are far more beautiful than I imagined they would be. Your entire body is magnificently put together. I could not have dreamed you would be this beautiful."

I lay back on the bed and Big Quack took off his clothes. He didn't look that big with no clothes on. He lay beside me, and said, "I won't do anything that you don't want."

"Please, take my mind off what I am going through."

He smiled and made trails on my breasts. With each trail, my body yearned for more. The more he tempted my body, the more I wanted him. He went further down, and stopped, and said, "If you don't want me to taste you I won't, but if you allow me to taste you, I promise I would be as gentle as any you have ever had." No words were said, for I parted my legs, and he slid down between them. He first placed what felt like his nose on me, and then he said, "You smell good and I'm too eager to do this."

I shook my ass, and he began to taste me like I knew he would. Big Quack was slow and gentle with his tongue fucking. Whenever I would glance down between my legs, I would see the motion of his head, going side to side taunting me to want more. He would tease me as he kisses the clit and the way he sucks on the pussy lips drives me in a furry. For odd reasons enough, my legs had a mind of their own as they spread in each direction.

When I couldn't hold them up, Big Quack would use his forearms to keep them up as he licked my pussy all the way to my ass. This is too damn awesome for a girl like me to intake. Big Quack is like a lover, far beyond his years. However, the more that lean muscle in his mouth bathed inside me, the wetter my pussy mouth became.

Honestly, he lives up to his name as the International Pussy Eating Champion but that did not stop him from bringing me to my explosive peak. He was putting me into overdrive as he plucked and tucked on each pussy lip. My body yearned for his round fat ass in ways I never knew of.

Without warning my body ruptured an orgasmic feeling of pleasure but that did not stop him. He continued until there was nothing left. My legs were weak and so was breath. Big Quack looked up, and said, "Now I will take my time and take you like a man takes a woman."

Big Quack lifted himself up over me. I, as well as I could, I lifted my legs for his entry. It was different no doubt because he isn't hard as Mr. Dildo and he isn't long as my husband, but his dick is desirable and strong. They say fat men can't fuck but Big Quack made that lie a lie. He moved his body as if he were a small man. His libido is dynamite and his love making is the most kind and, at this moment, the most sought after I had ever had.

The more he twirled my body, the more our bodies found its own rhythm. Big Quack cried out as he fills me. It was actually beautiful, and I will not ever forget this night with him. He was sweating and so was I. He looked down at me as sweat slowly dripped onto me. Big Quack smiled as his dick was still erected inside me.

We continued to stare in each other's face. He, from what I saw, had tears in his eyes. Not moving his body, he continued to hold himself upon me to say, "I can't get off you. As much as I want to, but I can't because the pussy is too damn good."

I could only smile, and he got beside me. All night he was next to me, holding me and rubbing the baby. He was a complete gentleman. For the first time in a while, I slept happy. When I woke up, I was in the same spot. I put on my house coat, took a shower, and went to see my car. I wished I hadn't seen it. I cried the more.

That time, someone had dead animals in my car and the appearance of red blood seemed to cover everything from the windshield to the trunk. I hollered and cried unstoppable. Big Quack walked outside to see why I was crying, and his first words were, "I'll be dipped in shit. Who the hell is doing this shit to you? Fuck! I just had this car repainted and fixed just for you and the baby. I'm going to get to the bottom of this bullshit. Hell no! Come here, Shondia."

Barely did his words reach my ears, for I was hurt extremely. I didn't move, either. I was in disbelief and anguish. "How could someone do this to me? I don't bother anyone, Big Quack, I promise, I don't. All I want is to be happy and have my baby, but…"

The sentence could not be finished, for tears were embedded in my eyes. He walked over and placed his arms around me as I cried onto his expensive shirt. The more I thought about my life and how fucked up it has become, I cried.

"It's going to be ok, I promise it is. Just stay here and take it easy, ok? I got you, girl. You hear me? I'm here for y'all. I am here and that counts for more than you have right now. It doesn't matter if your husband doesn't believe you, I do."

Still, I could not l respond to him as I listened to him profess his words. My life was in chaos and every turn deemed the wrong one. Crying was the only thing I could do. I continued to stand there in tears as Big Quack stood beside me and held me very gentle. I didn't know how long I was there, but I felt light headed as my boss tried to cheer me up all the more.

CHAPTER 13 (November)

My mind reminisced on the events that had occurred in my life and since my husband did not want me. My boss Big Quack; who has gone out his way to help me and the baby from lending me money, allowing me to stay in his man cave, driving his car, to moving into his house, and cheering me up as I cried over my husband's fuck buddy. My thoughts could not rationalize what all that meant. Thinking of making love to Big Quack, I cheesed like a pro. The fat fucker knew how to make love to a woman and not just eat pussy, which is an art.

I sighed deeply because I thought about my husband. If he flipped about me getting my pussy ate, he would fly the coop if he knew I actually did fuck. No delight was found in that thought, for his actions had told me that he had moved on with my love, Shay.

Sitting up, I sighed again and wiped more tears away. A familiar knock was heard. I still had my clothes on from the previous night. "Come in."

Big Quack stuck his head in the door, and said, "Can we talk?" I pat the bed beside me and he sat there. I dropped my head because I did not want him to see me crying. Big Quack lifted my chin with his huge hands and rubbed the tears from my eyes with his thumb. My boss stared deep into my eyes to say, "Talk to me. You can always talk to me, I need you to know that I'm here as I've always been and I won't give you advice as me, Big Quack. I will give you advice as your friend, Clark."

"Your government name is Clark?" I said as I

smiled a little.

"Hell yeah. At least you smiled, and yes, it is, so don't go around telling it."

"I won't," I spoke as I dropped my head.

"Good, so tell me what is going on with you?" Closing my eyes, I began to cry again but with more intent. "Sssh, don't cry."

"It hurts too bad and I just don't get it."

"What is there to get?" he asked.

"To begin with, he couldn't see the baby because he married me. Then, I told him about what happened between you and me before I met him."

"Which shit you tell him?" Big Quack spoke in a scream.

"Not about last night, of course, which happens to have been good, but when you only ate my pussy. I had been trying to tell him since I found out that you two knew each other. I know it was before him, but I know now that it is pregnancy hormones. Anyway, I told him, and he flipped out. He told me about how he flipped out my home girl a few times."

"What home girl?"

"They call her Snow Queen from 397"

He jumped up laughing like he heard something funny. Big Quack looked back at me, and said, "She was your home girl? The one that…"

Cutting into his excitement I sparred, "Yeah, don't tell me you have had her, too?"

"Hell no. I know her, and I've seen the way the boys work her out," Big Quack proclaimed.

Sitting back down beside me, I spoke, "You ready now?"

"Yes, go on"

"Anyway, he didn't think about him fucking Michelle, but he only focused on how you ate my pussy."

"Oh my," Big Quack said with a boyish face.

"That's not funny at all."

"I'm not laughing."

"No, you aren't, but that smile on your face says otherwise."

"No comment," Big Quack said as he looked at me.

"He then kicks me out and moves Shay in. He tells me that the night he kicked me out, he fucked her."

"The motherfucker did what? He actually told you that?"

"Yes, he fucked the other bitch that has caused chaos in my life since I've met her."

"You sure he said that? You sure you didn't read more into it than what you are telling me?"

"Yes, he told me if he finds out anything has happened between us, he will kill me and you both."

"The fucker won't do shit but put his thumb in his ass and spin."

"Please, know that I didn't make love to you because of that."

"I know. You hadn't been made love to in a minute and I was there to help ease your mind." For the first time, I laughed a hearty laugh. "You laughing, but I'm serious. He wants you in his life, he needs to come get you and do better by you than what he has."

"That is why I am crying. He put my heart in my hand by fucking Michelle. I can handle the Shay part; it is the Michelle part that bothers the fuck out of me."

"I'm sorry that has happened to you, but crying won't change anything. Shit, if that were true, I'd cry a river, the mighty Mississippi River for that matter. Girl, get with the program. You have a baby being born and the little man inside you should be your primary focus. I know you want your husband, but right now it hurts you. Use this opportunity to find out who Shondia is and what or who can make her happy."

We paused for a moment, and then I spoke ever so softly, "I love him and if I didn't, I would be long gone, long gone."

"Shondia, concentrate on the baby for now and everything else will fall in place. If you are not well, how can you expect the baby to be well? You can't, and right now he depends on you to be healthy. Think of it this way, when you cry, he cries. You don't want your baby to be born with red eyes, do you?"

That was too funny. I laughed at the thought of my baby being born with red eyes. Once I sniffled again, I lifted my hands to wipe my eyes. "I told him that if I ever stop crying over him, I am finish with him and there isn't anything else he could tell me."

"Do you want to be finished with him? I mean, really be finished with him?"

"I really don't know anything anymore. I also have someone trying to damage my life on purpose. They damaged my car, cut the brakes on your car, put dead

227

animals on my car, and burned down your man cave."

"Don't leave out you've been fighting like a damn bull." I laughed again, for it was true. Since the baby, I had not been the same. "See, you laughing. That is the smile I love to see. Soon, those big brown eyes will dry up and you will feel better. It just takes some time to go in any direction you choose."

"Thanks for the listening and giving me your advice."

"Anything for you, Shondia, I would do anything for you. I hope you know that. Just stay here, and consent me to help you and the baby,"

Before I could answer, a knock was at the front door. He left out the room. The way he said he would do anything for me gave me chills. I heard voices coming from the living room. It was Michelle.

"The feelings are not mutual. Let me step in and so we can do this."

Big Quack said, "You are a sick bitch. Get the fuck out, Michelle."

"Please, let me rephrase it," she mounted out.

"No, you stay the hell away, do you hear me?"

Then, their voices were lowered. Becoming off balance, I fell into the wall and Big Quack ran to my room to say, "Is everything alright?"

"Yeah, I'm ok thanks for asking. Who is at the door?"

"Michelle and she were just leaving."

He left out my room door and I walked behind him trying to see what was going on because of the way he spoke. Something must be up for him to talk the way he did. We reached the living room and Michelle was still by the front door. Big Quack pointed as he spoke to her, "I thought I told you to get out?"

Michelle stared at him, walked by the door, and said, "You in this with me and you haven't heard the last of me."

I clapped my hands, and spoke tauntingly, "About time she realized you are full of shit."

She did not get out the door on her own. Big Quack grabbed her by the arm and pushed her out. She leaned by him to snarl at me, "Bitch, if you only knew, if they…" was all she said before Big Quack pushed her out and slammed the door in her face.

Moments later, she sped off headed toward the dirt end of the road. When he walked from the door, he pulled out a chair for me, and I closed my gown and sat down. When he sat down, my button popped off and exposed my huge breasts. With embarrassment, I covered my breasts as much as I could with my hand. "What is she talking about?" I asked Big Quack.

"Nothing of importance, she just mad because I don't want anything else to do with her."

"Oh, if you need to talk to someone, I am here," I spoke as a friend.

It was that moment he came up to me, and said, "No matter what happens, think of me as your dearest friend, the one that has showed you love and kindness. And, please, believe me when I say that you and the baby are important to me. You have no idea how rare you are and how just being around you is joy. You, by far, are the most remarkable person I have ever known. Popcorn doesn't realize how special you are. He is crazy to leave you in the cold. You will always have a place here, just remember that."

"Where is all this coming from? I'm thankful that you put up with me and my silly ways. Big Quack, I do believe you, but what is this all about?"

"Nothing just had one of your crazy moments that I finally know what I need in my life and how it has always been there in my face." He touched my shoulder as he turned around and went outside, got in his car, and left.

The baby started kicking and I grabbed my stomach. I couldn't walk. I had to stand there in that position. When the pain let up, I got my cell and for the first time, I didn't call Popcorn.
"Big Quack, can you come back to the house?"

"What is it?" Big Quack asked sadly.

"I'm hurting again, and I can't move."

"Hold on, I'm coming." As if he had never left, he was back that quick. He came in and rushed to me.

"The baby is kicking, and I believe I have dilated more."

"You need to go back to the hospital?"

"Yes, please."

Helping me up off the couch, he placed his arms around me and guided me to his 2011 Tahoe. He helped me in and drove madly.

"You taking me to Winston General?"

"You want to die?" he spoke. I could only laugh.

I let the seat back and closed my eyes. Seconds later, I

felt his strong right hand on my stomach, soothing a baby that wasn't his. It was wonderful to have his hand on the baby, and for some reason the baby responded to his touch and his tone. "My baby knows you; you know that?"

Sadly, Big Quack nodded his head as he glanced at me. Moments later, the baby calmed down, but we were here at Oktibbeha General Hospital. Big Quack got out and went inside. It appeared to be a routine. The nurse walked out with him as he lifted me in the air to place me in the wheelchair. He kindly pushed me inside. They took me to the back, and she asked him to leave.

"I'm not leaving her, so do what you must, but I am not leaving."

"It's ok. They are going to get me undressed and check me below," I said to Big Quack.

"Oh, I guess I can leave for that, but I will be outside if you need me."

"Thanks. I will be fine and once they are finished; you can come back in."

He left out, and the nurse said, "He really loves his wife, and you should be happy to have that kind of care."

I jolted my head back from her saying he loved me. I had never noticed anything before and to recollect everything, it did appear that I had missed all the signs. He had told me on more than one occasion, I just did not know it. My heart raced. I never knew anything but him being a friend. *Now my situation is really fucked up*, I thought as I slid down to the edge of the table to be examined.

"Mrs. Collier, you have dilated up to two centimeters. You can go home, but if you feel more pressure of any kind come back and we will admit you. As for now, go home and rest."

"Ok, thanks."

Big Quack walked in, and asked, "Well, what they say?"

"I've dilated up to two and I need to rest but if I come back, they are going to keep me."

"Ok, let me bring the truck around so we can get you back to the house and off your feet."

"Big Quack, thank you for being here for me, it means a lot to me."

He glanced in my direction, and spoke, "Shondia, I will go out my way just to make you happy." When I glanced up at him, he spoke on, "Even though I've been losing money like there's no tomorrow, your ass needs to get to work."

Laughing, I said, "Go get your truck so I can get out here."

When I got in the car, he said, "You want bird, right?"

"I do, but I don't want to waste anymore of your money like I did the last time we were here, and I forgot to eat. Popcorn blew my mind."

"Well, its day light and you haven't eaten."

"Fine." I dragged on to speak, "Take me where you want."

Leaning over, he leaned down to the baby, and spoke, "Champ, what you want to eat? It's not about her, anyway."

I laughed, and said, "Since he can't talk and I can, it's whatever I say."

Leaning up, Big Quack pulled off and I looked at him. For the first time, I actually thought about why it couldn't be his baby and not my husband's. What would my life be like if I had married him and not Popcorn?"

"Snap out of it," Big Quack spoke as he snapped his fingers at me.

"Sorry, I didn't think I was daydreaming again."

"Yes, you were. Hope it was about me because you seem to do that a lot lately."

"You wish, don't you?" I spoke with tease.

"Girl, stop, you silly," he spoke in a pretend girl voice as he drove to the light.

"Where we going?"

"How about Christy's?" he asked.

"Yeah, guess we can eat chicken strips and crinkled fries," I spoke as I rubbed my stomach. Out loud, I spoke to my baby as I pulled up my shirt to reveal my stomach, "My son, you want tenders and crinkled fries?"

We pulled into Christy's, and Big Quack said, "You have transformed right before my eyes. You went from not showing to showing just like that."

"It's the baby, and I've been eating the WIC stuff I get from the health department."

"You are still beautiful and you're glowing." I pulled the sun visor down to check my face out. I could see my neck getting darker, but as for glowing, I could not tell for I'd always been that color. "Yes, you are brighter and beautiful."

"You are just saying that because you are thoughtful and nice."

"Shondia, have you ever known me to be a big liar?"

"No, cheap, but not a liar."

"So, it's like that?"

"Wait, buy my food then we can have this conversation over, ok?" I spoke as he laughed and went in to get our food.

I thought *he has a habit of leaving his cell phone around me*. I picked it up and saw that Shay texted him. *I need to chop it up with you soon. Get at me when you free.* Big Quack responded, O*K*.

Easing the phone back in the holster, I was about to get out, but Big Quack came out with our food. He came to my side, and said, "Where your ass trying to go? You just got out the hospital, and didn't the doctor tell you to stay off your feet?"

"Babysitter, I'll be fine."

"Call me what the fuck you like. I am your protector, and I will not have you do anything to harm you or the baby."

"Awe, how sweet, the Grinch does have a heart," I teased.

"Mrs. Scrooge McQuack" he responded, and we laughed.

He placed his food in the back, but he handed me mine. He got in and we pulled off heading to Highway 25. When we passed the shed buildings on the right, I spoke, "You care about me?"

At first, he did not answer. He looked at me as if his eyes were saying, "Isn't it obvious?" He tilted his head toward me to say, "You have some ketchup on the side of your mouth."

We laughed. That was his way of avoiding the conversation. I had known him for a while and had grown accustomed to how he acted. I wiped the ketchup from my mouth, to say, "Can we stop by the spring to get some water?"

"We don't have any jugs, but if we don't have a lot going on today at the restaurant, I'll get T. to go get you some."

"You don't have to make a special trip. I'm thankful for the water we have at the house."

"Shondia, you are pregnant, and you are supposed to be spoiled. You are dear to me and if I can do anything you ask, I will. I know you are Popcorn's wife, but you are my friend, and friends do stuff like this for each other."

Adding humor to a thick atmosphere, I said cheerfully, "Well, since you want to play daddy, sure. Go get my water and for supper, I want some KFC chicken with baked beans and mashed potatoes along with McDonald's sweet tea."

"That is just like a nigga. Give'em an inch and they'll take a mile."

"I'm just playing."

"No, be quiet about it and let me do this."

We looked at each other and grinned. I started eating my chicken and the baby agreed with it. The next thing I knew, I was waking up. We had made it back to Zion Ridge, the feeling someone was looking at me made me open my eyes. When I did, Big Quack was watching me.

"Yeah, sleepy head, you've been snoring like

crazy."

"Really? I didn't know I was out."

"We been here about half an hour," he said as he checked his wristwatch.

"Half an hour? Why didn't you wake me up?" I said as I sat straight up.

"You were resting so good; I didn't want to wake you up."

"Well, let me get out."

"Yeah, get the fuck on out. I, unlike you, have to go to work if I plan to keep up with this lifestyle I have."

He got out and helped me out the truck. As if I would break, he handled me fragile.
"I am not glass," I teased.

"No, you aren't, your stained glass because you're pregnant," he teased back.

We laughed harder as he unlocked the door, and we went inside. "You need to go to your bed to rest or you going to sit upfront?"

"I'll sit here and rest on the couch."

"Ok, get comfortable and if you need me, call me."

"Stop being so overprotective. I'll be fine."

"You sure?" Big Quack asked as if he didn't want to leave me alone.

"Go. I'll be alright and I again, I appreciate you coming to my every whim."

"Here is the remote control. You want some lemonade or something before I leave?"

"I want you to leave so I can bathe and get undressed."

"Go on and shower. I won't leave until you come out."

"I am going to be fine, and the baby knows that you are near, so he won't be giving me any problems for now," I said, trying to reassure him.

"You might be, but I don't want you to fall, and no one is here to help you. I don't know what I would do if something happened to either one of you or I was not here to shelter you."

"You are being kind, over the top, and, ok, you win. I won't be in there long."

I went in my room and got a house coat and gown out. Walking across the hall to the bathroom, I locked the door behind me and began to shower. Once I finished, I looked in the mirror and saw how big I had gotten in a matter of time. My appearance was huge, and my hair had grown. "The baby has given me some hips," I said with a small smile.

"You alright in there?" I heard Big Quack's voice from the other side of the door.

Turning my head to the door I smiled, for I forgot he was waiting on me so he could leave. "Yeah, I'm coming out. I was just looking at myself in the mirror."

"What the mirror tell you?" he whispered through the door.

"It told me to leave before I lose more than I bargained for, like my heart and my respect."

He was quiet. I wrapped my towel around me, swung open the door, and Big Quack was standing there looking down on me. I breathed deep as my eyes took in his sight.

He is a round, chunky dark brown skinned guy, but somewhat tall with it. His eyes and smile were never noticeable before until now.

I never recognized just how his hair is nicely cut and how his beard is trimmed to match. He always wore fitted caps to hide his hair and eyes; but you could always see his white smile. My boss above all is handsome. Walking closer to him, my hair clung to my face as I stared up at him. From the way he looked into my soul, I felt something. We did not speak, only stared. It was intense and heavy. Our eyes seemed to talk as we glared into the other's face.

Breaking the attraction was his cell phone going off. I felt that he was wanted to kiss me but was reluctant to do so. Half of me wanted to. It was because he had been good to me, but I was married and knew that I loved my husband, even if he did not love me enough to stay faithful. A part of me wanted to, but I knew that I could not do it.

Licking his lips, he spoke silently, "I better go."

I wanted to reach up and touch his fat face, but the thought of being low down like my husband crossed my mind. I stepped back, and responded, "Yeah, you better go. I'll be fine and if I need you, I will call you."

Big Quack dropped his head and walked off. I stared behind him. I started to call him back and let him please me, but that would not be right. I didn't need to add him to the mix when my life was in a spiral. I just stood there trying to figure out what the hell just happened. I heard the door closed and seconds later, he drove off. I sighed against the door frame where he once stood and gathered my thoughts.

Taking off the towel, I put on my night gown and house coat. I reached for the remote control, but didn't touch it. "What the hell just happened between Big Quack and me?" I could not shake it. The nurse said he was in love with me. He had always been nice to me and caring. For the nurse to say that she must have seen something I didn't. With the incident happening, I was beginning to see it. It seemed that he was getting emotionally attached over another man's wife.

CHAPTER 14

I sat on the couch thinking. I actually needed to talk to my husband. I needed to know how he felt, although, his actions told me he didn't want me. I just needed to be sure before I made another fuck up.

The doorbell rang and I eased off the couch to peep outside. The smile that came on my face was priceless. "Who is it?" I asked as if I didn't know.

"Open up, Shondia, it's me," the voice said.

"Who is me? Never mind, I'm coming," I said as I got up and unlocked the door. Without opening the screen door, I asked, "May I help you, Sir? Are you lost?"

"Can I talk to you?" Popcorn asked desperately.

"I don't know. Can you?"

"I'm sorry. May I please talk to you, Shondia?"

That was really nice and sincere. I nodded as I unlocked the screen door. He walked in soon as stepped aside. Closing the door behind me, I walked back to the couch and left him standing. Seeing that he was not sitting, I said, "You may sit."

Sitting on the edge on the recliner part of the wrap around couch with his legs opened and holding his own hands with his head slightly tilted upward toward the left, he spoke, "How you been? I mean, how you and the baby are doing?"

Keeping it short, I replied, "We good."

"That's good."

He kept looking at me but wouldn't say anything. I finally said, "Ok. What is it? You didn't come here to be social with me. Evidently, something is on your mind. That is why you came, right?"

"Yeah, there is."

"Well, I am listening."

"Well, first of all, Shay has moved into her apartment by the Louisville High School."

When he spoke that, my heart leaped out my chest, but I didn't know exactly what that meant for him and me. For the most part, I didn't really care.

"Now I want us to talk about you and Big Quack."

I was completely caught off guard. "Duh, you claim she just moved out and I know that you were bonding with her, so let us have a conversation about you, Shay, Michelle, and God know whoever the flavor is this week."

"I didn't come here to talk about me, but I just wanted you to know that no one is living with me."

"Back up. I guess things did not work out with you and her, so you come in here asking about me and my boss. Popcorn, this may not be about you or what you want, but you opened the door for me to question you as well."

"Have you fucked him?"

"Damn, jack in the box; you come out wanting to know shit that is no more your concern."

"You are my concern and if I want to know about you fucking another motherfucker, I will and gone ask."

"Nigga, please. You can and will ask all you want, but I don't have to answer you. In fact, I had hoped to talk to you, but now you are making me hurt. Please, leave," I point blank made known to him.

"Can I at least touch him?"

241

"Why touch a child you didn't want?"

"Shondia, it wasn't like that, and you know it."

"Lately, I don't know what to think anymore. You have changed my entire way of thinking and to know about the stuff you have done while we were are married."

"Please, Shondia let me feel him."

I gathered that he was being earnest, so I permitted him to touch my belly. Once he put his hand on it, the baby began to move like never before. It was like he knew that his dad was touching him. With surprise, I said, "He is acting up by moving and kicking me."

"He knows that daddy is here."

"Daddy? I thought you didn't believe me?"

"It matters not what I believe; all people know is that you are my wife and that is my baby."

"So, it's not that you believe he is yours, it's just that people will think he is yours even if you don't? Is that right? Is that what you are telling me?"

"Yes, they are going to think what they want to think." Snatching his hand off me, I began to ache like never before. "Shondia, you, ok? Is it the baby?"

Gathering my senses and as loud as I could, I declared, "Get your ass out and stay the fuck away from me and my baby. We don't need your "the community will think" ass near us."

"What the hell you talking about?"

Sitting up straighter than before, I said, "You only think this is your child because of what others will think. It is not what you believe. If you did not think that others would believe it is yours, you would not be here."

He was silent, and then exploded, "Wait! Shondia, that's not exactly it."

"Yes, it is. I finally get it. I really get it, now you have it. Get out and stay the fuck out."

"I come here to talk to you, and I intend to do just that."

"Not today, you have me hurting now and I need to lie down."

It was quiet for a few seconds between us. I was actually distraught because of how things had turned out. He knew that I was not going to back down, so he spoke softly, "I don't want to leave you here alone. I will be quiet and let you rest, but don't ask me to leave you here alone."

"Big Quack will be back in a few," I told my husband as his face went almost pale.

"Big Quack, huh?"

"Yes, he knows I've been hurting and…"

"And his fat ass left you?" Popcorn finished my sentence.

"No, he had business to take care of and I hadn't been long come from the ER."

"You went to the ER? When? What's wrong?"

"Right now, it's you."

Swallowing hard, I lay back on the couch and began taking those breaths that the nurse told me to whenever the baby has me in the position.

"What the doctor say?"

"Just leave. I don't want to talk about it. I'll be alright until he gets here."

"Until he gets here? I see that he and I are going to

have a conversation about my wife." Looking back at me, he spoke, "I will wait until he gets back before I leave you alone. I will not talk to you about anything, but I will in time and very soon, for that matter."

I did not say a word as I laid on my right side. I must have dozed off, for I felt relaxed. Memories of my life with my husband emerged. I recalled times when I would get off work and he would rub my tired, aching feet if it was his day off. It felt real as the baby was calmed and my feet felt relaxed, even though they were slightly swollen.

"What the hell is going on?"

Causing me to lurch out my sleep and almost falling off the couch was Big Quack's voice. However, to my amusement my husband had my feet in his lap and was rubbing them like he used to. I wanted to smile, for it felt wonderful to have him touch me.

"Not that it is your business, but I came by to see my wife and she was hurting. She would not rest until you got here. You are here, I guess I can leave, but rest assure that I will be checking in on her more."

Big Quack stood at the door as I turned my head slightly toward him. My boss stared at us. Popcorn eased up and placed my feet on the couch. I eased onto my right side just in time. Popcorn, whom stood taller than Big Quack, whispered lightly, "You and I are going to have a talk real soon about my wife."

Not showing any sign of weakness, Big Quack said even quieter, "Any time you feel that you need to talk to me about your wife, have your wife with you. As for discussing my friend that was kicked out of her house and humiliated, feel free. You know where I stay."

Popcorn left out the door and sped off. Big Quack locked the door behind him. He stood by me, and said, "I see you feeling better."

"Actually, he came here to talk, but I was hurting, and he didn't want to leave me alone. He was waiting on you to come."

"Well, he didn't have to rub your feet."

I sat up, and spoke, "He is still my husband, and I love him. Honestly, I fell asleep and him rubbing my feet was needed, although, I didn't tell him to. What is wrong with you?" Big Quack began to walk off without answering me, and I said, "What was the problem with him coming to see me?"

He stopped, and said, "There is no problem. You are married to it."

"It?" I echoed.

"Yes, it, for if he was any kind of husband or man, for that matter, he would have you in his life and never let you go as far as I am concerned."

"Yes, but you sound like you didn't want him here at all."

"Why would you think that, Shondia?"

"Boss, I detected a problem because of the way you spoke it to me. You acted rude and dazed to see him here with me."

He must have recognized that he let on more than he thought, for he tried to recant by saying, "No, you misunderstood my words and read more into it than you think."

"No, boss, I didn't misunderstand anything. I saw how you reacted when you saw him here."

"Just leave it alone, Shondia."

"No, I want to know why it was a problem for him to have been here. He said Shay has moved into her apartment at Ivy."

"What? He tells you that in hopes that you will spring back to him to pick up where she left off?"

"I don't know about all that."

"Shondia, let us talk about this later, I have to get ready for work," he demanded in a tone unlike him.

Getting up off the couch, I stood between him and the hall, to say, "Tell me what I think I already know that's what you do."

He was quiet as he heaved a sigh. "What is it that you think you already know?" he asked me as turned his head away from me.

"I want you to tell me. We are both grown individuals."

"Fine! But, can you handle it?"

"The question is can you tell me?" I questioned back.

He looked down into my eyes with tears in his, to say, "I love you, and I wish you and the baby were mine alone."

I knew it, but it sounded almost contagious to hear him come out and say it. As forgiving as I could, I stared at him and spoke with sincerity, "I never intended for this to happen. I had an idea, but never really knew you felt this way. I assumed that this was a friendship level that might have gotten out of hand. I just didn't know. Please, believe me."

"How could you not? How could you not see my love for you time after time? How could you not see the way I react whenever he would come down here?"

"I just didn't. I thought it was because we were working associates and friends. I didn't see you act any different toward him."

"Bullshit. I went face to face with him just for you. Like that night I gave you the money and he was kicking your car. I was ready to kick my boy ass over his damn wife" I nodded my head.

"Do you think I would trip with my boy over some bullshit?" I did not answer, for I really did not know. "I was there for you when you own husband wasn't. I was there when you didn't have anyone. When you needed someone for anything, you called me, and I was eager to come to you no matter what. All you had to do was ask me and it was yours. I didn't give a damn whoever needed me nor needed anything I had, you came first."

He turned away from me, headed back into the living room and sat in his favorite the love seat. Closc in tow, I spoke casually, "And I will always be internally grateful to you and your kindness."

He looked up at me as I sat in front of him on an ottoman. Out of nowhere, he, with a sly grin, announced, "You never thought it strange that I offered to just taste you the first time?"

When he said that, I felt funny as that night in the hotel flooded me. My legs were spread a part, and he had his head between my legs. I was nervous and had never had that done before with a man. The moment was intense as my nerves shook within me. It was unusual that I could never remember what it was like until he said that.

"No, I assumed that you did that to many women, and I was no different."

"Shondia, how naïve will you continue to be to see when a man loves a woman?"

"I'm just stunned, that's all. I've been doing things, getting pregnant, and since I met Michelle, my life has been upside down."

"Stunned?"

"Yeah, lost for words, flabbergasted, and many other words in that framework. Big Quack, I am actually at a dead end."

"I have always loved you and I have exhibited it every day you have been here. Not just that but having you somewhere in my life was better than not having you at all. It was something about you. I knew you had never had a man to taste you before and I had the privilege to have been your first. You kind of disappointed me when you would not let me suck all the juice your sweet tasting pussy had to offer that night. Yet, I was thankful for what you allowed me to do."

I dropped my head some, and said as I lifted it up, "How did you know that much about me? That is an intimate detail that you could not have known?"

"A man is like a woman, when we meet someone, we want we find out all we can about them. Popcorn got lucky and he carried your heart. When I found out that he was the one you were in love with I was crushed but knew that he wasn't a bad guy until he pulled that bullshit stunt and did what he did to you."

"Yeah, that caught us both off guard, but you never tried to pursue me."

"No, I didn't because I was getting myself together and getting rid of all the bitches that didn't mean shit, so when you found out about my feelings you wouldn't be so hesitant about being with me. I just moved too slow, but you were worth the wait."

"I have never looked at you in any other way but a friend, even after that night in the hotel."

"Shondia, I took you to a five-star hotel, took you out to eat, we danced, and had a real good time. I was wining and dining you because you were not the others. You meant something to me."

"I thought you did all your female friends like that. I had no clue."

"Hell no! I have a three-bedroom house, for that matter. I didn't need to take them anywhere. I needed you to see that you were different and special. It gave me honor to taste you, to feel your body, to lose myself in between your legs, and I will never forget how you taste. I will never forget the way we made love the other night. It meant more to me than you know."

"Since I have been here has those feelings changed any?"

"It is like this. When you got with Popcorn, I put them aside because you are my boy's wife, so yeah, I let it ride. When he kicked you out and you came to me, I had nothing but good intentions of helping you no matter how much I wanted you. I knew that you would not want me the way you did him or the way I would deserve."

"So, you had let go of how you felt about me?"

"Yeah, I did but I didn't realize how much the feelings were still there until the brakes went out and I held you safely in my arms. I didn't know what I would have done if you had gotten hurt. I have always put you on a pedestal and I have nothing but mad love for you. Popcorn is your husband, but he can't make you happy like I can. These last few weeks have been great. I didn't have to go home to a lonely house. You were always into something and needed something. You brought me back to life. Shouldn't it have occurred to you that no woman ever came by?"

"Michelle did."

"Oh, that bitch? We were working on a project, but I backed out. I couldn't do it and she was, and still is, pissed at me, but she will be alright."

"No, it never occurred to me about you and other women, I just thought you were meeting them elsewhere."

"No, it was because you were here and in my sick ass mind, I pretended that you were mine, even if for a short while. I had you and every time that fucker would fuck up, I was there for you to pick up the pieces. It stirred me senseless to see him touching you the way you won't let me."

"That is why you had an attitude about him rubbing my feet as I slept?"

"Do you know how many times at night I would stay awake, waiting on you to invite me into your bedroom? I didn't have to do anything but just see you. It made my day and night. I have Mike running the restaurant when I am not there."

"Oh, Big Quack, I had no idea it was that deep for you."

"Remember that night we sat on your bed?"   I nodded my head as tears filled my eyes as well as my heart for my dearest friend. "I wiped the tears away from your eyes. I vowed to never make you cry, but to be the one to make you smile and let you not want for nothing. You do something to my heart and I no matter how I tried to stop it, I couldn't. I wanted so badly for you to leave because my feeling were getting strong and I knew it was wrong, then I thought about how he was wrong for placing you in my care the way he did. Then, I knew if you left that you had nowhere to go, and I would rather you stay here where I know you would be safe."

"Oh, Big Quack."

"You in my life have been a dream come true, and the baby is a bonus. I've always wanted children and when y'all came along, it gives me purpose. I put away those tired ass tricks. It was time for me to grasp a hold of something that is real, something I could feel, and you did that to me. You have no sign as to how deep I feel for you, and yes, it would hurt me if you left, but I know that you have an ungrateful husband that doesn't know what he has in his hands."

Big Quack had tears in his eyes, and it gripped my being to see my friend like that. He was in love with an idea. I loved my husband and at a time like those, I wished

251

I didn't love him because there before me stood a man that was willing to make me his everything. All I could do was cry because as long as I was married, friendship was all it could go.

The more I stared at him, the sorrier I felt. As he wiped his tears away, he said, "Could you have loved me? I mean, if you decide to go back home one day, could I be in you and the baby's life?" I just listened because I was at a loss for words. "Would you still come see me? I'll say it again that having a piece of you is better than not having you at all in my life."

Getting up, he walked over to where I sat, got on his knees, and said, "Let me vow to always be there for you and the baby. Let me be a part of your world and take care of you like a man should."

I reached up and touched his teary face, to speak, "I can only love you as a friend, even though we have participated in sexual manner." He dropped his head, and I lifted it up to speak to his soul. "My heart belongs to Popcorn. I love my husband and to know he has cheated on me breaks me down, but I love him. I can only have a friendly love for you and nothing more. I can't see myself with you, not the way you need me to be, you understand?" He placed his head on my lap and cried. At that point, I could only rub his head as I continued, "You are a wonderful man, and any woman would be overjoyed to have you in her life. I know from personal experience that you are a kind man. You have been perfect to us, and you are the ideal man for any woman, but not for me. I wish it were easy for me, and I could drop my husband and be with you, but it will not be fair, nor will it be right."

Moments passed us by, and we did not say a word, but I broke the silence. "If it is going to hurt you more that I stay, tell me and I will go. I will find somewhere else to go. I don't want to grieve you more than I already have."

"Shondia, you leaving without a proper place to go will hurt me to the core."

"Well, I will stay and once the baby is born, I will leave, I have to. You don't see it, but me being here is only hurting you and giving you false hope of a relationship that won't happen."

Getting up, he said, "I understand. I have to get ready to go. I will lock the door behind me; you just go in your room and relax. If you need me, call me."

"I will."

"I am going to have a talk to your so-called husband. He needs to step the fuck up, if not, you need to do what you have to do. I know it means you may not be here, but you won't be there, either."

I didn't say a word. I went in my room and went to sleep.

CHAPTER 15

I thought I heard Popcorn come in the house and the kicking of the baby assured me that it was daddy. Waking up with pains all over me, I eased out of bed with my hands on my stomach. The deep breaths were not soothing me as they once were, but I continued to be calm. Before I could make it to the door, my pain went away because I heard my husband say, "I want my wife and son back, and I don't intend to leave here until I talk to her."

"She sleep right now, you can come back later."

"What time?" Popcorn asked.

"Half past the monkey's ass, a quarter to his balls."

They laughed, and Popcorn spoke, "For real, I want to talk to her."

"Get the fuck out of here, you don't mean it."

"I do," Popcorn faintly said.

"It's me, man, tell me the truth. You only want her back because shit with Shay ass didn't work out."

"I could have made it work out with her, but I just couldn't do it."

"For real?"

"Yeah, but I fucked up and fucked Shay once. When I did it, I knew it was a mistake."

"After you got that nut, you knew it was a mistake, motherfucker?"

They laughed again, and then my husband said with sincerity, "I opened my eyes and saw that I was throwing away the one woman that has been there for me."

Making a comedy, Big Quack said, "You saw all that

after one night of getting all the pussy you want along with getting your dick sucked?"

They laughed again. Popcorn broke the laughter, by stating, "I don't even remember it all. Shit, I was drunk and pouting over Shondia ass."

"You a damn lie and your nickname shit. What man does not know how the ass was he got? How many men liked it and only got it once? Your ass was fucking that pussy on a regular basis. I'm surprised you moved the pussy in."

"She needed somewhere to go, and I couldn't see my child out on the street."

"I feel ya on that one, but shit, your other child was out on the streets. How the hell you exchange one for one?"

"I didn't know she was pregnant."

"Let me rephrase it, you moved one pussy out for another pussy, and how the fuck could you not know?"

"I didn't do it like that, but shit, I just didn't know she was pregnant, or at least by me."

"So, you don't pay attention to her?"

"I do, but a baby was the last thing we were thinking about."

"I am going to be honest to you. She and the baby are special to me, and they mean a lot to me."

"Like Michelle does?" Popcorn said.

"That bitch doesn't mean shit to me. If you knew the bullshit you would kick her ass, plus, you the one that fucked her and got caught on camera about it, not me."

"That was some fucked up shit. I never wanted to hurt Shondia like that. I was going to tell her, but the time was never right."

"How the hell you plan to tell the woman you love about you fucking another woman? Pop, the shit gets harder with each passing day; it doesn't get easier, especially when you lie over and over in her face."

"True."

"Look man let me give you some advice," Big Quack said.

Out of anger, Popcorn said, "How the hell you going to give me advice and your ass single with no damn kids?"

"I may be single, but your wife and kid have been living in my house." Popcorn didn't say a word. "Man, do you love her, or you just want to cause her more grief?"

"I have always loved Shondia. It was never a time in my life that I did not love her."

"How the hell did you fuck Michelle and that dyke ass Shay then?"

"I was amped up and ready to fuck the shit out of Shondia, but she was tripping. I came down with Chug and when you drunk, pussy is pussy. All I wanted to do was release this pressure."

"So, the pussy wasn't good? Don't lie to me. I've had it before from the back."

"It was good, but not as good as Shondia and that is no lie."

"Nigga, get the fuck out of here."

"Real talk, I don't tell what my wife and I do or don't do in the bedroom, but I will say this, the pussy is number one and that is why I will fuck her up and any man that has had her since me."

"Well, if you two work it out, start over and don't let your past hurt your new future."

"I know, man. That is why I am here. I know you love her. I see, and don't think I didn't."

"A woman like her you can't help but to love, and that's real shit."

"I know, but I have to bring her back. I have to make it up to her."

"She not going to stay in that damn place after you was fucking in it."

"I know she won't stay, that is why I am getting something else. I will even move to 397 if she wants to."

"Have you lost your everlasting mind?"

"Yeah, for my baby. Quack, I knew I loved her, but now I know that I truly love her and no amount of friendship or head, pussy for that matter, will make me leave home."

"Hell yeah, a motherfucker is stupid if he leaves home. Wait, your ass didn't just leave home, you kicked your pussy out and moved in a more experienced pussy. You a bad dog, Pop," Big Quack said.

"Out of all the time she has been at my house, I only fucked it once and I ate the pussy once," Popcorn said with humor.

"You a dam lie."

"For real, when I woke up the next morning and realized what I did, I couldn't do it. I didn't say she didn't try to tempt me, for she did, and it was a good try, but my dick wouldn't get up for shit. I only thought about how Shondia was going to feel when she finds out."

"She stayed with you as long as your wife been here with me."

"Yeah, but I know you hadn't fucked my wife."

"You sure about that? I am Big Quack."

"I am sure of that. I know my wife and I am happy that she has still been faithful to me after all I put her through."

"You mean to tell me that you didn't get that dick sucked by Shay?"

I waited on the answer as my tears were muffled and pains began to grip my lower half again.

"She said she doesn't suck dick, and her lover wears a strap on, but after it all said and done, she sucked mine."

"You knew that was a damn lie. What bitch gets her pussy ate and don't want to suck that dick? I don't know any whores, for that matter."

I wanted to die. Ever since I met Popcorn, he showed me what tasting a man was all about. I always thought of oral sex as intimate between those that love and to hear that it had been taken lightly by my husband made me look at him differently. My first thought was, *how could he take something so sacred and share it with my bitch?* What they may have done before our marriage was on them, but it was after our marriage and a part of me wanted to die.

Then, I heard, "Shondia and the baby need someone to love them, and not brush them aside because they want to play games."

"Believe it or not, I have grown up since she has been away. I never knew that loving someone would hurt like hell, but it did. Each time I saw her I wanted to beg her to come home, but pride got in my way."

"Pride? Motherfucker, you moved another woman in the house she helped you get."

"I did that. I made that mistake and every day for the rest of my life, I will be grateful that you stepped in and watched over them, but now I am here. I am willing to pick up where you left off. That is, if she will have me back."

"Sorry, man, I just can't let you do that."

"You love her, don't you? Your ass has fallen in love with my wife."

"Yes, she grows on you, and you can't help but to love her. She is truly remarkable in every way. She isn't Shay or any of those tricks you were fucking around with."

"I know that, and it took not having her for me see that I need my family back. I have been at a lost without her," Popcorn spoke with his voice cracking.

"So, mounting Shay and hitting Michelle is the kind of love you intend to give her?"

"Hell no. Michelle and Shay both were mistakes. I was thinking with the wrong head. I fucked up and to know that I was tricked, that shit hurts like a motherfucker. I love my wife always have, and no one can take her place."

"Even when you were out fucking, and she was homeless? How about when you kicked her out and the same night you were fucking? Did you think of her then? I can tell you that you weren't, you were only thinking about yourself, being a greedy pussy motherfucker. That is what you were doing."

"It doesn't matter what the fuck I was doing. I love her."

"Nigga, get on down. You loved her, but not enough to stay faithful, even when she was faithful to you."

"She is my wife, not yours. Why the hell you so concerned about how I do mine any fucking way?"

"I am concerned because she is worth more than you have to offer, and what the fuck that means that she is your wife if you don't treat her like one? Tell me what the fuck does it mean when she is here in my house crying over a nigga that has his cake and eating it, too?"

"It doesn't matter. Shit, I told you I love her, and I know she still loves me."

"You also remember that she told you that once she stopped crying over you that she is done."

"Yeah, but she hasn't, has she?" Popcorn questioned, unsure.

"I wouldn't tell you because I can say she deserves more than what you are giving her. She is standing by a man that did not stand by her."

"I made that mistake, what the fuck else is there to do? I was confused and lonely when I fucked Shay, as for Michelle, I was just doing something to get a nut off."

"Doing something? What if she does something?" Big Quack asked Popcorn.

"I can't take it if I knew she has fucked someone since we been together. I would simply lose my damn mind. I can't take it and if you or any other has fucked her, I will come unglued, and God forbid." It was quiet, and Popcorn said, "The baby in her stomach is mine. I am the daddy, not you. I know you going around here pretending to be the daddy and shit."

Big Quack butted in to say, "I'm going around her being the daddy. Didn't your ass make her believe that it was not your baby?"

"That was my mistake."

"Seems like you are making a lot of damn mistakes, homie."

"Mistakes that she can forgive me for, if she chooses to," Popcorn added.

"Your ass not here and you haven't been trying to be there. You decided to turn your back on her. You neglected her and she was alone, but did she cheat? Nooo, she didn't, she hung in there and wanted to tough it out, but you weren't satisfied, you had to kick her out all because I tasted the pussy before you."

"Listen, motherfucker, I'm already not coping too well with that fact, so don't say that shit again, for if you do, I will blank out and fuck your world up!"

"You act like you have never been behind me. Shit, who you think was fucking Shay before her ass got pregnant? I was eating the pussy, and she was sucking my dick like a pro. Did I get mad? No. I was cool because she is a whore and I expected that of her, but not of you. I didn't think the bitch had a heart."

"Big Quack, Shay was just a woman, a trick, anybody's bitch. Shondia is my wife and that makes her more special, more special than she will ever know. I plan to make it up to her and be there for her and our son."

"Now you claiming him because he is almost born, that's just like a motherfucker," Big Quack spoke.

"You would probably have kids if you didn't eat the

bitches up."

With a smirk in his tone, his reply was, "You would probably have your wife and child if you weren't such an ass, chasing ass. She needs someone to love her and to treat her as the queen she really is. Your broke ass can't do shit for her. You didn't even want her until you realized that she is worth more than anything in the world. The way she smiles brightens up your day and her laugh make you feel at ease. She hasn't done that for you because you were too caught up in your own world throwing a pity party when you should have been believed her and stood by her side. But, no, you chose to freelance with bitches and tricks, and not giving a fuck about the woman that desires to be in your world more than anything. You see she can actually be happy and have a life, and you can't stand it."

"I was weak, but she is strong."

"So, she loves you more?" Big Quack asked.

"Yeah, she does, but don't get it twisted, I love her to death. I realize now that a fuck partner ain't about shit if you don't have the one that loves you in spite of your fucked up ways. Quack, you can't ever begin to please her or truly make her happy. Money isn't everything and for her to take me back, that will be enough for me."

"Naw, motherfucker, you ain't about shit and the only shit in your life lives in my motherfucking house," Big Quack stated to my husband.

"You better get the fuck on down, Quack. You run around town thinking you the shit, you the one not about shit. People can't stand your cheap; wanna be it ass, thinking you everything when you ain't shit. I may not

262

have money like you, but I have real love and that is something you crave but can't find because you are too busy buying pussy and eating it up."

"I will give your wife anything that I have just to eat that good smelling, pretty pussy again and this time, I won't stop until her juice is all over me."

It sounded like they were tussling, for I heard mumbles of their voices. The pains began to hit me continuously, so I stumbled out the room. Popcorn had Quack in a headlock and Quack's arms were around Popcorn. They stared at me with my hand on my stomach. All of a sudden, we all looked down and a puddle of water drenched the floor.

I spoke, "its coming!" They both were still in their positions, looking like dummies, so I screamed loudly, "The baby is coming!" I could not move another step, but Popcorn let go of Quack and ran over to me while Big Quack stood up frozen.

"You have a bag packed?" Popcorn asked rapidly.

"Fuck a bag, get me to Winston General"

"Hell no! We going to Oktibbeha."

He helped me, so Popcorn faced Quack, and asked, "Bitch, where your keys?"

Quack was still frozen for a moment. Before we could walk out the door, he spoke, "They are in the truck, let's go!"

The men were on each side of me and helped me into the truck. I lay back with each leg outstretched and hollering as the pain gripped my pussy. It was unbearable agony beyond my wildest dreams. Every time I cried out, Big Quack looked back at me to check on me as Popcorn drove frantically.

"Hold on, baby, I'm going as fast as I can," Popcorn called out to me. "Turn around and see if the baby is coming. Tell me what the hell you see."

"You want me to see her pussy?" Big Quack asked slowly.

"Damn, nigga, it's about the baby, so yeah, look and tell me what the hell you see." Somehow, Big Quack turned around and when he looked between my legs, he flipped around making the b sound over and over again. "Quack, what the fuck is it?" I heard my husband ask him.

Big Quack still did not say anything but the b sound and looking straight ahead. From nowhere, Popcorn reached over and slapped Big Quack. As if he was awakened from a dream, he yelled out, "I saw the head, fuck, I saw the head. The damn baby is almost out. Shit, it's almost out. I saw it! I saw it! I fucking saw it!"

"Damn, please don't let nothing happen to them, Lord," I heard Popcorn say as he drove faster.

Popcorn got on his cell and called the hospital. He told them that he was almost there and what was going on with me. Before I knew it, we pulled up to the ER. I hurt so bad, I could not move or cry out anymore. I was silent with my baby's head in the canal.

The doctors met us at the ER with a stretcher. They had to help me on it, for I could not move. Popcorn left the truck to Big Quack as he ran in behind me. They took me to the ER room and saw the head was crowning. The doctor walked in and when I pushed a few times, the baby was out and crying.

"You want to cut the cord?" I heard the doctor say to Popcorn.

I could hear him crying as he said, "Yes, I will do the honors in cutting my son's cord."

He walked back over to me, and said, "I cut the cord, Shondia. He is wonderful and he is all mines."

I turned to the sound of his voice and closed my eyes.

CHAPTER 16

When I awakened, I was in the room and the baby was in Popcorn's arms. Smiling, I said with a cracked voice, "Hey."

Wearing a smile so wide, Popcorn got up and walked over to me with the baby in his arms. I sat up as much as I could, for I was sore and weak. "Take it easy. The doctor said you will be like this, but you have to start moving around if you want to go home within a day or two."

I reached for my son, and he placed him in my arms. "Hey, you, mommy loves you," I said to my son.

He looked more like his dad, but a mixed version with Choctaw and black from me, and black from his dad. His hair was black and curly looking. My son is gorgeous and the most beautiful thing I had ever seen.

"What are you going to name him?"

"I don't know. I really haven't thought about it."

"You can name him after his father so he could be a junior or the second."

"How about no?" I said point blank as I placed my breast into my son's mouth.

"What? You don't want to name him after me?"

"Why? You denied him the short time I was pregnant. You didn't want anything to do with us, so why give you the fame?"

"I know I was wrong for..."

Cutting him off, I spoke, "You were more than wrong. You threw me out over shit I tried telling you about for months and when I told you, your ass kicked me out and moved Shay's ass in."

"Please, let us talk about it calmer. Our son can pick up when people are arguing."

At that time, the baby started crying at the top of his lungs. I put my breast up and spoke to my son in my Choctaw language, "Hello, your mother is here, and I will take good care of you." Surprisingly, he became quiet again and I placed the breast back into his mouth.

Popcorn said, "I don't like it when you speak your language because I don't understand it."
"He is going to hear it because my native language is important, and he won't forget it. I kindly told him that I am here for him, and I will take good care of him."

Picking up my son, I placed him on my shoulder and burped him. Putting my breast up, I placed my son back in my arms, and said to Popcorn, "I will not argue in front of my son, no matter how old he is. He will not hear me disagree with anyone, for that matter. He knows when things are out of sync, even at this early age, like you said."

"And I agree."

Before he could finish talking, Chug's mom walked in happily speaking Choctaw, and I had to respond in Choctaw, for her English was very rusty. "My darling niece, you are finally a mother."

"Yes, I am. I'm a mom." Popcorn looked at us, and I told him what we just said to each other.

"Well, I am going to leave out and let y'all talk about girl things. I will be back because I am not leaving your side."

Popcorn left out and my aunt stayed for almost three

hours. She was more excited about the baby than I was. From time to time, Popcorn peep his head in, and then left out the room. She asked me what I was going to name him, and I really didn't know. I wanted him to have a heritage name that stood proud and reflected the kind of man I wanted him to become. I also knew that it would mean the world for him to be named after his dad. Sighing, I hugged my aunt goodbye as she left me alone.

Soon as she left, my phone rang, and I got up and grabbed it quickly. "Hello."

"I see you finally had a baby, bitch."

I knew that it was Shay's voice. "What do you want?"

"I just want you to be happy and if leaving me the fuck alone is what you want, then I guess I have to obey."

"Really, what is the catch?"

"Since Popcorn won't tell you because he is all caught up in that baby, I might as well tell you that I am pregnant." My world stopped. I became quiet to listen to her. "Yeah, all those nights you were away, I was fucking in your house with your husband and Big Quack. Every time he would finish fucking me, he would regret it because he knew he was fucking up on you."

"And you are telling me this because?" I spoke with confidence.

"I just thought you should know before you decide to come and fuck up my world."

"Your world? You moved into my home with my husband," I added.

"Look, if he didn't want me there, he could have told me to go. I know him. He wants to do the right thing and that, I must say, gets him fucked up every time."

"You a part of me and I will always love you, but I have to let things go," I said to her as I slammed the phone down. The nurse walked in and got my son. I could not look at her, for tears were all on me.

Popcorn walked in, and said, "They done took little man back?"

When I heard his voice, I could no longer contain my anger. Using the tears that flowed from my eyes and the pain that squeezed my heart, I spoke, "You bastard. You had me fooled, and to think, I almost considered going back to you,"

"Huh? What are you talking about?"

"You and Shay that is what I am talking about." I faced him, and he saw the red eyes and the dried traces of tears on my face.

"What you mean me and Shay?"

"She called me and told me, since you haven't told me, that she is pregnant."

"What?"

"Yeah, looks like you don't have a wife anymore."

"She lying, Shondia. The bitch lying. If she is pregnant, it's not mine."

"How funny that you call her a bitch, but when you fucking her, she not a bitch."

"She has always been a bitch. She's mad because I only fucked her once and that was it. I hadn't touched her since then, regardless of what it looks like."

"Well, from my point of view, it's fucked up. So, if you don't mind, leave me and my baby alone. Go back to the woman you were playing house with."

"Shondia, please believe me. I don't love her."

"You may not love her, but she was living with you and let me not forget y'all fucked in our house. You see it as a friend, but to me, that is a relationship, and she was your lover."

"The bitch was not my lover, and she is not pregnant. She is lying!"

"I know what she told me and because of such, I can't have any part of it."

He got on his knees in front of me as I lay in bed, to say, "You know that I love you."

"Huh? I know you used to love me."

Shaking his head, he said again, "I love you, Shondia, and I messed up. I realized what I did and how fucked up it all looked. Believe me. I have never stopped wanting you or loving you. I just got confused and was hurt when you finally told me about your incident."

"Bitch, I tried to tell your sorry ass on numerous occasions, and it was all before you! Not after you, like what you did."

"Baby, please, don't turn me away. I love you."

"It's time for you to leave and don't come back."

He stood up, and spoke, "You don't think it's strange that we started having problems soon as you told Chug that he needs to do better with his life? Then, Shay comes along finds out about your baby before me? She poisons me about the baby before you talk to me. How about Michelle? Soon as that went down between us, all of a sudden, she fucking Big Quack, I kick you out, and he takes you in? This shit

270

just didn't happen. People don't want to see us together."

"No. I think it is strange that you want to blame others, but not you for what you were caught doing and if things weren't different, you would have kept it all going."

"Shondia, I was wrong, and I admit it, but soon as shit hit the fan, Big Quack is there like a pocket on a damn shirt, and handy at that."

"What does he have to do with this? You did that, not him. He has been a friend to me and has shown kindness to the baby and me."

"He has been a snake in the damn grass, slithering around and waiting on a chance to strike. Why are you fooled? Don't you see he loves you?"

"Why are you fooled? If he loves me, then I know it without adding other bitches to the mix. As for him having a chance to strike, you gave him one."

"I didn't give him a damn thing, but Shay is going to get the damn business once and for all."

He stormed out the room with tears and anger on the inside. What he said did have weight, but I didn't want to believe him any more than I believed he loved me. Shattering my thoughts was the phone ringing again. I didn't want to answer, but I did, anyway.

"Hello." There was a silence, and I spoke again, "Hello."

"Yeah, this is Michelle."

"What is this, bitch day?"

"Say what you want, but I want to tell you something."

When she said that, I looked up and it was Big Quack.

271

I said, "What do you fucking want, Michelle?" In a flash, Big Quack hung up the phone.

"What ya do that for?"

"Today is your special day and I don't want you to be bothered with tricks."

"Thanks for being concerned, but how about this. Shay called me and said she is pregnant."

"No, the hell she didn't."

"Yes, she did."

"What you say?"

"I told him to leave and don't ever talk to me again."

"How did he take that?"

"He didn't, he smashed out and left out here angry."

"Damn," he said as he got up from the chair.

"What is it?"

He paused before saying, "Nothing. It's nothing at all."

"You look like something is wrong."

"Yeah, but it will be ok. Let me come back later."

"Ok."

"Before I go, tell me how the baby is?"

"He is good. You want to see him?"

"I will the next time I come back."

"Before you go, can I tell you something?"

"Yeah."

"I may move out and move back to 397. With all this stuff going on, I think it might be best for me to move back home. All this is too much for me to handle at one time."

"If that is what you want, ok. I hope you wouldn't

go, but I won't stop you. You being happy means the world to me and it would be wonderful to have that little man in the house. Just remember, anytime you need to come back, you are welcomed."

"Thanks."

He left out. Things were beginning to add up and it was puzzling to me how things looked. Deciding to take a nap, I got settled in before they were to bring the baby back in. *Fuck, what am I going to name him?* I thought as I went to sleep with the idea that the first name come to mind will be his name.

When I opened my eyes, the nurse was there with my son. "Have you gotten a name yet?" she asked.

"Not really."

"The lady that does the birth certificate will be by this morning, and a name is a must."

Sitting up, I placed my breast in his mouth, and he began to suck hungrily. She left out and when I looked up, Popcorn was in my vision. "This is a beautiful sight," he exclaimed.

"What do you want?"

"I told you that I am not leaving your side, and I am not."

The baby became agitated, and I spoke, "Remember what we said."

Speaking lightly, he said, "Yes, and someone is going to call and tell you something."

"Who is going to call me and what are they going to tell me?"

"Shay is going to call you, and she is going to tell

you the truth."

"Oh, ok," I said to sound calm as possible because I did not want my son to pick up on anything. Seconds later the phone rang. I was hesitant to answer, but I did. "Hello."

"Hi, this is Shay."

"Yeah, what do you want?" I asked as if I didn't know what she had to say.

"I didn't tell you everything."

"Why?" I said to play dumb.

"I guess a piece of me still wants to hold on and about me being pregnant."

"Oh, that. What about it?"

"I am pregnant, but it is not Popcorn's, its Big Quack's."

"Well, does he know that or is this just another one of your tricks?"

"He knows."

"Well, what does this have to do with me?"

"I wanted you and Popcorn broken up at first because he had more of you than I did, but I see that you want a male and female household, and I can't blame you. I also must make amends."

"Amends?"

"Look, I was a part of something, and I can only tell you my part in everything, and now I see a different light."

"I see."

"Yes, I want to do the right thing and that is to come clean about everything."

"Everything?"

"Yes, I have told you and I will not bother you

unless you need me."

"Ok, but I don't think that would happen."

"Popcorn is there listening, isn't he?"

"Yes, and I am ending this conversation." I hung up and the lady with the birth certificate came in. Popcorn looked at me, and I told her, "Chadwick Isaiah Collier, Jr."

Popcorn almost jumped out his seat to hear that I was naming our son after him. We both signed the papers, and she left. Popcorn's phone vibrated. He said, "I need to go take this call."

He left out the room and was gone for about ten minutes. When he walked back in, he acted different. He sat there on the couch and did not say a word. I knew something was wrong from his posture. Opening my mouth, I said, "Are you ok?"

Taking his time to lift his head, he said, "You like eating pussy?"

"What are you talking about?"

"Don't play dumb with me. You heard what the fuck I said. Now, answer the damn question." I didn't say anything. He got up and came toward me, to say, "All this time you were pretending not to like Shay. All this time you were eating her pussy and fucking her, you damn dyke."

"It's not true."

"Cut the bullshit. I know it's true like you know it's true. Tell me that you didn't play me."

"I didn't play you. I love you."

"No, dyke bitch, I loved you. Where the hell did I play in all this? Tell me that much?" he asked with anger boiling by the minute.

"I met you, but didn't know it was you. I fell in love with you and when I did, I let Shay go."

"Really? You were just fucking her in our damn trailer."

"And you fucked her in our damn trailer. So, fucking what. I'm straight now."

"Dykes don't ever be just straight."

"Popcorn, please, listen to me," I begged.

"You know, I'm fucking tired of just listening. Everywhere I go, some damn body has a damn story they want me to hear. Fuck you and your story. I don't give a shit about what you have to say."

"Don't do this to Jr.; he needs you in his life. He needs both of his parents in his life."

"Just like Shay's daughter needs me in her life? When were you ever going to tell me that the little girl may not be mine? I have been paying for her because I really thought she was mine, even when I didn't do a blood test. You and your dyke ass lover can rot in hell and take your baby tickets with you."

"Shay's may not be yours, but mine is."

"I've already asked for a blood test, but the saddest part is, I believe he is mine more than anything. I loved you and gave yo ass my last name. Where was the fucking love you showed back?" I could not answer. He continued to stare at me as if he desired to hit me.

"You want to hurt me, don't you?" I asked between the tears and sniffles.

"The only thing I want to do is take you to court and have parental rights. I want to be able to see my son as much as possible. I desire to teach him how to be a man to the kind of man you are to Shay."

"Please, don't do this. In spite of everything, I love you and I want us to have a life together, put our lives back together," I stated to my husband.

"You bitch, what the fuck you thought I was doing? Playing hide and go seek?"

"You only focused on what I did. You never discussed about what you did. Besides, we haven't had any talking about what all has happened since we have been separated."

"I fucked your lover once in our home, fucked Michelle and ate the pussy, and moved your lover into our home, not my heart. You, on the other hand, only wanted me because you found out about me and your lover, Shay. You also knew the child may not be mine and you kept it from me, then you moved in the house with a pie eating pussy champion, which you more than likely fucked him, and you continued to fuck Shay. If you add it up, what you did outweighed anything that I had done."

"You know I love you and I can be good to you," I plead to my heartbroken husband.

"No, I loved you and was going insane without you. Now I wished I would have fucked her and a few more, but that won't do any good because deep down I am a better man than you will ever be."

He wiped the tears from his face and before he made it to the door, he turned to say, "You silly bitch, you had me hook, line, and sinker. I was too blind by you letting him taste you when all along, that bitch had tasted you too."

"Shay was my first relationship, but I knew it had to end when I met you."

Suddenly, he screamed at me, "Shut that hole in your damn face before I forget that you are my son's mother and put a whipping on your damn ass. Don't ever contact me unless it has to do with Jr. When you get out, let me know where you will be living at so I can come see him." He opened the door, and said, "Now, when I finish crying over you, I'm done with you."

I sat beside the bed and wept sorrowfully. I never thought that losing his love completely would hurt so badly. I now knew that Shay wanted to tell me that she told my husband about her and me. The nurse brought Jr. in, and I nursed him as I cried. Those hours seemed to drag by as I was there alone with only my son to hold and talk to.

CHAPTER 17 (December)

I decided to put everything behind me. I was a mother, and my son would need me as much as I needed him. Getting up, I began to pack my bags when the door of my hospital room swung open. To my surprise, it was Chug. I was so glad to see him, and yet, his lies flooded me, too.

"Yeah, motherfucker, bring your tied ass in here."

"Is that any way to greet your cousin who just made it out of boot camp?"

Giving him a hug, I spoke, "A lot of shit has gone down since you been gone."

"Oh shit, like you having a damn baby. I never would have seen that coming."

"Me either, but that is not the shit I am talking about."

"I already know what shit, but you go first," he spoke as he sat on the bed beside me.

"To top it off, I know about you seeing Popcorn fucking Michelle."

He grins his usual boyish grin, to say, "Oh, about that."

"Yeah, motherfucker, about that?"

"You see, I was in another world that night and I forgot all about that. I was too busy getting my dick suck and playing in ya girl's pussy."

"I bet you did."

"All truths, I did, but I got some news to share with you and I don't know how you gonna take it."

Tilting my head to the right, I said, "Let me have it."

"I talk to Michelle last night. You know I had to

have my big bitch before coming here and she told me some things that you need to know."

"Like?" He paused as if he had to get his thoughts together. I knew whatever it was; he was trying his hardest to tell me as nice as he could. I knew him and it was his serious face. "Out with it," I demanded.

"How all your dirty secrets came out because you tried to wreck her life?"

"How is that?"

"You were the one giving me advice on leaving her alone because she is married."

"Well, she is married, and you don't need to be with a married woman."

"Yeah, but at the same time, you're married, and you were still fucking off with Shay. The pot calling the kettle black."

I became silent, for I knew he was telling the truth. "How you know that?"

"Wake the fuck up cuz and fucking listen with your damn ears. Michelle knew that she did not know enough on you, so she got Big Quack in on it."

"Popcorn was right!" I exclaimed.

"Well, she found out that Big Quack was in love with you and wouldn't stop until he had you. So, she got him to help her come between you and Popcorn."

"So, Popcorn finding out that I was pregnant was no accident?"

"No, Michelle has a home girl that works in the Health Department. She had knowledge of you, so she called Michelle and told her. She, on the other hand, had her friend tell Shay that you were pregnant by Big Quack."

"So, Shay didn't know?"

"Wait, let me finish."

My heartbeat rapidly as he said to let him finish. Silently, I spoke, "Go on."

"Shay didn't know then, but somehow that was not good enough. So, Michelle messed up your car with the animals and shit. Big Quack cut the brakes more than he thought and it hurt him to know that he almost killed you."

I started crying and Chug placed his left arm around me for comfort. It was too much. The only one I believed was a friend to me was in on it to get me. *How could I have been so blind? I even made love to him,*

"Shush. It is going to be alright. Now you have to get on your shit and fuck all those Zion Ridge motherfuckers. Get yo ass back in those sticks and stay the fuck there."

"Chug, but I love my husband, and I want to be with him and only him."

"At some point, he loved you, too, but you fucked that up by staying involved with Shay and lying about Shay's baby."

"Yeah, you right. I brought all this on myself," I spoke as I sniffled.

"No, you didn't. It was uncalled for having your life be made public because you gave me sound advice. I got in her ass for that. She says she was only trying to break you and your husband up, and that she never knew you were into women until word got on the street."

"No one really knew."

"Hell, I was stunned that you were getting the pussy I been wanting for a minute."

I laughed, and he said, "Michelle burned down the man cave just to get you in the house with Quack. She also said that day he kicked her out, Big Quack told her that he couldn't do it to you anymore and that he had already done enough."

"I remember that day. He told her to get out and she told me that if I only knew. I had no idea that this is what she is talking about."

"Yeah, that is what she was saying."

"How Shay plays into all this?" I needed to know if she was one of the trio.

"She became a joker. She was involved and didn't really know. She was playing on her emotions for you, and she didn't want to leave you. She really wants you and Popcorn. Damn bitch," Chug said as he got up.

"Thanks for letting me in on this. I don't know what to do."

"Well, there is no real proof, so you can't go to the police. I say you let the shit ride and get the fuck on down. Now you know, so do what you have to do to raise your little man."

For the first time, my cousin actually made sense. The entire experience had made me realize that you couldn't trust the fuckers you came across, no matter how innocent and nice they were. My damn world blew up in my face because I could not leave pussy alone and, mostly, because I gave advice.

I got up, dried my eyes, and finished packing. I knew

that home was where I was going and from that day forward, I would not give anyone damn advice about shit. I was going to let them figure it out on their own like the fuck I did.